THE PROOF OF THE PUDDING

"I 'M NOT LOSING ANYTHING; AND BESIDES, I 'M
HAVING A MIGHTY GOOD TIME"

THE PROOF OF THE PUDDING

By MEREDITH NICHOLSON

AUTHOR OF
"Otherwise Phyllis," Etc.

With Frontispiece
By C. H. TAFFS

A. L. BURT COMPANY

Publishers   New York

Published by Arrangements with HOUGHTON, MIFFLIN COMPANY

TO

CARLETON B. McCULLOCH

CONTENTS

CONTENTS

THE PROOF OF THE
PUDDING

CHAPTER I

A YOUNG LADY OF MOODS

I⊤ was three o'clock, but the luncheon the Kinneys were giving at the Country Club had survived the passing of less leisurely patrons and now dominated the house. The negro waiters, having served all the food and drink prescribed, perched on the railing of the veranda outside the dining-room, ready to offer further liquids if they should be demanded. Such demands had not been infrequent during the two hours that had intervened since the party sat down, as a row of empty champagne bottles in the club pantry testified. The negroes watched with discreet grins the antics of a girl of twenty-two who seemed to be the center of interest. She had been entertaining the company with a variety of impersonations of local characters, rising and moving about for the better display of her powers of mimicry. Hand-clapping and cries of "Go on!" followed each of these performances.

She concluded an imitation of the head waiter — a pompous individual who had viewed this impiety with mixed emotions — and sank exhausted into her chair amid boisterous laughter. The flush in her cheeks was not wholly attributable to the heat of the June day, and the eagerness with which she gulped a glass of champagne one of the men handed her suggested a familiar acquaintance with that beverage.

"Now, Nan, give us Daddy Farley. Do old Uncle Tim cussing the doctor — put it all in — that's a good little Nan!"

"Go to it, Nan; we've got to have it!" cried Mrs. Kinney.

"I think it will kill me to hear it again," protested Billy Copeland, who was refilling the girl's glass; "but I'd be glad to die laughing. It's the funniest stunt you ever did."

The girl's arms hung limp, and she sat, a crumpled, dejected figure, glancing about frowningly with dull eyes.

"I'm all in; there's nothing doing," she replied tamely.

"Oh, come along, Nan. We'll go for a spin in the country right afterwards," said Mrs. Kinney — who had just confided to a guest from Pittsburg, for whom the party was given, that Nan's imitation of Daddy Farley abusing his doctor was the killingest thing ever, and that she just must hear it.

Their importunities were renewed to the accompaniment of much thumping of the table, and suddenly the girl sprang to her feet. She seemed immediately transformed as she began a minute representation of the gait and speech of an old man.

"You ignorant blackguard! you common, low piece of swine-meat! How dare you come day after day to torture me with your filthy nostrums! You've poured enough dope into me to float a battleship and given me pills enough to sink it, and here I am limpin' around like a spavined horse, and no more chance o' gettin' out o' here again than I have of goin' to heaven! What's that! You got the cheek to offer to give up the case! Just like you to want to turn me over to some other pirate and keep me movin' till the undertaker comes along and hangs out the crape! There's been a dozen o' you flutterin' in here like hungry sparrows lookin' for worms. You don't see anything in my old carcass but worm-food! Hi, you! What you up to now? Oh, Lord, don't leave me! Come back here; come back here, I say! Oh, my damned legs! How long you say I'd better take that poison you sent up here yesterday? Well, all right" — meekly — " I guess I'll try it. Where's that nurse gone? You better tell her again about the treatment. She forgets it half the time; tell her to double the dose. If I've got to die, I want to die full o' poison to make it easier for the embalmer. I guess you're all right, doc; but you're slow, mighty damned slow. Hi, Nan, you grinnin' little fool, who told you to come in here? Oh, Lord! Oh, my poor legs! Oh, for God's sake, doctor, do something for me — do something for me!"

She tottered toward her chair, imaginably the bed from which the old man had risen, and glanced at her audience indifferently, as they broke into hilarious applause. The vulgarity of the exhibition was mitigated somewhat by her amazing success in sinking herself in another personality. They all knew that the man she was imitating was her foster-father and benefactor; that he had rescued her from obscure, hopeless poverty, educated her and given her his name; and that but for his benevolence they never would have known or heard of her; but this clearly was not a company that was fastidious in such matters. The exhibition of her cleverness had been highly diverting. They waved their napkins and demanded more.

She continued to survey them coldly, standing by her chair and absently biting her lip. Then she turned with an air of disdain and moved among the tables to the nearest door with languid deliberation. They watched her dully, mystified. This possibly was a prelude to some further contribution to the hour's entertainment, and they craned their necks to follow her, expecting that at any moment she would turn back.

The screen door banged harshly upon her exit. She crossed the veranda, ran down the steps toward the canal that lay a little below the clubhouse, and hurried away as though anxious to escape pursuit

4

or questioning. She came presently to the river, pressed through a tangle of briars and threw herself down on the bank under a majestic sycamore.

A woodpecker drummed upon a dead limb of the tree, and a kingfisher looked down at her wonderingly. She lay perfectly quiet with her face buried in the grass. Hers was not a happy frame of mind. Torn with contrition, she yielded herself to the luxury of self-scorn. She had no intention of returning immediately to the clubhouse, and she was infinitely relieved that none of her late companions had followed her. She wished that she might never see them again. Then her mood changed and she sat up, flung aside her hat, dipped her handkerchief in the river and held it to her burning face.

"You little fool, you silly little fool!" she said, addressing her reflection in the water. She spoke as though quoting, which was indeed exactly what she was doing. It was just such endearing terms that her foster-father applied to her in his frequent fits of anger.

Then she stretched herself at ease with her hands clasped under her head and stared at the sky. Beneath the cloud of loosened black hair that her various exertions had shaken free, her violet eyes were fine and expressive. Her face was slender, with dimples near the corners of her mouth: a sensitive face, still fresh and girlish. Her fairness was that of her type — a type markedly Irish. The wet handkerchief that had brought away a faint blotch of scarlet from her rather full lips had left them still red with the sufficient color of youthful health. Lying relaxed for half an hour, watching the lazily drifting white clouds, she became tranquillized. Her eyes lost their restlessness as she gazed dreamily at the heavens.

The soft splash of oars caused her to lift her head guardedly and glance out upon the river. A young man was deftly urging a cedar skiff toward a huge elm that had been uprooted by a spring storm and lay with half its trunk submerged. He jumped out and tied the skiff to a convenient limb and then, standing on the trunk, adjusted a rod and line and began amusing himself by dropping a brilliant fly here and there on the rippling surface. It was inconceivable that any one should imagine that fish were to be wooed and won in this part of the stream; even Nan knew better than that. But failures apparently did not diminish the pleasure the fisherman found in his occupation.

He was small and compactly made and wore white flannel trousers, canvas shoes, and a pink shirt with a four-in-hand to match. He moved about freely on the log to give variety to his experiments; he was indeed much nimbler with his feet than with his hands, for his whipping of the stream lacked the sophistication of skilled fly-casting. He lighted a cigarette without abating his efforts, and commented audibly upon his stupidity when a too-vigorous twist of the wrist sent the fly into a sap-

6

ling, from which he extricated it with the greatest difficulty.

He was not of her world, Nan reflected, peering at him through the fringing willows. She knew most of the young gentlemen who attended dances or played tennis and golf at the Country Club, and he was not of their species. Once in making a long cast his foot slipped, and he capered wildly while regaining his balance, fell astraddle of the log, and one shoe shipped water. He glanced about to make sure this misfortune had not been observed, shook the water out of his shoe and lighted a fresh cigarette.

She admired the dexterity with which he held the rod under his arm, manipulated the "makings" and had the little cylinder burning in a jiffy and hanging to his lip — a fashion of carrying a cigarette not affected by the young gentlemen she knew. It was just a little rakish; but he was, she surmised, a rather rakish young man. A gray cap tilted over one ear exaggerated his youthful appearance; his countenance was still round and boyish, though she judged him to be older than herself.

The patience and industry with which he plied the rod were admirable: though there was not the slightest probability that a fish would snap at the fly, he continued his futile casting with the utmost zeal and good humor. His sinewy arms were white — which, being interpreted, meant that their exposure to the sun had not been as constant as might

7

be expected of one who was lord of his own time and devoted to athletics. She was wondering whether he intended to continue his exercise indefinitely, when his efforts to extricate the fly from a tangle of water-grass freed it unexpectedly, and the line described a semicircle and caught a limb of the sycamore under which she was lying.

His vigorous tugs only tightened it the more, and she began speculating as to whether she should rise and loosen it or await his own solution of the difficulty. If it became necessary for him to leave the fallen tree to effect a rescue, he must find her hiding-place; and her dignity, she argued, would suffer if she allowed him to discover that she had been watching him. He now began moving toward the bank with the becoming air of determination that had attended his practice with the rod. She rose quickly, jumped up and caught the bough that held the fly, and tore it loose with a handful of leaves.

"Lordy!" he exclaimed, staring hard. "Did you buy a ticket for this show, or did you stroll in on a rain-check?"

"Oh, I was here first; but it is n't my river!" she replied easily. "They don't seem to be biting very well," she added consolingly.

"Biting? Well, I should say not! There has n't been a minnow in this river since the Indians left. I'm just practicing."

"You've done a lot of it," said Nan, looking

8

about for her hat and picking it up as an earnest of her immediate departure.

He dropped his rod and walked toward her guardedly and with an assumed carelessness, his hands in his pockets.

"That's one good thing about fly-fishing," he observed detainingly; "you don't need to bother about the fish so long as there's plenty of water."

He noted the handkerchief that she had spread on a bush to dry, and eyed her with appreciation as she thrust the pins through her hat.

"Country Club?" he asked casually.

She nodded affirmatively, glancing toward the red roof of the clubhouse, and brushed the bits of bark and earth from her skirt. If he meant to annoy her with further conversation, it might be just as well to make it clear that the club afforded an easily accessible refuge.

"Excuse me, but you're Miss Farley, — yes? It's kind o' funny," he continued, still lounging toward her, "but I remember you away back when we were both kids — my name being Amidon — Jeremiah A., late of good old Perry County on La Belle Rivière — and I've seen you lots o' times downtown. I'm connected in a minor capacity with the well-known house of Copeland-Farley Company, drugs, wholesale only — naturally sort o' take an interest in the family."

It was still wholly possible for her to walk away without replying; and yet his slangy speech amused

9

her, and his manner was deferential. She remembered the Amidons from her childhood at Belleville, on the Ohio, and she even vaguely remembered the boy this young man must have been. Within three yards of her he paused, as though to reassure her that he was not disposed to presume upon an acquaintance that rested flimsily upon knowledge that might have awakened unwelcome memories; and seeing that she hesitated, he remarked: ⌣

"A good deal has happened since you sat in front of me in the public school down there. I guess a good deal has happened to both of us."

This was too intimate for immediate acceptance; but she would at least show him that whatever changes might have taken place in their affairs, she was not a snob.

"You are Jerry; the other Amidon boy was Obadiah. I remember him because the name always seemed so funny."

"You're playing safe! Obey died when he was ten — poor little kid! Scarlet fever. That was right after the flood you floated away on."

She murmured her regret at the death of his brother. It was, however, still a delicate question just how much weight should be given to these slight ties of their common youth.

The disagreeable connotations of his introduction — the southward-looking vista that led back to the poverty and squalor to which she was born — were rather rosily obscured by the atmosphere of assured blitheness he exhaled. He seemed to imply that both had put Belleville behind them and that there was nothing surprising in this meeting under happier conditions. He was a clean-cut, well-knit, resolute young fellow. His brownish hair was combed back from his forehead with an onion-skin smoothness; indeed, he imparted a general impression of smoothness. His gray eyes expressed a juvenile innocence; his occasional smile was a slow, reluctant grin that disclosed white, even teeth. A self-confident young fellow, a trifle fresh, and yet with an unobtrusive freshness that was not displeasing,'Nan thought, as she continued to observe and appraise him.

"I broke away from the home-plate when I was sixteen," he went on, "about four years after you pulled out; and I've been engaged in commercial pursuits in this very town ever since. Arrived in a freight-car," he amplified cheerfully, as though she were entitled to all the facts. "Got a job with the aforesaid well-known jobbing house. Began by sweeping out, and now I swing a sample-case down the lower Wabash. Oh, not vulgarly rich! but I manage to get my laundry out every Saturday night."

"You travel for the house, do you?" she asked with a frown of perplexity.

"That's calling it by a large name; but I can't deny that your words give me pleasure. They're just trying me out; it's up to me to make good.

I've seen you in the office now and then; but you never knew me."

"If I ever saw you, I did n't know you, of course," she said with unaffected sincerity; "if I had, I should have spoken to you."

"Oh, I never worried about that! But of course it would be all right if you did n't want to remember me. I was an ugly little one-gallus kid with a frowsy head and freckled face. I should n't expect you to remember me for my youthful beauty; but you saved me from starvation once; I sat on your fence and watched you eat a large red apple, and traded you my only agate — it was an imitation — for the core."

She laughed, declaring that she could never have been so grasping, and he decided that she was a good fellow. Her manner of ignoring the social chasm that yawned between members of the fashionable Country Club and the Little Ripple Club farther down the river, to which young men who invaded the lower Wabash with sample-cases were acceptable, was wholly in her favor. Her parents had been much poorer than his own: his father had been a teamster; hers had been a common day laborer and a poor stick at that. And recurring to the maternal line, her mother had without shame added to the uncertain family income by taking in washing. His mother, on the other hand, had canned her own fruit and been active in the affairs of the First M.E. Church, serving on committees with the wives of men who owned stores and were therefore of Belleville's aristocracy; she had even been invited to the parsonage to supper.

If Nan Corrigan's parents had not perished in an Ohio River flood, and if Timothy Farley, serving on a flood sufferers' relief committee, had not rescued her from a shanty that was about to topple over by the angry waters, Nan Farley would not be standing there in expensive raiment talking to Jerry Amidon. These facts were not to be ignored and she was conscious of no wish to ignore them.

"I've been fortunate, of course," she said, as though condensing an answer to many questions.

"I guess there's a good deal in luck," he replied easily. "If one of our best tie-hoppers had n't got killed in a trolley smash-up, I might never have got a chance to try the road. I'd probably have been doing Old Masters with the marking-pot around the shipping-room to the end of time."

His way of putting things amused her, and her smile heightened his admiration of her dimples.

"I suppose you're going fishing when you learn how to manage the fly?" she asked, willing to prolong the talk now that they had disposed of the past.

"You never spoke truer words! It's this way," he continued confidentially: "When I see a fellow doing something I don't know how to do, my heart-action is n't good till I learn the trick. It used to make me sick to have to watch 'em marking boxes at the store, and I began getting down at six A.M. to practice, so when a chance came along I'd be ready to handle the brush. And camping once over Sunday a few miles down this romantic stretch of sandbars, I saw a chap hook a bass with a hand-made fly instead of a worm, and I've been waiting until returning prosperity gave me the price of a box of those toys to try it myself. And here you've caught me in the act. But don't give me away to the sports up there." He indicated the clubhouse with a jerk of the head. "It might injure my credit on the street."

"Oh, I'll not give you away!" she replied in his own key. "But did the man you saw catch the fish that time ever enter more fully into your life? I should think he ought to have known how highly you approved of him."

"Well, I got acquainted with him after that, and he's taken quite a shine to me, if I may say it which should n't. The name being Eaton — John Cecil — lawyer by trade."

Her face expressed surprise; then she laughed merrily.

"He's never taken a shine to me; I think he dis-approves of me. If he does n't" — she frowned — "he ought to!"

"Oh, nothing like that!" he declared with his peculiar slangy intonation. "He is n't half as frosty as he looks; he's the greatest ever; says he believes he could have made something out of me if he'd caught me sooner. He works at it occasionally, anyway; trying to purify my grammar — a hard job; says my slang is picturesque and useful for commercial purposes, but little adapted to the politer demands of the drawing-room. You know how Cecil talks? He's a grand talker — sort o' guys you, and you can't get mad."

"I've noticed that," said Nan, with a rueful smile. "You ought to be proud that he takes an interest in you. I suppose it's your sense of humor; he's strong for that."

This compliment, ventured cautiously, clearly pleased Amidon. He stooped, picked up a pebble and sent it skimming over the water.

"He says a sense of humor is essential to one who gropes for the philosophy of life — his very words. I don't know what it means, but he says if I'm good and quit opening all my remarks with 'Listen,' he'll elucidate some day."

Her curiosity was aroused. The social conjunction of John Cecil Eaton and Jeremiah A. Amidon was bewildering.

"He's not in the habit of wasting time on people he does n't like — me, for example," she remarked, lifting her handkerchief from the bush and shaking it out. "I suppose you met him in a business way?"

"Not much! Politics! I room in his ward, and we met in the Fourth Ward Democratic Club. He tried to smash the Machine in the primary last spring, and I helped clean him up — some job, I can tell you! But he's a good loser, and he says it's his duty to win me over to the Cause of Righteousness. Cecil's a thinker, all right. He says thought is n't regarded as highly nowadays as it used to be; says my feet are well trained now, and I ought to begin using my head. He always wears that solemn front, and you never know when to laugh. Just toys with his funny whiskers and never blinks. Says he tries his jokes on me before he springs 'em at the University Club. I just let him string me; in fact, I've got to; he says I need his chastening hand. Gave me a copy of the Bible, Christmas, and told me to learn the Ten Commandments; said they were going out of fashion pretty fast, and he thought I could build up a reputation for being eccentric by living up to 'em. Says if Moses had made eleven, he could n't have improved on the job any. Queer way of talking religion, but Cecil's different, any way you look at him."

These revelations as to John Cecil Eaton's admiration for the Ten Commandments, coming from Amidon, were surprising, but not so puzzling as the evident fact that Eaton found Copeland-Farley's young commercial traveler worth cultivating. Amidon was quick to see that he rose in Nan's estimation by reason of Eaton's friendly interest.

"Well, I never get on with him," she confessed, willing to sacrifice herself that Amidon might plume himself the more upon Eaton's partiality.

"Lord, I don't *understand* him!" Amidon protested. "If I was smart enough to do that, I would n't be working for eighteen per. I guess he just gets lonesome sometimes and looks me up to have somebody to talk to — not that *anybody* would n't be tickled to hear him, but he says he finds in me a certain raciness and tang of the Hoosier soil — whatever that means. He took me over to the Art Institute last Sunday and gave me a lecture on the pictures, and me not understanding any more than if he'd been talking Chinese. Introduced me to a Frenchman fresh from Paris and told him my ideals were distinctly post-impressionistic. Then we bumped into a college professor, and he made me talk so the guy could note the mellow flavor of my idiom. Can you beat that? Cecil says the hostility of the social classes to each other is preposterous. Got me to take him to a dance the freight-handlers were throwing. It was funny, but they all warmed to him like flies to a leaky sugar-barrel. Wore his evening clothes, white vest and all, and he was the only guy there in an ironed shirt! I thought they'd sure kill him; but not on your life!"

The John Cecil Eaton thus limned was not the austere person Nan knew. Her Eaton was a sedate gentleman who made cryptic remarks to her at parties and was known to be exceedingly conservative in social matters. Amidon, she surmised, was far too keen to subject himself unwillingly to Eaton's caustic humor, nor was Eaton a man to trouble himself with any one unless he received an adequate return.

"I must be going back," she said, glancing at her watch. Her casual manner of consulting the pretty trinket on her wrist charmed him. He was pleased with himself that he had been able to carry through an interview with so superior a person.

He had never been more at ease in his most brilliant conversations with the prettiest stenographer in the drug house, whose sole aim in life seemed to be to "call him down" for his freshness. Lunch-counter girls, shop-girls, attractive motion-picture cashiers, were an alluring target for his wit, and the more cruelly they snubbed him the more intensely he admired them. But the stimulus of these adventures was not comparable to the exaltation he experienced from this encounter with Nan Farley. If she had pretended not to remember him he would have hated her cordially; as it was, he liked her immensely. Though she lacked the pert "come-back" of girls behind desks and counters, he felt, nevertheless, that she would give a good account of herself in like positions if exposed to the bold raillery of commercial travelers. He was humble before her kindness. She turned away, hesitated an instant, then took a step toward him and put out her hand. There was something of appeal in the look she gave him as their hands touched — the vaguest hint of an appeal. Her eyes narrowed for an instant with the intentness of her gaze as she searched his face for

— sympathy, understanding, confidence. Then she withdrew her hand quickly, aware that his admiration was expressing itself with disconcerting frankness in his friendly gray eyes.

"It's been nice to see you again," she said softly. "Good luck!"

"Good luck to you, Miss Farley; I hope to meet you again sometime."

"Thank you; I hope so too."

She nodded brightly and moved off along the path toward the clubhouse. He felt absently for his book of cigarette-papers as he reviewed what she had said and what he had said.

He did not resume his whipping of the river, but restored his rod to its case and turned slowly downstream, not neglecting to lift his eyes to the clubhouse as he drifted by.

CHAPTER II

THE AFFAIRS OF MRS. COPELAND

IN a quiet corner of the club veranda Fanny Copeland and John Cecil Eaton had been conscious of the noisy gayety of Mrs. Kinney's party, and they observed Nan Farley's hurried exit and disappearance.

"Nan does n't seem to be responding to encores," Eaton remarked. "She's gone off to sulk — bored, probably; prefers to be alone, poor kid! It's outrageous the way those people use her."

"They have to be amused," replied Mrs. Copeland, "and I've heard that Nan can be very funny."

"There are all kinds of fun," Eaton assented dryly. "She's been taking off Uncle Tim again. I don't see that he's getting anything for his money — that is, assuming that she gets his money."

"If she does n't," said Mrs. Copeland quickly, "she won't be the only person that's disappointed."

Eaton lifted his eyes toward a stretch of woodland beyond the river and regarded it fixedly. Then his gaze reverted to her.

"You think Billy wants to get back the money he paid Farley for the drug business?" he asked, in a colorless, indifferent tone that was habitual.

John Cecil Eaton was nearing the end of his

thirties — tall, lean, with a closely trimmed black beard. He was dressed for the links, and his waiting caddy was guarding his bag in the distance and incidentally experimenting at clock golf. Eaton's long fingers were clasped round his head in such manner as to set his cap awry. One was conscious of the deliberate gaze of his eyes; his drawling voice and dry humor suggested a man of leisurely habits. He specialized in patent law — that is to say, having a small but certain income, he was able to discriminate in his choice of cases, and he accepted only those that particularly interested him. He had been educated as a mechanical engineer, and the law was an afterthought. His years at Exeter and the Tech, prolonged by his law course at Harvard, had quickened his speech and modified its Hoosier flavor. He passed for an Eastern man with strangers. He was the fourth of his name in the community, and it was a name, distinguished in war and peace, that was well sprinkled through the pages of Indiana history. Though the Eatons had rendered public service in conspicuous instances they had never been money-makers, and when John heard of the high prices attained by Washington Street property in the early years of the twentieth century he reflected that if his father and grandfather had been a little more sanguine as to the city's future he might have been the richest man in town.

Eaton's interests were not all confined to his

profession. He read prodigiously in many fields; he observed politics closely and was president of a club that debated economic and social questions; he was the best fly-fisherman in the State. His occasional efforts to improve the tone of local politics greatly amused his friends, who could not see why a man who might have been pardoned for looking enviously upon a seat in the United States Senate should subject himself to the indignity of a defeat for the city council. To the men he lunched with daily at the University Club his interest in municipal affairs was only another of his eccentricities. He had never married, but was still carried hopefully on the list of eligibles. By general consent he was the best dinner man in town — a guest who could be relied upon to keep the talk going and make a favorable impression on pilgrims from abroad.

Mrs. Copeland's ironic smile at his last remark had lingered. Their eyes met glancingly; then the gaze of both fell upon the distant treetops. Theirs was an old friendship that rendered unnecessary the filling in of gaps. Eaton was thinking less concretely of her reference to Billy Copeland's designs upon the Farley money than of the abstract fact that a divorced woman might sit upon a club veranda and hear her former spouse's voice raised in joyous exclamation within, and even revert without visible emotion to the possibility of his remarrying.

Times and standards had changed. This was no

longer the sober capital it had been, where every one went to church, and particular merit might be acquired by attending prayer-meeting. It was a very different place from what it had been in days well within Eaton's recollection, before the bob-tail mule cars yielded to the trolley, or the automobile drove out the sober-going phaëtons and station-wagons that had satisfied the native longing for grandeur. The roster of the Country Club bore testimony of the passing of the old order. The membership committee no longer concerned itself with the ancestry or reputation for sobriety of applicants, or their place of worship, or whether their grandfathers had come to town before the burning of the Morrison Opera House, or even the later conflagration that consumed the Academy of Music. You might speak of late arrivals like the Kinneys with all the scorn you pleased, but they had been recognized by everybody but a few ultra-conservatives; and if Bob Kinney was something of a sport or his wife's New York clothes were a trifle daring for the local taste, such criticisms did not weigh heavily as against the handsome villa in which these same Kinneys had established themselves in the new residential area on the river bluff. Curiosity is a stern foe of snobbishness; and when Mrs. Kinney seemed so "sweet" and had given a thousand dollars to the new Girls' Club, besides endowing a children's room in the Presbyterian Hospital, many very proper and dignified matrons felt fully justified in crossing the Rubicon (otherwise White River) for an inspection of Mrs. Kinney's new house. Eaton had accepted such things in a philosophic spirit, just as he accepted Kinney's retainer to safeguard the patents on the devices that made Kinney's cement the best on the market and the only brand that would take the finish and tint of tile or marble.

"It seems to be understood that they're waiting for Farley to die so they can be married comfortably," Eaton remarked. "But Farley's a tough old hickory knot. He's capable of hanging on just to spite them."

"He was always very kind to me. I saw a good deal of him and his wife after I came here. He was proud of the business and anxious that Billy should carry it on and keep developing it."

"I always liked the steamboating period of Farley's life," said Eaton, ignoring this frank reference to her former husband, in which he thought he detected a trace of wistfulness; "and he's told me a good deal about it at times. It was much more picturesque than his wholesale-drugging. He never quite got over his river days — he's always been the second mate, bullying the roustabouts."

"He never forgot how to swear," Mrs. Copeland laughed. "He does it adorably."

"There was never anything like him when he's well heated," Eaton continued. "He never means anything — it's just his natural way of talking.

His customers rather liked it on the whole — expected him to commit them to the fiery pit every time they came to town and dropped in to see him. When he got stung in a trade — which was n't often — he 'd go into his room and lock the door and curse himself for an hour or two and then go out and raise somebody's wages. A character — a real person, old Uncle Tim!''

The thought of the retired merchant seemed to give Eaton pleasure; a smile played furtively about his lips.

"Then it must have been his wife who used to lure him to church every Sunday morning."

"Not a bit of it! It was the old man himself. He had a superstitious feeling that business would go badly if he cut church. He never swore on Sundays, but made up for it Monday mornings. He's always been a generous backer of foreign missionaries on the theory that by Christianizing the heathen we 're widening the market for American commerce. We 've had worse men than Farley. I suppose he never told a lie or did an underhanded thing through all the years he was in business. And all he has to leave behind him is his half million or more — and Nan."

"And Nan," Mrs. Copeland repeated with a shrug of her shoulders. "I suppose Mr. Farley knows what's up. He's too shrewd not to know. Clever as Nan is, she could hardly pull the wool over his eyes."

THE PROOF OF THE PUDDING

"She's much too clever not to know she can't fool him; but he's immensely fond of her, just as his wife was. And we've got to admit that Nan is a very charming person — a little devilish, but keen and amusing. She's too good for that crowd she's running with — no doubt of that! If Uncle Tim thought she meant to marry Billy, he would take pains to see that she did n't."

"You mean he would n't leave her the money?" she asked in a lower tone. "I suppose he'd have to."

Eaton shook his head.

"He's under no obligation to give it all to Nan. If he thought there was any chance of her marrying Billy —"

"She's been led to believe that it would all be hers. The Farleys educated her and brought her up in a way to encourage the belief. It would be cruel to disappoint her; he would n't have any right to cut her off," Mrs. Copeland concluded with feeling.

"It might be less cruel to cut her off than to let her have it all and go on the way she's started. She came about ten years too late upon the scene. It's only within a few years that a party like we've listened to in there would have been possible in this town. If Nan had reached her twentieth year a decade ago, she'd have been the demurest of little girls, and there would have been no question of her marrying a man who had divorced his wife merely to be free to appropriate her."

THE AFFAIRS OF MRS. COPELAND

Mrs. Copeland opened and closed her eyes quickly several times. No other man of her acquaintance would have dared to speak of her personal affairs in this blunt fashion. Eaton had referred to the divorce that had severed her ties with Copeland quite as though she were not an interested party to that transaction. He now went a step further, and the color deepened in her face as he said: —

"I don't understand why you did n't resist his suit. I've never said this to you before, and it's too late to be proffering advice, but you ought n't to have let it go as you did. Billy's whole conduct was perfectly contemptible."

"There was no sense in making a fight if he wanted to quit. The law could n't widen the breach; it was there anyhow, from the first moment I knew what was in his mind."

"He acted like a scoundrel," persisted Eaton in his cool, even tones; "it was base, rotten, damnable!"

"If you mean" — she hesitated and frowned — "if you mean that he let the impression get abroad that I was at fault — that it was I who had become interested elsewhere — it's only just to say that I never thought Billy did that. I don't believe now that he did it."

He was aware that he had ventured far toward the red lamps of danger. This matter of her personal honor was too delicate for veranda discussion;

in fact, it was not a matter that he had any right to refer to even remotely at any time or place.

"Of course, unpleasant things were said," she added. "I suppose they're always bound to be. Manning was his friend, not mine."

Eaton received this impassively, which was his way of receiving most things.

"By keeping out of the way, that gentleman proved that he couldn't have been any friend of yours. If he'd been a gentleman or even a man —"

She broke in upon him quietly, bending toward him with tense eagerness.

"He offered to: I have never told that to any one, but I don't want you to be unfair even to him. My mistake was that I meekly followed Billy when he began running with the new crowd. I knew I was boring him, and I thought if I took up with the Kinneys and the people they were training with, he might get tired of them after a while and we could go on as we had begun. But I hadn't reckoned with Nan. I allowed myself to be put in competition with a girl of twenty — which is a foolish thing for a woman of thirty-five to do."

She carried lightly the thirty-five years to which she confessed, but sometimes, in unguarded moments, a startled, pained look stole into her brown eyes, as though at the remembrance of a blow that might repeat itself. There was a patch of white in her hair just at one side of her forehead. Its effect was to contribute to her natural air of distinction.

THE AFFAIRS OF MRS. COPELAND

She was of medium height and her trim figure retained its girlish lines. Her face and hands were tanned brown, and the color was becoming. She wore to-day a blue skirt and a plain blouse, with a soft collar opened at the throat. She had walked to the clubhouse from her home, a mile distant, and her meeting with Eaton had been purely incidental. After her divorce she had established herself as a dairy farmer on twenty acres of land that she had inherited from her father, a banker in one of the smaller county seats, who had been specially interested in dairying and had encouraged her interest in the diversion he made profitable. To please him she had taken a course in dairying at the State Agricultural School and knew the business in all its practical aspects. Copeland had first seen her at a winter resort in Florida where she had gone with her father in his last illness, and their common ties with Indiana had made it easily possible for him to cultivate her better acquaintance later at home. Billy Copeland was an attractive young fellow with good prospects; his social experience was much ampler than hers, and the marriage seemed to her friends an advantageous one. When after ten years she found herself free, she rose from the ruins of her domestic happiness determined to live her life in the way that pleased her best. She shrank from adjusting herself to a new groove in town; the plight of the divorced woman was still, in this community, not wholly comfortable. There was little consola-

tion in the sympathy of friends — though she had
many; and even the general attitude, that Copeland's conduct was utterly indefensible, did not
help greatly. She realized perfectly that in following Copeland's lead unprotestingly when he caught
step with the quicker social pace set by the Kinneys,
— a name that stood as a synonym for noisier functions and heavier libations than the community had
tolerated, — she had estranged many who were
affronted by the violence with which the town was
becoming kinneyized.

Two years had passed and her broken wings
again beat the air with something of their early
rhythm. The pathos of her isolation was more apparent to her old friends in town than to herself.
Whether she had dropped out of the Kinney crowd,
or whether it was more properly an ejectment, there
was all the more reason why women who had regarded the intrusions of that set with horror should
manifest their confidence in her. If she had been
poor, a *divorcée* lodged in a boarding-house and in
need of practical aid, she might have suffered from
neglect; but having an assured small income which
her investment in the dairy farm in no wise jeop-
ardized, it was rather the thing to look in on her
occasionally. Young girls in particular thought her
handsome and interesting-looking, and risked their
mothers' displeasure by going to see her. And there
were women who sought her out merely to em-
phasize their disapproval of Copeland and the

scandal of his divorce, which they felt to be an affront
to the community's dignity in a man whose father
had been of the old order of decent, law-abiding,
home-keeping, church-going citizens. They admired the courage and dignity with which she met
misfortune and addressed herself uncomplainingly
to the business of fashioning a new life.

"I've been keeping you from your game," she
said, rising abruptly; "and I must be getting home."

They walked down the veranda toward the entrance and reached the door at a moment when
Copeland, who had been keeping company with a
tall glass in the rathskeller below, waiting impatiently for Nan's return, lounged out.

He stopped short with a slightly challenging air.
Eaton bowed and tugged at the visor of his cap.
Copeland lifted his straw hat and muttered a good-
afternoon that was intended for one or both as they
chose to take it. Mrs. Copeland glanced at him
without making any sign; she did not speak to
Eaton again, but as they parted near the first tee
and she started across the links toward the highway, she nodded quickly and smiled a forlorn little
smile that haunted him for some time afterward.

Half an hour later, standing erect after successfully
negotiating a difficult putt, he said, under his breath:—

"By George! She's still in love with him!"

He glanced around to make sure no one had over-
heard him, and crossed to the next tee with a look
of deep perplexity on his face.

THE PROOF OF THE PUDDING

Nan, having returned to the clubhouse, sauntered down the veranda toward Copeland, wearing a demure air she had practiced for his benefit. Her indifference to his annoyance at her long absence added to his vexation.

"Well, what have you been up to?" he demanded irritably. "The others skipped long ago."

"Oh, I was tired and went down to the river to rest. I'm going home now."

"You can't go home; Grace expects us to stop at her house; they'll all be there in half an hour."

"Sorry, but I must skip. You run along like a good boy, and I'll hop on the trolley. I must be home by five, and I'll just about make it."

"That's not treating Grace right, to say nothing of me!" he expostulated. "I'm getting sick of all this dodging and ducking. I'm coming up to the house to-morrow and have it out with Farley."

"You're a nice boy, Billy, but you're not going to do anything foolish," she replied.

He found the kindness of this — even its note of fondness — unsatisfying. He read into it a skepticism that was not flattering.

"We've been fooling long enough about this; we've got to announce our engagement and be done with it."

"But, Billy, we're not engaged! We're just the best of friends. Why should we stir up a big fuss by getting engaged?"

"What's got into you, anyhow!" he exclaimed,

eyeing her angrily. "This talk about not being engaged does n't go! I'm getting tired of all this nonsense — being kicked about and held off when I've staked everything I've got on you."

"You mean," she said steadily, "that you divorced your wife, thinking I would marry you; and now you're angry because I'm not in a hurry about it, and don't want to trouble papa, who has been kinder to me than anybody else ever was —"

"For God's sake, don't cry here! We've been talked about enough; I don't understand what's got into you to-day."

"I just mean to be sensible, that's all. We've had some mighty fine times, and you've been nice to me; but there's no hurry about getting married —"

"No hurry!" He stared at her, unable in his impotent rage to deal with the situation as he thought it deserved. "Look here, Nan, I can stand a lot of this Irish temperament of yours, but you're playing it a little too far."

"My Irish temperament!" she repeated poutingly. "Well, I guess the Irish is there all right; I don't know about the temperamental part of it. A good many people call it something very different."

"When am I going to see you again?" he demanded roughly.

"How should I know! You see me now and you don't like me. You'd better go downtown and do some work, Billy; that's what I should prescribe for you. And you've got to cut out the drink; it's getting too big a hold on you. I'm going to quit, too."

Standing near the entrance, they had been obliged to acknowledge the greetings of a number of new arrivals. It was manifestly no place for a prolonged serious discussion of their future. Mrs. Harrington, whose husband's bank, the Phœnix National, was the soundest in the State, climbed the steps from her motor without seeing Nan and her companion. Until Farley retired, the Copeland-Farley account was carried by the Phœnix; when Billy Copeland took the helm he transferred it to the Western, as likely to grant a more generous credit.

Copeland flushed angrily at the slight; Nan bit her lip.

"I'm off!" she said. "Be a good boy. I'll see you again in a day or two. And for Heaven's sake, don't call me on the telephone; papa has an extension in his room, you know, and hears everything. Tell Grace I'm sorry —"

"Let me run you into town; I can set you down somewhere near home. The trolleys are hot and dusty. Besides, I want to talk to you; I've got a lot to say to you."

"Not to-day, Billy. Good-bye!"

Eaton found Nan waiting for him at the fourth green.

"I was praying for a mascot, and here you are," he remarked affably. "I can't fail to turn in a good card. Glad to see you've taken up walking; there's nothing like it — particularly on a humid afternoon."

"Sorry to disappoint you, but I hope to catch the four-thirty for town. What are my chances?"

"Excellent, if you don't waste more than ten minutes on me. You've never given me more than five up to date. How is Mr. Farley?"

"He's been very comfortable for a week; really quite like himself. You'd better come and see him."

"I meant to drop in often all winter, but was afraid of boring him."

"You're one of the few that could n't do that. He likes to talk to you. You don't bother him with questions about his health — a sure way of pleasing him."

"A rare man, Farley. Wiser than serpents, and stimulating. I've learned a good deal from him."

They reached his ball, that had accommodatingly effected a good lie, and after viewing it with approval he glanced at Nan and remarked: —

"You'd better urge me to come to see you, too. It's just occurred to me that it might be well for us to know each other better. I may flatter myself; but —"

"That's the nicest thing I've heard to-day! Please come soon."

THE PROOF OF THE PUDDING

"Thank you, Nan; I shall certainly do that."

"I met a friend of yours a while ago," she said, "who pronounced you the greatest living man."

"Ah! A gentleman, of course; I identify him at once; he's the only person alive I fool to that extent — Jeremiah A. Amidon! I can't imagine why he has n't mentioned his acquaintance with you. I shall chide him for this."

He viewed her in his quizzical fashion through the thick-lensed spectacles he used for golfing. In his ordinary occupations these gave place to eye-glasses that twinkled with a sharp, hard brightness, as though bent upon obscuring the kindness that lay behind them.

"I had n't seen him lately — not since I was a child. We used to be neighbors when we were children, and he was a very, very naughty boy."

"I dare say he was," Eaton remarked, with his air of thinking of something else. "I suppose you did n't find him at all backward in bringing himself to your notice. Shyness is n't his dominant trait."

"On the other hand, he was rather diffident and wholly polite. I thought his manners did you credit — for he said you had been coaching him."

"He must be chidden; his use of my name in that connection is utterly unwarranted. He was one of Mrs. Kinney's party, I suppose, — very interesting. I'm glad they have taken him up!"

He was watching, with the quick eagerness that

36

made him so disconcerting a companion, the passing of a motor toward the clubhouse, but she understood perfectly that this utterance had been with
ironic intent. She laughed softly.

"How funny you are! I wish I were n't afraid
of you."

"I 've made a careful study of the phobias, and
there is nothing in the best authorities to justify a
fear of me. I'm as tame as buttered toast."

"Well, it's clear Mr. Amidon is n't afraid of
you!"

"I'm relieved — infinitely; I'm in mortal terror
of *him*. He's fixed standards of conduct for me that
make me nervous. I'm afraid the young scoundrel
will catch me with my visor down some day; then
smash goes his poor idol. I'm glad you spoke of
him; if he was n't at your luncheon — a guess
you scorned to notice — I suppose you met by
chance, the usual way."

"It was just like that," she laughed. "Very
much so!"

"H'm! I warn you against accepting the attentions of just any young man who strolls up the
river. A girl of your years must be discreet. Your
early knowledge of Mr. Amidon in the loved spots
your infancy knew won't save you. You'd better
refer all such matters to me. Pleasant as this is,
you're going to miss your car if you don't rustle.
And Harrington's bawling his head off trying to
fore me away. Good-bye!"

THE PROOF OF THE PUDDING

With a neat stroke he landed his ball on the green and ran after it to raise the blockade. When Nan had halted the car and climbed into the vestibule, she waved her hand, a salute which he returned gallantly with a sweep of his cap.

CHAPTER III

MR. FARLEY BECOMES EXPLICIT

THE Farleys had lived for twenty years in an old-fashioned square brick house surrounded by maples. The lower floor comprised a parlor, sitting-room, and dining-room, with a library on the side. The library had been Farley's den, where he smoked his pipe and read his newspapers. The bookcases that lined the walls had rarely been opened; they contained the "Waverley Novels," Dickens's "Works" complete, and a wide range of miscellaneous fiction, including "Uncle Tom's Cabin," most of Mark Twain, Tourgée's novel of Reconstruction, "A Fool's Errand," Helen Hunt Jackson's "Ramona," and a number of Mrs. A. D. T. Whitney's stories for girls — these latter reminiscent of Nan's girl-hood. The brown volumes of "Messages and Papers of the Presidents" were massed on the bottom shelves invincibly with half a dozen "Reports" of the State Geological Survey. The doors of the black-walnut bookcases were warped so that the contents were accessible only after patient tugging. Half the books were upside-down — and had been since the last house-cleaning. The room presented an inhospitable front to literature, and the other arts fared no better elsewhere in the house. A steel engraving of the Parthenon on the dining-room wall confronted a crude print of the JANE E. NEWCOMB, an Ohio River packet on which Farley had been second mate — and an efficient one — in '69–'70.

Mrs. Farley had established in her household the Southwestern custom of abating the heat by keeping the outer shutters closed through the middle of the day, and the negro servants who still continued in charge had not changed her system in this or in any other important particular. Nan had not lacked instruction in the domestic arts; in her school vacations she had been thoroughly drilled by Mrs. Farley. Cleanliness in its traditional relationship to godliness had been deeply impressed upon her; and she had been taught to sew, knit, and crochet. She knew how to cook after the plain fashion to which Mrs. Farley's tastes and experience limited her; she had belonged to an embroidery class formed to give occupation to one of Mrs. Farley's friends who had fallen upon evil times; and Nan had been the aptest of pupils.

But Nan had never been equal to the task of initiating changes in the Farley household, with its regular order of sweepings, scrubbings, and dustings; its special days for baking, its inexorable rotation in meats and vegetables for the table. And if she had needed justification she would have given as her excuse Farley's long acceptance of his wife's domestic routine, and the fear of displeasing him by altering it. The colored cook's husband did the

heavier indoor cleaning and maintained the yard;
and the dining-room and the upper floor were cared
for by a colored woman. Hardly any one employed
a black second girl, and Nan would have changed
the color scheme in this particular and substituted a
neatly capped and aproned white girl of the type
that opened the door of her friends' houses, but the
present incumbent was a niece of the cook and not
to be eliminated without rending the entire domestic fabric.

Nan reached home a few minutes after five.
She ran upstairs and found Farley in his room,
bending over a table by the window playing soli-
taire. The trained nurse who had been in the
house for a year appeared at the door and withdrew. Nan crossed the room and laid a hand on
Farley's shoulder. He had nearly finished the
game, and she remained quietly watching his tremulous hands shifting the cards until he leaned back
with a little grunt of satisfaction at the end. He
put up his hand to hers and drew her round so that
he could look at her.

"Still wearing that fool hat! Take it off and sit
down here and talk to me."

His small, round head was thickly covered with
stiff white hair, though his square-cut beard had
whitened unevenly and still showed traces of brown.
While he lay in the chair with a pathetic inertness,
his eyes moved about restlessly, and his bleached,
gnarled fingers were never wholly quiet.

THE PROOF OF THE PUDDING

"Let's see what you've been up to to-day?" he asked.

"Mamie Pembroke's; she was having a luncheon for her cousin."

"Just girls, I suppose?" he asked indifferently. "You must have had a lot to eat to be gone all this time."

"Well, we went for a motor run afterward and stopped at the Country Club on the way back."

"More to eat, I suppose. My God! everybody seems able to eat but me! I told that fool doctor awhile ago I was goin' to shoot him if he did n't cut off this gruel he's feedin' me. You can lay in corn' beef and cabbage for to-morrow; I'm goin' to eat a barrel of it, too. If I can get hold of some real food for a week, I'll get out of this. I understand they've got Bill Harrington playin' golf. My God! he's two years older than I am and sits on his job every day. If I'd never knuckled under to the doctors, I'd be a well man!" The wind rustling the maple by the nearest window attracted his attention. "Open that blind, and let the air in. Things have come to a nice pass when a man with my constitution can be shut up in a dark room without air enough to keep him alive."

It was necessary to lift the wire screen before the shutters could be opened, and he watched her intently as she obeyed him quickly and quietly.

"Been to luncheon, have you?" he remarked as she sat down. "Well, eatin' your meals outside

does n't save me any money. Those damned nig-
gers cook just as much as if they had a regiment in
the house. What did they give you to eat at the
Pembrokes' — the usual bird-food rubbish?"

Before his illness he had scrupulously reserved his
profanity for business uses; and it was only when
his pain grew intolerable or the slow action of his
doctor's remedies roused him to fury that he had
recourse to strong language. He allowed her to
change the position of his footstool, which had
slipped away from him, and grunted his appreciation as he stretched his long, bony figure more comfortably.

"Well, go on and tell me what you had to eat."

It seemed best to meet this demand in a spirit of
lightness. Having lied once, it might be well to
vary her recital by resorting to the truth, and she
counted off on her fingers, with the mockery that
he had always seemed to like, the items of food that
had really constituted Mrs. Kinney's luncheon.

"Grape-fruit, broiled chicken, asparagus, pota-
toes baked in their jackets and sprinkled with red
pepper, the way you like them; romaine salad, ice-
cream and cake — just plain sponge cake — coffee.
Nothing so very sumptuous about that, papa."

It had always been "papa" and "mamma" since
her adoption. When she came home from a boarding-school near Philadelphia where she had spent
two years, her attempts to change the provincial
"poppa" and "momma" to the French pronuncia-

tion had been promptly thwarted. Farley hated anything that seemed "high-falutin'"; and having grown used to being called "poppa," his heart was as flint against the impious substitution.

"Of course there were no cocktails or champagne. Not at the Pembrokes'! If all the women around here were like Mrs. Pembroke, we would n't have nice little girls like you swillin' liquor; nor these sap-headed boys that trot with you girls stewin' their worthless little brains in gin. What do you think these cigarette-smokin' swine are goin' to do! Do you hear of 'em doin' any work? Is there one of 'em that's worth a dollar a week? My God! between you girls runnin' around half-naked and these worthless young cubs plantin' their weak, wobbly little chins against cocktails all night, things have come to a nice pass. Well, why don't you go on and tell me who was at your party? Here I am, lyin' here waitin' for the pallbearers to carry me out, and never hearin' a thing, and you sit there deaf and dumb! Who was at that party?"

"Well, papa, there were just seven girls, counting me: Mary Waterman, Minnie Briskett, Marian Doane, and Libby Davis, and Mamie and her guest — a cousin from Louisville. Of course, there was nothing to drink but claret cup, with sprigs of mint in the glasses."

"So the Pembrokes are comin' to it, are they? They've got to have something that looks like liquor — well, they'll be passin' the cocktails before long. Claret cup dressed up like juleps; and how much did you get of it?'

"Oh, I had one glass; nobody had more, I think; there was some kind of mineral water besides. It was all very simple."

"Just a simple little luncheon, was it? Well, I suppose it's not too simple to get into the newspapers. Nobody can put an extra plate on the table now without the papers have to print it."

He had never quizzed her like this, and his reference to the newspaper alarmed her. His usual custom was to ask her what she had been doing and whom she had seen and then change the subject in the midst of her answer. If he had laid a trap for her she had gone too far to retreat; and while she had lied to him before, she had managed it more discreetly. She had escaped detection so long that she believed herself immune from discovery.

He began tugging at a newspaper that had been hidden under his wrapper, and her heart throbbed violently as he opened it and thrust it toward her. It was the afternoon paper, folded back to the personal and society items.

"Just read that aloud to me, will you? I may have been mistaken. Maybe I did n't get it straight. Go ahead, now, and read it — read it slow."

She knew without looking what it was; the reading was exacted merely to add to her discomfiture. The newspaper was delivered punctually at four o'clock every afternoon, so that before she left the

45

Country Club he had known just where she had been and the names of her companions. She read in a low, monotonous tone: —

"'Mrs. Robert Smiley Kinney entertained at luncheon at the Country Club to-day for Mrs. Ridgeley P. Farwell, of Pittsburg, who is her house guest. The decorations were in pink. Those who enjoyed Mrs. Kinney's hospitality were Mr. and Mrs. Frederic Towlesley, Miss Nancy Farley, Miss Edith Saxby, Mr. George K. Pickard, and Mr. William B. Copeland.'"

She refolded the paper and placed it on the table beside him. Instead of the violent lashing for which she had steeled herself, he spoke her name very kindly and gently, with even a lingering caress.

"I lied to you papa," she faltered; "but I didn't mean to see him again. I — "

"Let's be square about this," he said, bending forward and clasping his fingers over his knees. "You promised me a year ago that you'd not meet or see Copeland; I didn't ask you to drop Mrs. Kinney, for I don't think she's a particularly bad woman; she's only a fool, and we've got to be charitable in dealin' with fools. You can't ever tell when you're not one yourself; that means me as well as you, Nan. Now, about that worthless whelp, Copeland! I want the whole truth — no more little lies or big ones. You know that piece of carrion wouldn't dare come to this house, and yet you sneak away and meet him and leave me to find

46

it out by accident! Now, I want the God's truth; just what does all this mean?"

His quiet tone was weighted with the dignity, the simple righteousness, that lay in him. She could have met more courageously a violent tirade than his subdued demand. She was conscious that he had controlled himself with difficulty; throughout the interview his wrath had flashed like heat-lightning on far horizons, but he had kept himself well in hand. He was outraged, but he was hurt, troubled, perplexed by her conduct. The adoption of Nan had marked a high altitude in the married life of the Farleys, and they had lavished upon her the pent love of their childlessness. The very manner in which she had been flung upon their protection made her advent in their household something of an adventure, broadening their narrowing vistas and bringing a welcome cheer to their monotonous existence. They had felt it to be a duty, but one that would repay them a thousand-fold in happiness.

Farley patiently awaited her explanation — an explanation she dared not make. She must satisfy him, if at all, by evasions and further lies.

"Mrs. Kinney made a point of my coming; she was always very nice to me, and I have n't been seeing her, — honestly I have n't, — and I was afraid she'd be offended if I refused to go. And I did n't know Mr. Copeland would be there. The luncheon was in the big dining-room, where everybody could see us. I did n't see any more of him than of anybody else. In fact, I got tired and ran away — down to the river and was there by myself for an hour before I came home on the trolley. When I got back to the clubhouse, they had all gone motoring and I did n't see them again."

"Left you there, did they? Well, Copeland waited for you, did n't he?"

"Yes," she admitted quickly. "But I saw him only a minute on the veranda and told him I was coming home. He understands perfectly that you don't want me to see him."

"H'm! I should hope he did! All that crowd understand it, don't they? They've been puttin' you in his way, have n't they, — tryin' to fix up something between you and that loafer! Look here, Nan, I'm not dead yet! I'm goin' to live a long time, and if these fool doctors have been tellin' you I'm done for, they've lied. And if Copeland thinks my money's goin' to drop into his lap, he's waitin' under the wrong tree. Never a cent! What you got to say to that?"

"I don't think he ever thought of it; it's only because you don't like him that you imagine he wants to marry me. I tell you now that I have never had any idea of marrying him. And as for your money — it is n't my fault that you brought me here! You don't have to give me a cent; I don't want it; I won't take it! I was only a poor, ignorant little nobody, anyhow, and you've been disappointed in me from the start. I've never pleased

48

you, no matter how hard I've tried. But I've done the best I could, and I'm sorry if I've hurt you. I never told you an untruth before," she ran on glibly; "and I would n't to-day if I had n't guessed that you knew where I'd been and were trying to trick me into lying. You don't love me any more, papa; I know that; and I'm going away —"

Her histrionic talents, employed so successfully in imitating him in his fury, for the pleasure of Mrs. Kinney's guests, were diverted now to self-martyrization to the accompaniment of tears. She had been closer to him than to his wife: what Mrs. Farley denied in the way of indulgences he had usually yielded. He had liked her liveliness, her keen wit, the amusing cajoleries with which she played upon him. The remote Irish in his blood had been responsive to the fresher strain in her.

"For God's sake, stop bawlin'!" he growled. "So you admit you lied, do you? Thought I had laid a trap for you, eh?"

It was difficult for him to realize that she was twenty-two and quite old enough to be held accountable for her sins. Her appeal to tears had always found him weak, but her declaration that she had suspected a trap when be began to quiz her was a trifle too daring to pass unchallenged. He repeated his demand that she sit up and stop crying.

"We may as well go through with this, Nan. I want to know what kind of an arrangement you have with Copeland. Are you in love with that fellow?"

"No!"

"Have you promised to marry him?"

"No!"

"Then why are you goin' places where you expect to see him?"

"I've explained that, papa," she replied with more assurance, finding that he did not debate her answers. "I didn't like to refuse Mrs. Kinney when I'd been refusing so many of her invitations. She asked me a while ago to come to her house to spend a week; and a little before that she wanted me to go on a trip with them, but you were sick and I knew you didn't like her, anyhow, so I refused. You've got the wrong idea about her, papa," she continued ingratiatingly. "She's really very nice. The fact that she hasn't been here long is against her with some of the older women, but that's just snobbishness. I always thought you hated the snobbishness of some of these people who have lived here always and are snippy to anybody else."

He was conscious that she was eluding him, and he gripped his hands with a sudden resolution not to be thwarted.

"I don't care a damn about the Kinneys; I'm talkin' about you and Copeland," he rasped impatiently.

"Very well, papa; I've told you all there is to know about that —"

MR. FARLEY BECOMES EXPLICIT

"I don't care what you say 'about that,'" he mocked; "that worthless scoundrel seems to have an evil fascination for you. I don't understand it; a decent young girl like you and a whiskey-soaked, loafin', gamblin' degenerate, who shook his wife — a fine woman — to be free to trail after you! That slimy wharf-rat has the fool idea that I took advantage of him when I sold him my interest in the store — and just to show you what a fool he is I'll tell you that I sold him my interest at a tenth less than I could have got from three other people — did it, so help me God, out of sheer good feelin', because he's the son of a father who'd given me a hand up, and I thought because he was a fool I wouldn't be just fair with him — I'd be generous! I did that for Sam Copeland's sake.

"That was four years ago, and I hadn't much idea then that he'd make good. He's already cashed in everything Sam left him but the store. And I've still got his notes for twenty-five thousand dollars — twenty-five thousand, mind you! — that he'd like damned well to cancel by marryin' you. A man nearly forty years old, who gambles and soaks himself in cocktails and runs after a feather-head like you while the business his father and I made the best in the State goes plumb to hell! Now, you listen to what I'm sayin': if you want to marry him, you do it, — you go ahead and do it now, for if you wait for me to die, you'll find he

won't be so anxious; there ain't goin' to be anything to marry you *for!*"

His voice that had been firm and strong at the
beginning of this long speech sank to a hoarse
whisper, but he cleared his throat and uttered his
last words with sharp distinctness.

"I never meant to; I never had any idea of
marrying him," she said. "And I've never thought
of the money. You can do what you like with it."

"Well, a man can't take his money with him to
the graveyard, but he can tie a pretty long string
to it; and it's my duty to protect you as long as I
can. I'd hoped you'd be married and settled before
I went. Your mamma and I used to talk of that;
you'd got a pretty tight grip on us; it could n't
have been stronger if you'd been our own; and I
don't want anything to spoil this, Nan. I want you
to be a good woman — not one of these high-flyin',
drinkin' kind, that heads for the divorce court, but
decent and steady. Now, I guess that's about all."

She stood beside him for a moment, smoothing
his hair. Then she knelt, as though from an acces-
sion of feeling, and took his hands.

"I'm so sorry, papa! I never mean to hurt you;
but I know I do; I know I must have troubled
mamma, too, a very great deal. And you've both
been so good to me! And I want to show you I appreciate it. And please don't talk of the money
any more or of my marrying anybody. I don't
want the money; I'm not going to marry: I want

us to live on just as we have been. You've been cooped up too long, but you're so much better now you'll soon be able to travel."

"No; there's no more travel for me; I'll be glad to hang on as I am. There's nothing in this change idea. About a year more's all I count on, and then you can throw me on the scrap-heap."

She protested that there were many more comfortable years ahead of him; the doctors had said so. At the mention of doctors his anger flared again, but for an instant only. It was a question whether he had been mollified by her assurances or whether the peace that now reigned was attributable to his satisfaction with the plans he had devised to protect her from fortune-hunters.

She hated scenes and trouble of any kind, and peace or even a truce was worth having at any price. She had grown so accustomed to the bright, smooth surfaces of life as to be impatient of the rough, unburnished edges. It was not wholly Nan's fault that she had reached womanhood selfish and willful. In their ignorance and anxiety to do as well by her as their neighbors did by their daughters, there had been no bounds to the Farleys' indulgence.

"I'm going to have dinner up here with you," she said cheerfully, after an interval. "I'm tired of eating alone downstairs with Miss Rankin; her white cap gets on my nerves."

She satisfied herself that this plan pleased him,

and ran downstairs whistling — then was up again in her room, where he heard her quick step, the opening and closing of drawers.

She faced him across the small table in the plainest of white frocks, with her hair arranged in a simple fashion he had once commended. She told stories — anecdotes she had gathered while dressing, from the back pages of "Life." He was himself a capital story-teller, though at the age when a man repeats, and she listened to tales of his steamboating days that she had heard for years and could have told better herself.

Soon a thunder-shower cooled the air, and made necessary the closing of windows, with a resulting domestic intimacy. The atmosphere was redolent of forgiveness on his part, of a wish to please on hers.

At nine o'clock, when she had finished reading some chapters from "Life on the Mississippi," — a book that he kept in his room, — and Miss Rankin appeared to put him to bed, he begged half an hour more. He had n't felt so well for a year, he declared.

"Look here, Nan," he remarked, when the nurse had retired after a grudging acquiescence, "I don't want you to feel I'm hard on you. I guess I talk pretty rough sometimes, but I don't mean to. But I worry about you — what's goin' to happen to you after I'm gone. I wish I'd gone first, so mamma could have looked after you. You know we set a lot by you. If I'm hard on you, I don't mean —"

MR. FARLEY BECOMES EXPLICIT

She flung herself down beside him and clasped his face in her hands.

"You dear old fraud! — there can't be any trouble between you and me, and as for your leaving me — why, that's a long, long time ahead. And you can't tell! I might go first — I have all kinds of queer symptoms — honestly, I do! And the doctor made me stop dancing last winter because my heart was going jigglety. Please let's be good friends and cheerful as we always have been, and I'll never, never tell you any fibs any more!"

She saw that her nearness, the touch of her hands, her supple young body pressed against his worn knees, were freeing the remotest springs of affection in his tired heart.

Nan wanted to be good — "good" in the sense of the word that had expressed the simple piety of her foster-mother. She had the conscience of her temperament and from childhood had often been miserable over the smallest infractions of discipline. Her last words with Copeland on the club veranda had not left her happy. It had been in her mind for some time that she must break with Billy. She had never been able to convince herself that she loved him. She had liked his admiration, and had overvalued it as coming from a man much older than herself; one who, moreover, stood to her as a protagonist of the gay world. No one but Billy Copeland gave suppers for visiting actors and actresses or chartered a fleet of canoes for a thousand-dollar picnic up the river. It was because he was different and amusing and made love to her with an ardor her nature craved that she had so readily lent herself to the efforts of the Kinneys to throw them together.

Being loved by Copeland, a divorced man rated "fast," had all the more piquancy for Nan as affording a relief from the life of the staid, colorless household in which she had been reared. There were those who, without being snobs, looked down just a little upon a girl who was merely an adopted child to whom her foster-parents gave only a shadowy background. The Farleys were substantial and respectable, but they were not an "old family." She was conscious of this, and the knowledge had made her the least bit rebellious and the more ready to surrender to the blandishments of the Kinneys, who were even more under the ban.

As she undressed and crept wearily into bed, she pondered these things, and the thought of them did not increase her happiness.

CHAPTER IV

NAN AND BILLY'S WIFE

FARLEY improved as the summer gained headway. He became astonishingly better, and his doctor prescribed an automobile in the hope that a daily airing would exercise a beneficent effect upon his temper. Farley detested automobiles and had told Nan frequently that they were used only by fools and bankrupts. A neighbor who failed in business that spring had been one of the first men in town to fall a victim to the motor craze, and Farley had noted with grim delight that three automobiles were named among the bankrupt's assets.

When the idea of investing in a machine took hold of him, he went into the subject with his characteristic thoroughness. He had Nan buy all the magazines and cut from them the automobile advertisements and he sent for his friends to pump them as to their knowledge of various cars. Then he commissioned a mechanical engineer to buy him a machine that could climb any hill in the State, and that was free of the frailities and imperfections of which his friends complained.

Farley manifested a childlike joy in his new plaything; he declared that he would have a negro chauffeur. It would be like old steamboat times, he said, to go "sailin' around with a nigger to cuss."

Nan or the nurse went out with him daily — preferably Nan, who was immensely relieved to find that they were now on better terms than for several years. Life had n't been a gay promenade since she ceased to share the festivities of the Kinneys and their friends. Copeland she had dismissed finally, and the rest of them wearied of calling her on the telephone only to be told that it was impossible for her to make engagements. It may have been 'that Farley realized that she was trying to meet his wishes; at any rate, she had no cause to complain of his kindness.

"This would have tickled mamma," he would say, as they rolled through the country in the machine. "She was always afraid of horses; these things don't seem half as risky when you get used to 'em. If I keep on feelin' better, we 'll take some long trips this fall. There 's a lot o' places I 'd like to see again. I 'd like to go down and take another look at the Ohio."

He spoke much of his wife, and at least once every week drove to the cemetery, and watched Nan place flowers on her foster-mother's grave.

After one of these visits he ordered the chauffeur to drive north. He had read in the papers of the sale of a farm at what he said was a record price for land in that neighborhood, and he wanted to take a look at the property. After they had inspected the farm and were running toward home, Nan suggested that they stop at the Country Club for a cool drink.

"Let's drive to Mrs. Copeland's place," he remarked casually. "I've always meant to look at her farm."

He watched her sharply, as though expecting her to object. Possibly he had some purpose in this; or the suggestion might be due to malevolence; but she dismissed any such idea. He was always curious about people, and there was, to be sure, no reason why he should not call on Mrs. Copeland.

"Certainly; I shall be very glad to go, papa," she answered.

"Nan," he said, laying his hand on her wrist, "there was never any trouble between you and that woman about Copeland, was there? If it's goin' to make you uncomfortable to stop at her house, why, we won't do it."

"Of course not, papa. I hope she understood that I couldn't help the gossip. It wasn't my fault."

"Well, it was nasty, anyhow," he remarked. "And as you've got rid of Copeland, it wouldn't be a bad idea to let her know it. I guess it won't be long before that worthless scamp goes to the dump. I've got a pretty good line on him and the store. If I was ten years younger, I'd go down there and kick him out and put the house on its feet again."

THE PROOF OF THE PUDDING

He had frequently told her that Copeland-Farley was doing badly, but she supposed this to be only the wail of a retired pilot who thinks his old ship is doomed to disaster without his hand at the wheel. No communications had passed between her and Billy since the day of Grace Kinney's party. She persuaded herself that she could face Billy Copeland's former wife with a good conscience.

"That hound," began Farley after an interval of silence, "had the brass to try to put her in the wrong — did n't dare go into court with it, but let it be whispered on the outside to save his own face! There was a man somewhere used to visit here, a friend of his. I guess nobody took any stock in that scandal."

"Of course, nobody would believe it of her," said Nan. "I hardly —"

She had begun to say that it was incredible that Billy would have done such a thing, but she caught herself in time.

"What?" demanded Farley sharply. "Well, I guess nobody but the lowest cur would have done it."

Mrs. Copeland's brown bungalow was set upon the highest point on her farm, and from her veranda and windows she could view every part of it. The veranda was made to be lived upon; there was a table with books and periodicals; a work-basket lay in a swing seat as though some one had just put it down; there were wall-pockets filled with fresh flowers. Along the veranda rail nasturtiums bloomed luxuriantly.

As Nan waited for an answer to her ring, the lower floor of the house lay plainly in view through the screen door: a large raftered living-room with a broad fireplace and a dining-room beyond. Here at least were comfort and peace. Perhaps Billy Copeland's wife had n't fared so ill after all!

The maid said Mrs. Copeland was out on the farm, and an observation from the veranda discovered her in the barn lot.

Nan had counted on Farley's presence to ease the shock of the meeting, and she did not wholly relish being sent off alone to meet a woman who might be pardoned for wishing to avoid her. Farley said he would wait in the car, and Nan left him contentedly studying the house and its encompassing landscape.

When Mrs. Copeland saw Nan approaching, she started across the lot to meet her. A handsome collie trotted beside her. She had not yet identified her visitor, and was flinging back an injunction to a workman as she moved toward the gate. She wore a dark skirt, blue waist, and heavy shoes, and a boy's round felt hat. A pair of shabby tan driving-gloves covered her hands.

"Good-afternoon!" said Nan. "Papa and I were passing, and he thought he'd like to see your place. If you're busy, please don't bother."

"Oh, I'm glad to see you, Miss Farley; I was just

coming to the house. My pump works badly and we are planning some changes. I'm glad Mr. Farley is able to be out again."

She set the pace with a quick, eager step. Several times she turned smilingly toward Nan; the girl saw no trace of hostility. To all appearances Fanny Copeland was a happy, contented woman. The tempests might vent their spite on her, but she would still hold her head high. Nan, little given to humility, experieced suddenly a disturbing sense of her inferiority to this woman whose husband she had allowed to make love to her.

"Yes, I get a great deal of fun out of the farm," Mrs. Copeland was saying. "I don't have any time to be lonesome; when there's nothing else to do, I can fuss around the garden. And now that I've taken up poultry there's more to do than ever!"

"I believe I'd get on better with chickens than with cows," said Nan. "They would n't scare me so much."

"Oh, cows are adorable! Are n't these in this pasture beauties!"

A calf thrust its head through the bars of the fence, and Fanny patted its nose. Nan asked if they all had names and Mrs. Copeland declared that naming the calves was the hardest part of her work.

"I think it's a mistake for a girl to grow up without knowing how to earn her own living, and I don't know a thing!" said Nan impulsively.

NAN AND BILLY'S WIFE

Fanny looked at her quickly. If it was in her mind that the obvious and expected thing for Nan to do was to marry Billy Copeland, she made no sign. Nan was amazed to find that she was anxious to appear to advantage before this woman who had every reason for disliking and distrusting her, and she was conscious that she had never seemed so stupid. Her modish gown, her dainty slippers with their silver buckles, contrasted oddly with Fanny's simple workaday apparel. She was self-conscious, uncomfortable. And yet Fanny was wholly at ease, talking light-heartedly as though no shadow had ever darkened her life.

They reached the house and found that Farley had braved the steps and established himself on the veranda. The maid had brought him a glass of milk which he was sipping contentedly while he ran his eye over a farm paper.

"Mrs. Copeland, what will you take for your place?" he demanded. "If I'd moved into the country when I quit business, the doctors would n't be doggin' me to death."

"But Miss Farley tells me you are almost well again! It's fine that you've taken up motoring — a new world to conquer every morning."

"I got tired o' bein' hitched to the bedpost; that's all. But I want to talk farm. It's a great thing for a woman to run a place like this and I want you to tell me all about it."

He examined and cross-examined her as to the

63

joys and sorrows of dairying. She replied good-
naturedly to most of his questions and parried the
others.

"Of course, I'm not going to tell you how much I
lose a year! Please keep it a dark secret, but I'm
not losing anything; and besides, I'm having a
mighty good time."

"Well," he warned her, "don't let it put you
in a hole. The place may be a leetle too fancy.
You don't want to make your butter too good;
your customers won't appreciate it."

"You preach what you never practiced," laughed
Nan. "Your rule at the store was to give full
measure."

"Well, I guess I held trade when I got it," he
admitted.

"I've been adding another department to the
farm," said Mrs. Copeland. "I started it early in
the summer in the old farmhouse back there that
was on the place when father bought it. Real
homemade canned fruit, pickles, and so on. I've
set up four girls who'd found life a hard business,
and they're doing the work with a farmer's wife to
boss them. It's my business to sell their products.
I've interested some of the farmers' daughters, and
they come over and help the regulars on busy days.
We're having a lot of fun out of it."

Farley was immensely interested. Nan had not
in a long time heard him talk so much or so ami-
ably; he praised and continued to praise Mrs. Cope-

land's enterprise and success; for he had satisfied himself fully that she was successful. He clearly liked her; her quiet humor, her grace and prettiness. In his blunt way he told her she was getting handsomer all the time. She knew how to talk to men of his type and met him on his own ground.

He began telling stories and referred to Old Sam Copeland half a dozen times, quite unconscious that the sometime daughter-in-law of Old Sam was sitting before him. Nan grew nervous, but Mrs. Copeland met the situation with perfect composure.

Finally, when they were about to leave, Eaton appeared. He had walked over from the Country Club merely, he protested, to refresh himself at Mrs. Copeland's buttermilk fountains. He addressed himself cordially to Farley, whose liking for him was manifest in a brightening of the old man's eyes. It was plain that Eaton and Mrs. Copeland were on the friendliest terms; they called each other by their first names without mincing or sidling.

Nan suspected that Eaton had come by arrangement and that in all likelihood he meant to stay for dinner; but already the lawyer was saying, as he saw Farley taking out his watch: —

"I'm going to beg a lift into town from you plutocrats. I thought I could stay me with flagons of buttermilk and catch the interurban that gallops by at five fifty; but I made a miscalculation and have already missed the car."

65

THE PROOF OF THE PUDDING

"I can send you in," said Mrs. Copeland, "if it is n't perfectly convenient for Mr. Farley."

"Of course Eaton will go with us," said Farley cordially. "It's time to move, Nan."

While Eaton helped him down the steps, Mrs. Copeland detained Nan for glimpses of the landscape from various points on the veranda.

"It was nice of you to stop; I think we ought to know each other better," said Fanny.

"Thank you!" said Nan, surprised and pleased. "It won't be my fault if we don't!"

As they crossed the veranda their hands touched idly, and Mrs. Copeland caught Nan's fingers and held them till they reached the steps. This trifling girlish act exercised a curious, bewildering effect upon Nan. She might have argued from it that Mrs. Copeland did n't *know* — did n't know that she was touching the hand of the woman who was accused of stealing her husband's affections.

"I don't see many people," Mrs. Copeland was saying; "and sometimes I get lonesome. You must bring your father out again, very soon. He can ride to the barn in his machine and see my whole plant."

"He would like that; he's one of your warmest admirers, you know."

"We always did seem to understand each other," she laughed; "probably because I always talk back to him."

"He's much gentler than he looks or talks; and he means to be kind and just," replied Nan, knowing in her heart that she had frequently questioned both his kindness and his justice. "I hope you will stop and see us, very soon. Papa's getting too much of my company; it would cheer him a lot to see you."

"I never make calls, you know," said Mrs. Copeland, smiling, "but I'm going to accept your invitation."

Bitterness and resentment, traces of which Nan had sought in this cheery, alert little woman, were not apparent. Her kindness and sweetness and tolerance, as of the fields themselves, impressed Nan deeply.

In saying good-bye Nan impulsively put out both hands.

"I wish we could be good friends!" she exclaimed.

Her face flushed scarlet the moment she had spoken, but Fanny's manner betrayed no agitation.

"Let's consider that we're already old friends," she responded, smiling into the girl's eyes.

CHAPTER V

A COLLECTOR OF FACTS

WHEN Jerry came in "off the road" Saturday, he found a note from Eaton asking him to call at his office that evening. To comply with this request, Jerry was obliged to forego the delights of a dance at the Little Ripple Club to which he had looked forward with the liveliest anticipations all the week. But Eaton was not, in Amidon's estimation, a person to whom one telephoned regrets with impunity, and at eight o'clock he knocked at Eaton's door on the fifteenth floor of the White River Trust Building and was admitted by the lawyer in person.

Eaton's office always exerted a curious spell on Jerry's imagination. This was attributable in some measure to the presence of cabinets filled with models of patentable and unpatentable devices — queer contrivances with each its story of some inventor's success or failure. The most perfect order was everywhere apparent. Books from the ample library were never strewn about in the manner of most law offices, and Eaton's flat-top desk in the last room of the suite was usually clear; or if papers were permitted to lie upon it, they were piled evenly and weighted with a smooth stone that was never visible unless in use. The file-cases (of the newest

68

and most approved type) contained not only letters, legal papers, and receipts, but, known to no one but the girl who cared for them, newspaper clippings and typewritten memoranda on a thousand and one subjects that bore no apparent relation to the practice of law.

Facts were Eaton's passion; with facts, one might, he believed, conquer the world; indeed, he was capable of demonstrating that all the battles in history were lost or won by the facts carried into the contest by the respective commanders. He had so often disturbed the office of the Commissioner of Patents with his facts that the public servants in charge of that department were little disposed to risk a brush with him on points that involved facts, facts that seemed, in his use of them, to glitter like the lenses of his eyeglasses.

He seated himself in his office chair — a leathern affair with a high back — and bade Amidon shed his coat and be comfortable.

"Smoke?" he suggested, opening a drawer containing cigars and cigarettes. Jerry hated readymade cigarettes, but he was afraid to produce the "makings" before Eaton, who had once complained that the odor of the tobacco he affected was suggestive of burning jimson weed. Eaton produced a glass ash-tray, and filled a pipe with the deliberation he brought to every act.

"Business is bad, I suppose, as usual," he remarked leadingly.

THE PROOF OF THE PUDDING

"Rotten! The shark that runs the credits has cut off one or two of my easiest marks; but I managed to end last month with a ten-per-cent advance over last year's business, and that helps some."

"You have spoken well, Amidon. I suppose you were received with joyous acclaim by the boss, and urged to accept a raise in wages?"

"Stop kidding me! I'm sensitive about my wages. They still pretend they're just trying me out — not sure I'll make good and that sort of piffle!"

"That sort of piffle" was a phrase he had taken over bodily from Eaton's familiar discourse. So sensitive was he to Eaton's influence that he imitated, with fair success, the unruffled ease that was second nature to the lawyer. He was also practicing Eaton's trick of blinking before uttering a sentence, and then letting it slip with a casual, indifferent air. Eaton had used this in the cross-examination of witnesses to good purpose. Amidon had exercised it so constantly in commercial and social conversation that he had to be on guard lest Eaton, whose discernment seemed to him to partake of the supernatural, should catch him at it and detect its spuriousness.

"Won a case somewhat in your line the other day; defended a trade-mark of the Pomona Velvet Complexion Cream, warranted to remove whole constellations of freckles in one night. Seductive

70

label, showing a lovely maiden unfreckling herself before a mirror; bottle of Pomona in her hand. Basely and clumsily imitated by a concern in Kansas that's been feloniously uttering a Romona Complexion Cream. The only original Pomona girl held the bottle in her right hand; label on Romona nostrum showed it clenched in her left."

"Hard luck!" said Amidon, deeply interested. "We've been pushing that Kansas beautifier — a larger discount for the jobber than the Pomona. Reckon we'll have to chuck it now. I suppose the judge did n't know Pomona removes the cuticle — has n't the real soothing effect of the Romona."

"I'll mention that to the district attorney and he can pass it on to the government inspectors. I'm annoyed by your revelation. Shock to my conscience — defending a company that poisons the young and beautiful of the republic."

"Now that you know what a swindle you defended, I suppose you'll turn back your fee — if you've got it?"

"Retainer of a thousand dollars," Eaton replied easily; "it would be immoral to return it, thus increasing the dividends of such an unscrupulous corporation. However, I'll consider giving half of it to the Children's Aid Society."

It was pleasant in any circumstances to sit in Eaton's presence, to enjoy his confidence; and yet nothing so far disclosed justified Jerry's relinquishment of the Little Ripple Club dance.

THE PROOF OF THE PUDDING

"Which of our noble streams did you follow this trip — the Pan-haunted Wabash or the mighty Ohio, sacred to the muses nine?"

Allusions of this sort, to which Eaton was prone, were Jerry's despair. He felt that it would be worth subjecting one's self to the discomforts of a college education to be able to talk like this, easily and naturally. But he was aware that Eaton was driving at something; and while it was the lawyer's way to lead conversations into blind alleys, he always arrived somewhere and fitted a key into the lock that had been his aim from the start.

"I shook hands with the trade along the Ohio this trip. I can tell you it's lonesome at night in those river burgs; the folks just sit and wait for the spring flood — and even *it* fails sometimes. They turn the reel once daily in the movies, and the whole town's asleep at nine-thirty."

"A virtuous and home-loving people, but crime occasionally disturbs the peace. Murders should always occur along navigable streams, so the victim can be sent cruising at once toward New Orleans and the still-vexed Bermoothes."

Amidon thought he caught a gleam; but experience had taught him the unwisdom of anticipating the unfolding of Eaton's purposes.

"Oh, there's always a lot of crooks loafing along the river; they keep their skins filled with whiskey and they fish and shoot muskrats and do a little murdering on the side."

A COLLECTOR OF FACTS

"Interesting type," said Eaton musingly. "If you were at Belleville this week, you must have heard of a murder down there — man found stabbed to death in a house-boat."

Jerry grinned, pleased with his own perspicacity in having surmised the object of the interview. Murder was not, Amidon would have said, within the range of Mr. John Cecil Eaton's interests; and yet this was not the first time that the lawyer's inquiries had touched affairs that seemed wholly foreign to his proper orbit.

"I was there the day after they found the body. They had already arrested the wrong man and turned him loose — as usual. They always do that; and they'll probably pick up some tramp who was visiting old college friends in New York when the murder was committed and indict him so the prosecuting attorney can show he's on the job."

"You shouldn't speak in that manner of sworn officers of the law," Eaton admonished. "Better that forty innocent men should be hanged than that one guilty man escape."

Jerry fidgeted nervously as Eaton's glasses were turned for a full minute upon the ceiling.

"A Cincinnati paper printed an item yesterday about that murder case, mentioning the arrest of a suspect at Henderson on the Kentucky shore." Eaton hesitated. "The suspect's name was Corrigan. You have known Corrigans, perhaps?"

There was a faint tinkle in the remote recesses

of Jerry's consciousness as the shot, so carelessly fired, reached the target.

"The name's common enough; I've known a number of Corrigans."

"But," the lawyer continued, "there have been instances of Corrigans ceasing to be Corrigans and becoming something else."

"You mean," Amidon replied, meeting Eaton's eyes as they were bent suddenly upon him, "that a Corrigan might become a Farley. Am I right?"

"Quite right. I was just wondering whether you had picked up anything about this particular case down along the river. I have no interest in it whatever—only the idlest curiosity. I happened to recall that Miss Farley had been a Corrigan; I have a note of that somewhere."

He swung his chair round and surveyed the file-cases back of him. His gaze fell upon a drawer marked *F*, as though he were reading the contents through the label — a feat which Amidon thought not beyond Eaton's powers.

Jerry resented the idea that Nan Farley might still be affected by the lawless deeds of any of her kinsfolk; he became increasingly uncomfortable the more he reflected that the lawyer, with all his indifference, would not be discussing this subject unless he had some reason for doing so.

"It was stated that this particular Corrigan had wealthy connections — that always sounds well in such news items, as though rich relations were a mitigating circumstance likely to arouse public sympathy. Mere snobbishness, Amidon; and snobbishness is always detestable. If that particular Corrigan hopes to obtain help from a sister now known as Farley, it occurred to me that I ought to possess myself of the fact. You understand that what we're saying to each other is entirely *sub rosa*. We've never happened to speak of Miss Farley; but having been connected with the Copeland-Farley Company before Farley retired, you probably have heard of her. A very interesting girl — slightly spoiled by prosperity, but really refreshingly original. Do you mind telling me whether you have any reason for believing that the particular Corrigan arrested down there as a suspect, and with those wealthy connections so discreetly suggested in the newspaper, is related in any way to Nan Farley?"

"Well, there was a Corrigan boy, considerably older than I am — probably about thirty now, and not much to brag of. I've asked about him now and then when I dropped off at Belleville, and I never heard any good of him — just about the kind of scamp that would mix up in a cutting scrape and get pinched."

"And who, having been pinched, — what we may call a pinchee, one who has been pinched, — might perhaps remember that he had a prosperous sister somewhere and appeal to her for help? Such things have happened; it would be very annoying for a young woman who had emerged — risen —

climbed away from her state of Corriganism, so to speak, to have her relationship with such a person printed in the newspapers of her own city. I merely wish to be prepared for any emergency that may arise. Not, of course, that this is any of my business; but it's remarkable how other people's affairs become in a way our own. Somebody has remarked that life is altogether a matter of our reciprocal obligations. There's much truth in that, Amidon."

Jerry did not wholly grasp this, but he confirmed it with a nod. Now that Nan Farley had been mentioned, he hoped Eaton would drop life's reciprocal obligations and talk of her; and he began describing his meeting with her, in such manner as to present his quondam schoolmate in the most favorable light.

Eaton listened to this recital with as much interest as he ever exhibited in anything that was said to him. He smiled at the young fellow's frank acknowledgment that it was in a spirit of the most servile imitation that he had gone forth with his fly-box. The ways in which Amidon aped him amused Eaton. He addressed him as "Amidon," or as "my dear Amidon," or "my dear fellow," and talked to him exactly as he talked to his cronies at the University Club; for while he was looked upon as an aristocrat, — the last of an old family that dated back to the beginnings of the town, — at heart he was the soundest of democrats. Jerry's meeting with Nan on the river bank seemed to him the most delightful of confrontations, and he sought by characteristic means to extract every detail of it.

"Well, sir, after she had been so nice and turned to go, she swung round and came back — actually came back to shake hands! I call that pretty fine; and me just a little scrub that was only a bunch of freckles and as tough a little mutt as ever lived when she used to know me. Why, if she'd said she never heard of me, she'd have put it over and I could n't have said a word!"

"She mentioned the meeting to me a little later," observed Eaton carelessly.

"Like thunder she did!" exploded Jerry. "So you knew all about it and let me go ahead just to kid me! Well, I like that!"

"Merely to get as much light on the subject as possible. We stumble too much in darkness; the truth helps a good deal, Amidon. Miss Farley spoke of you in terms that would not have displeased you. I assure you that she had enjoyed the interview; her description of it was flattering to your tact, your intuitive sense of social values. But it was all very sketchy — you've filled in important omissions. For instance, the giving of her hand, as an afterthought, was not mentioned; but I visualize it perfectly from your narrative. We may read into that act good-fellowship, graciousness, and all that sort of thing. She's a graceful person, and I can quite see her extending a perfectly gloved hand —"

THE PROOF OF THE PUDDING

"Wrong for once; she had n't on any gloves! But she had a handkerchief. It was drying on a bush."

"Ah! That is very important. Tears, perhaps? Her presence alone on the shore rather calls for an explanation. If she had gone down there by herself to cry, it is imaginable that life had n't been wholly to her taste earlier in the afternoon."

"She did n't look as though she had ever cried a tear in her life, and why should she?"

"The Irish," replied Eaton reflectively, "are a temperamental race. I had knowledge of her — remote but sufficient — before she sought the cool, umbrageous shore. Her companions were the gayest, and they doubtless bored her until a mood of introspection seized her — sorrow, regret, a resolve to do quite differently. Very likely you were a humble instrument of Providence to win her back to a good opinion of herself. So she seemed quite jolly and radiant? Conceivably your appearance caused her to think of her blessings — of her far flight from those scenes your presence summoned from the past."

"Well, she's a fine girl all right," Amidon commented to cover his embarrassment at being unable to follow Eaton in his excursion into the realm of psychology. "You would n't have thought that girl, born in a shack with as good-for-nothing folks as anybody ever had, would grow up to be about the finest living girl! I guess you'd hunt pretty hard before you'd find a girl to touch her."

A COLLECTOR OF FACTS

"I've thought of that myself, though not in quite your felicitous phrases."

"Don't rub it in!" Amidon protested. "I guess the less I think about a girl like that the better for me. And I guess there's plenty of fellows got their eye on her. I've heard some talk at the store about her and the boss."

"She doesn't lack admirers, of course. When you say 'boss,' you refer, I assume, to Mr. Copeland?"

Eaton looked up from the polishing of his glasses — a rite performed with scrupulous care. The vague stare of his near-sighted eyes, unprotected by his glasses, added to a disinterestedness expressed otherwise by his careless tone.

"Well," Amidon began, defensively, "Copeland is the boss, all right, — that is, when he's on the job at all. He's some sport, but when he calls me into his pen and goes over my orders, he knows whether I'm on the right side of the average. Only he doesn't do that with any of the boys more than once in two months. He doesn't quite get the habit; just seems to think of it occasionally."

"Capacity without application! Unfortunate, but not incurable. To be sure, an old business like Copeland-Farley is hard to kill. Billy Copeland's father had the constructive genius, and Farley had the driving power. It's up to Billy not to let the house die on his hands. Trouble is, the iron diminishes in the blood of a new generation: too easy a

79

time of it, soft-handed, loss of moral force, and that sort of thing."

"I guess Copeland travels a pretty lively clip, all right," ventured Amidon, not without a tinge of pride in his boss. "He and Kinney are pace-setters; they've got plenty of gasoline in the buggy and like to burn it. The boss may be a sport, but he's a good fellow, anyhow. I guess if he wants to marry Miss Farley he's got a right to."

He uttered this tamely, doubtful as to how his guide and mentor might receive it, but anxious to evoke an expression.

"A trifle weak, but well-meaning," remarked Eaton, as though he had been searching some time for a phrase that expressed his true appraisement of Copeland. "It's deplorable that fellows like that — who really have some capacity, but who are weak-sinewed morally — can't be protected from their own folly; saved, perhaps. Our religion, Amidon, is deficient in its practical application. A hand on your boss's shoulder at the right moment, a word of friendly admonition, might —er — save him from a too-wasteful expenditure of gasoline. If I had the gift of literary expression, I should like to write a treatise on man's duty to man. It's odd, Amidon," he went on, refilling his pipe, "that we must sit by — chaps like you and me — and see our brothers skidding into the ditch and never feel any responsibility about them. Doubtless you and I are known to many of our friends as weak mortals, in dire need of help, — or, perhaps, only a word of warning that the bridges are down ahead of us would suffice, — and yet how rarely do we feel that hand on the shoulder? We should be annoyed, displeased, hot clean through, if anybody — even an old and valued friend — should beg us to slow down. It's queer, Amidon, how reluctant we are to extend the saving hand. Timidity, fear of offending and that sort of thing holds us back. It becomes necessary to perform our Christian duty in the dark, by the most indirect and hidden methods."

Amidon frowned, not sure that he understood; and he hated himself when he did not understand Eaton. Not to grasp his friend's ideas convicted him of stupidity and ignorance. Religion in Amidon's experience meant going to church and being bored. He remembered that the last time he had visited a church he had gone to hear a girl acquaintance sing a solo. She sang very badly, indeed, and he had been depressed by the knowledge that she was spending for music lessons wages earned as a clerk at the soap and perfumery counter in a department store. Eaton's occasional monologues on what, for a better name, he called his friend's religion, struck him as fantastic; he was never sure that Eaton was n't kidding him; and the suspicion that you are being kidded by a man at whose feet you sit in adoration is not agreeable. But Eaton had become intelligible again.

"I've sometimes wondered whether Copeland

should n't be saved — a good subject for experiment, at least. To demonstrate that we have the courage of our convictions we must take a hard nut to crack. Queer thing, that religious effort, as we now see it, is directed solely to the poor and needy — the down-and-outers. Take a man of the day laborer type, the sort that casually beats his wife for recreation: gets clear down in the gutter, and the Salvation Army tackles his case — sets him up again; good work! Great institution — the Army. But you take the men who belong to clubs and eat course dinners; they don't beat their wives — only say upleasant things to them when the bills run too high; when such fellows get restless, absorb too much drink, neglect business, begin seeing their bankers in the back room — where's your man, society, agency, to put the necessary hand on that particular shoulder? What we do, Amidon, when we see such a chap turning up Monday morning with a hang-over from Saturday night, is to remark, 'Too bad about Tom' — or 'Dick' or 'Harry' — and then go to the club and order a cocktail. That's how we meet our reciprocal obligations!"

There seemed nothing that Amidon could add to this; but plainly it was "Billy" Copeland, who was in Eaton's mind, and no imaginary Tom, Dick, or Harry; so he ventured to remark: —

"Well, I guess the boss has n't let go yet; he'll pull up. He's the best man on the street to work for — when you can feel you *are* working for him."

A COLLECTOR OF FACTS

"Pleasanter to work for a boss than the boss's creditors, of course. And minor stockholders sometimes get anxious and cause trouble."

These utterances were like important memoranda jotted down on the margin of a page whose text is of little value in itself. Amidon stared blankly.

"Well, I don't know about that; I guess the house has always made money, We do more business than any other drug house in the State."

"An excellent business, of course. And we'd imagine that a man falling heir to it would take pride in holding on to it. But if he does n't, somebody else will take the job. I've seen the signs change on a good many business houses in my day. Your boss has taken several little flyers on the outside since his father died; he's rather fascinated with the idea of being vice-president of new concerns: minor trust companies, doubtful manufacturing schemes, and that sort of thing. All this is entirely in confidence; I'm using you as an incentive to thought. Kindly consider that my reflections are all *inter nos*. That murder business got us started — but of course, it has n't anything to do with your boss. It had occurred to me, though, that both you and I may have certain reciprocal obligations in some of these matters we have touched on. One never can tell where the opportunity to serve — to lay that friendly hand on a particular shoulder — may present itself!"

During a rather long silence Amidon pondered

this, wholly mystified as to just what he or John Cecil Eaton had to do with the affairs of William B. Copeland, a gentleman whose shoulder did not, on the instant, seem to present itself as a likely object for the laying on of hands. But Eaton was saying: —

"Coming to the matter of outside investments, there's Kinney's ivory cement. The Kinney Manufacturing Company's a client of mine, and it would n't be proper for me to express an opinion even to you, Amidon, on the stability of its patents."

"Well," said Amidon, "everybody thinks Kinney's making all the money there is; he'd have to, to put as much jam on his bread as he's spreading. I meet his road men now and then, and they sob because they can't fill orders. They're not looking for new business; they're shaking hands with the customers they've already got and telling 'em to sit at the freight house until the factory catches up with orders. And before he hit that cement, Kinney was bookkeeper in a brickyard!"

"Have a care, Amidon! You must be careful of your facts even in social conversation. Mr. Kinney had a small interest in a brickyard, which is very different. By the way, your opportunities for cultivating Mr. Copeland's acquaintance are rather restricted? Except on those rare occasions when he summons you to make sure your orders cover your expense account, you don't see much of him?"

84

A COLLECTOR OF FACTS

"Oh, he used to give me a jolly occasionally before I went on the road — ask me why our ball team was glued to the tail of the league and things like that. Once he asked me to look up a good chauffeur for him — and I got him a chap who'd been a professional racer. I guess that made a hit with him."

"An assumption not wholly unwarranted. I hope he finds the chauffeur satisfactory?"

"I guess he does; he must like him, for he bails him out about once a week when he gets pinched for speeding."

"Rather unfortunate that you're not an inside man, so you could observe the boss more closely; not, of course, to the extent of exercising an espionage — but it might be possible — er —"

"Well, I can have an inside job if I want it. My being on the road was just a try-out, and I'm not so keen about hopping ties with the sample-cases. If I'm going to tackle the reading you've laid out for me, I'll have to change my job. The head stock-man's quitting to go into heavy chemicals on his own hook; I guess I could get his place."

"Don't refuse it without full consideration. My attitude toward you thus far has been wholly critical; I've refrained from compliments; but it would interest me to — er — see what you can do with your brains. I suggest that you learn everything there is about the business outside and in: become indispensable, be tolerant of stupidity,

85

forbearing amid jealousy, and indifferent to con-
tumely; zealous, watchful, polite, without, let us
say, sissiness. Manners, my dear boy, are appraised
far too low in our commercial life."

The grin occasioned by these injunctions died on
Amidon's face as he realized that the lawyer was in
earnest; but he was very much at sea. Eaton was
a busy man, as his generous office space and the
variety of his paraphernalia testified; just why he
had sought an interview, for the sole reason, apparently, of extracting a little information and giving
a little advice, caused Amidon to wonder. He was
still wondering when Eaton rose and glanced at the
tiniest of watches, which he carried like a coin in his
trousers pocket and always looked at as though
surprised to find he had it.

"Time for me to be off; arguing a case in Pittsburg Monday."

He opened a bag that lay beside him on the floor,
pulled a packet from a drawer and dropped it in,
and told Jerry he might, if he had nothing better to
do, accompany him to the station.

CHAPTER VI

AN ERROR OF JUDGMENT

NAN stood at her window watching a man turn out of the walk that led from the front door to the street. Her eyes followed him until the hedge hid him from sight, and then she sat huddled in the window-seat, breathing hard from her run upstairs. She went to her desk and glanced at a page of the pass-book of a trust company that showed the withdrawal on June 29 of one thousand dollars from her savings account. There remained a balance of sixteen hundred, and she verified the subtraction before thrusting the book into the bottom of a drawer under a mass of invitations she meant at some time to file in a book she kept as a record of her social activities.

She knew that she had made a mistake, and she was considering the chances of discovery with a wildly beating heart. The man she had just closed the door upon had paid two calls on successive days. He had represented himself as the attorney for her brother, held on a charge of murder at Belleville. He had plausibly persuaded her that it was only fair for her to help her brother in his distress; that he was the victim of unfortunate circumstances, but that an investment of one thousand dollars for his defense would save her the humiliation of having one of her own flesh and blood convicted of a murder for which he was in no wise responsible. It had been intimated in discreet terms that her relationship to the prisoner could be hidden; it would even be denied if necessary.

She knew now that she should not have yielded; that in all fairness to her foster-father she should have reported this demand to him. In secretly giving money that represented Christmas and birthday gifts through half a dozen years, for the defense of a man she had not heard of since the beginning of her life with the Farleys, she justified herself with the thought that it was kinder to her foster-father, in his invalid condition, to keep the matter from him. She experienced a sudden revulsion of feeling the moment the money passed from her hands in the ten one-hundred-dollar bills the man had specified.

Farley had been seeing much of his lawyer since the row over the Kinney luncheon. While his wrath at her duplicity seemed to pass, she assumed that he had not forgotten his threat to disinherit her if she married Copeland.

She was unwontedly attentive, spending much time reading to him or playing cards. She knew that he liked having young people about, and she asked to his room some of the girls and young men who called on her. She exercised all her arts, which were many, to keep him cheerful, and if he realized that the change had been abrupt, and that it dated from his outburst against Copeland, he made no sign. She must n't stay in too much, he said; he did n't want to be a burden to her.

Eaton had called shortly after his talk with her on the golf links, but on a night when Farley was receiving the attentions of his masseur. He had spent the evening and had been at pains to make himself agreeable. Now that Copeland had been thrust into the background, it occurred to her that Eaton was worth cultivating. We all maintain more or less consciously a mental list of people on whom we feel that we may rely in difficulties; it had occurred to Nan that in a pinch Eaton would be a friend worth having.

While it was wholly unlikely that Farley would ever learn of her transaction with the stranger, it was nevertheless a possibility that would hang over her as long as he lived. She sought comfort in the reflection that the amount was small, and that Farley had never stinted her; moreover, that it was her own money, subject to her personal check; but there was little consolation to be had from such reasoning. She must talk to some one, and before dinner she telephoned Eaton and asked him to come up.

Farley had spent two hours with his lawyer that day, and from the fact that two of his old friends had arrived hurriedly in answer to telephonic summons, she judged that he had been making a new will and that these men had been called to witness it.

He ate his prescribed supper, grumbling at its slightness, and watched her consume her ampler meal with his usual expressions of envy at her appetite.

"If I could eat like that, I'd be well in a week; it's all rubbish, this infernal diet!"

" But we tried disobeying the doctor the other night when the nurse was out, and you did n't sleep a wink. You'll have to be good until the doctor discharges you!"

"Don't be silly!" he snapped. "They know mighty well they can't cure me; they're just hangin' on to me as long as they can for what they get out of it. But I may fool 'em yet! My grandfather lived to be ninety and died then from bein' kicked by a horse; and my own father got up to seventy-eight, and that gives me eight years more," he ended defiantly.

"But you worked harder than they did, papa; you never used to come home to dinner until seven."

"Of course I did n't!" he flared. "These young fellows that think four hours make a day's work are fools; you won't see them gettin' very far in the world, spendin' their time flyin' around in automobiles and playin' golf all day!"

"Well, of course, some of the young men don't amount to much," she admitted conciliatingly;

"but there are others who work like nailers. I suppose Mr. Eaton works as hard as any man in town; and he does n't need to."

"Does n't need to?" Farley caught her up. "Every honest man works; a man who does n't work 's a loafer and very likely a blackguard. John Eaton works because he has the brains to work with! He's a rare man, John Eaton. There ain't many men like John, brought up as he was, with everything easy; but he's bucklin' down to hard work just the same, like the man he is. You say he's comin' up? Well, we'll let him do the talkin'. Maybe he can get a laugh out o' me; he says some mighty funny things — and they're mostly true."

⸳ He began feeling about for the evening paper that he had dropped at his side when his tray was brought in.

"Just find the market page and read through the local stock list. I noticed they've put a new figure on White River Trust; I used to be a director in that company. What's that? Two hundred eighty-five? Let me see, that's fifteen dollars more than it was last January when I bought fifty shares at two-seventy. She'll go three hundred in five years. It's the safest buy in town."

His long conference with his lawyer had left him tired and irritable. His doctor had repeatedly counseled Nan and the nurse to keep him quiet. As they seemed to be on perfectly safe ground, she began reading the financial comment preceding the general stock and bond list, and finding that he was interested, she followed it with the letter of a firm of brokers that buoyantly prophesied a strong upward movement in the immediate future. She thought he was listening attentively when he began murmuring half to himself: —

"Two-eighty-five; she's bound to go to three hundred. Hey? What's that rubbish you're readin'? Wall Street letter? What do I care what a lot of infernal gamblers say about a better tone in the market! Those fellows down there don't produce anything; it's the boys out here that grow the corn and feed the pigs that put value in the paper those fellows down there gamble in! Put that paper down; I want to talk a little business. How much money you got?"

The question was like a blow in the face. Her wits danced nimbly in her effort to find an answer, to decide just how to meet the issue.

"Do you mean the housekeeping money?" she asked faintly.

Since Mrs. Farley's death she had paid the household bills from a sum deposited to her credit the first of every month. Beyond asking occasionally how the bills were running, Farley had never questioned her as to her expenditures. There was a special allowance and a generous one for her clothing, and when she asked for additions to the household money to renew linen or pay for repairs, it was always readily forthcoming.

AN ERROR OF JUDGMENT

"No, no!" he ejaculated impatiently. "I don't mean the house money. How much you got in the trust company — the savings you've been gettin' three per cent on? You must have over two thousand dollars there. I been meanin' to ask you about that; you've got too much to keep at three per cent, and we ought to put it into securities of some kind. Run along and get your pass-book. If you have n't got enough to buy ten shares of White River Trust stock, I'll bring it up a little so you can have an even number."

He was absorbed in mental calculations and did not notice the reluctance with which she rose and walked toward her room. The trust company required that books be presented when withdrawals were made, and she remembered the appearance of the teller's notation. Farley had never looked at her pass-book since the day she brought it home and proudly displayed it. It was the unkindest fate that had turned his mind upon it at this juncture, and she canvassed all possible explanations: necessary expenditures in excess of her household and personal accounts; unusual repairs which she might pretend she had not wanted to trouble him with in his illness; or benevolences — the latter, she fancied, more likely to appease than the others in view of his own generosity to causes that appealed to him. She decided that a frank confession followed by an appeal to sentiment was the likeliest means of staying his anger.

THE PROOF OF THE PUDDING

She waited twisting her hands nervously, while he examined the book.

"What's this? What's this mean, Nan? You took out a thousand dollars in one lump — to-day! My God, what does this mean? What kind of investments you makin', Nan? Yesterday you had with interest — lemme see — twenty-six hundred dollars, and now you've cut it down to sixteen hundred! What you spendin' that money for, girl?"

"Well, papa," she began with the best air of frankness she could summon, "something very strange and sad has happened. I meant to tell you all about it just as soon as you were stronger, but I'm glad to tell you now, for I know you will understand and sympathize — as you've always done whenever I've had my little troubles —"

He seemed to be taking this in good part until "troubles" caused him to sniff.

"Troubles! What troubles you ever had? I guess there ain't a girl in town that's had less trouble than you have!"

"Of course, I did n't mean it that way, papa; I mean only the little things, little mistakes and slips I've made that you and mamma have always been kind about. No girl was ever treated as kindly as you have treated me. And I mean always to be perfectly frank with you; and I'm going to be now."

"Well," he said impatiently.

94

AN ERROR OF JUDGMENT

She felt that her contemplated explanation had been well chosen, but she must be adroit, risking no word that might spoil the effect of her disclosure.

She knelt beside him and began in a tone that was eloquent of humility, yet with a confidence that she hoped would not be lost upon him.

"You see, papa, when you brought me home with you, and you and mamma began caring for me, I was just a poor little waif, ready for an orphan asylum. My father and mother would never have been able to do anything for me if they had lived; and if it had n't been for you and mamma, I 'd never have known any of the things I 've learned through you. I might have been a dining-room girl right now in some cheap hotel if you had n't opened your doors and your hearts to me. And that has made me appreciate my blessings — all the comforts and luxuries you have given me. And it has made me feel, more than you may imagine, for people not so lucky as I am — the under dog that gets kicked by everybody. And even when people are wicked and do evil things, I think we ought to think kindly of them and help them when we can. I know you and mamma always practiced that. And I 've tried to; I really have!"

She lifted her eyes and there were tears in them, that seemed to be born of a deep compassion, a yearning toward all the poor and erring among mankind. Farley was not unmoved by this demonstration; he shifted his legs uneasily under the light

95

pressure of her arms. Her spell upon him had never been more complete; she felt that she might risk much in the mood to which she had brought him.

"And you know, papa, I have thought a great deal about my brother — who drifted away with the flood. I have n't seen him since father and mother died. Tom is much older than I am, and the poor boy never had any chance. I had n't even heard of him since you brought me away until the other day. And he's in trouble, very deep, serious trouble, papa; he's been arrested — I'm sure not for anything he really did; but being poor and without friends it was perfectly natural for him to ask me to help him. I think you will agree to that. And he sent his lawyer to ask me for money to use in defending him. I meant to tell you all about it when you were well; I felt sure I was doing right and that you'd be glad to have me help him; and it's all so horrible —"

She felt his form grow rigid, felt his hands roughly push her away, as he blurted hoarsely: —

"Blackmail! My God, it's blackmail — or else you're lyin' to me!"

She rose and faced him tearfully.

"It's the truth!" she declared. "He's my brother — the only one of my family that's left. You would n't have me refuse to help —"

"Help him! Turn a thousand dollars of your savings over to a worthless whelp that's got into jail! How do you know he's your brother? — a

96

man that waits all these years before he shows
himself and then plumps down on you for a
thousand dollars! I tell you it's blackmail, blackmail! And you hide all this from me just as though
I had n't any right to know what kind o' trouble
you get mixed up in! Ain't you got sense enough to
know you're touchin' bottom when you give up
money that way? What's he threatened you with?
You tell me everything there is to know about this,
and I'll find out mighty quick whether a contemptible scoundrel can come to my house and
carry away a thousand dollars!"

Farley glared at her unpityingly while she told
her story, which seemed preposterously weak when
reduced to plain terms. She sobbingly admitted
her fear of newspaper notoriety, her wish to shield
him from the shame of her connection with a man
awaiting trial for murder. There was no mercy in
his eyes; he was outraged that she had again deceived him.

"Afraid o' havin' your name in the papers, were
you? Just as though blackmailers did n't always
use that club on the fools they rob! And how many
times do you think a man like that will come back,
now he knows you're easy — now you've gone into
business with him?"

The maid knocked at the door and announced
Eaton, but Farley gave no heed.

"Payin' blackmail! You've got yourself into a
nice mess! And after all I've done to protect you

97

and make a decent woman of you, you're scared to death of havin' some of your relations go to jail — just as though you had n't turned your back on the whole set when we brought you here and gave you our name. That *ought* to have made you respectable, if it did n't! Afraid of newspapers, afraid of jackleg lawyers! It's the rottenest case of blackmail I ever heard! And here I've been proud to think that we'd pulled you out of the river mud and made a high-minded woman of you, that could stand up with any girl anywhere!"

She waited listening to his deep breaths, watching his tremulous hands; and then without attempting to answer his indictment, she said meekly: —

"Of course, it was a mistake, papa. I ought to have told you about it; but it's my trouble —you must remember that! The shame of the exposure would be something I'd have to bear alone; that was the way I looked at it; and I did n't want you to have the worry of it when you were just beginning to get well."

His thoughts had wandered away from her, playing about her offense in its practical and legal aspects. When she ventured to remind him of Eaton's presence in the house, he made no reply. The silence became intolerable and she stole from the room.

CHAPTER VII

WELCOME CALLERS

NAN decided to explain to Eaton that Farley's illness had taken a turn for the worse and that he had been abusing her as a relief from his suffering. She was surprised to find two men in the parlor, the second of whom she did not at once recognize as Jerry.

"I've taken the liberty," Eaton began, "of bringing Mr. Amidon along. Thought you would n't mind, particularly as I could n't have come myself without him. He dropped in just as I was leaving and seemed greatly depressed; I had n't the heart to leave him. Depression is his normal state — no serenity, no hope, no vision!"

Amidon grinned during this explanation, realizing that its lack of veracity was, in the circumstances, peculiarly Eatonesque and attributable to his friend's wish to relieve Nan of embarrassment. They had been uncomfortable from the moment the maid admitted them and they became conscious of the discord above. Words and phrases of Farley's furious arraignment had reached them and there was no escaping the conclusion that she had been the object of the castigation. Jerry, acting on his own impulses, would have grabbed his hat and bolted. It was only the demeanor of his idol, placidly staring at the wall, that held him back. The call had been suggested by Eaton as a gay social adventure, but it was disconcerting to find a girl whose good fortune had seemed so enviable with tears in her eyes, nervously fingering a moist handkerchief, and Jerry's wits were severely taxed by his efforts to meet a situation without precedent in his experience. Once he had called on a girl whose father came home drunk and manifested an ambition to destroy the furniture and use the pieces in the chastisement of his daughter, and Amidon had enjoyed a brief, decisive engagement with the inebriated parent and had then put him to bed. But there was nothing in that incident that bore in the slightest degree upon the difficulties of people who lived in the best street in town, where, he had always assumed, the prosperous householders dwelt in peace and harmony with their fortunate families.

"I'm glad to see you, both of you," she said, with all the assurance she could muster. "Papa's been having a bad time; you must have heard him talking. He's very angry. I wish you'd go up, Mr. Eaton, and see if you can't talk him into a better humor."

"If you think it's all right —" Eaton began dubiously; but he was amused at Nan's cheerful willingness to turn her angry foster-parent over to him for pacification. It was like Nan!

"Oh, he'd been looking forward to seeing you,"

she answered quite honestly. "These spells don't
last long; the very sight of you will cheer him."

She did not, however, offer to accompany him to
Farley's room, but discreetly left him to test the
atmosphere for himself.

"Well," Jerry remarked, when he was alone with
Nan, "Pittsburg put it over on New York to-day.
Three to nothing!"

He gave the score with a jubilant turn to the
"nothing," as though Pittsburg's success called for
universal rejoicing.

Nan, intent upon catching some hint of the nature of Eaton's reception, merely murmured her
mild pleasure in this news. She was satisfied, from
the calm that reigned above, that Eaton had begun
well, and that under the spell of his presence Farley
would soon be restored to tranquillity.

"Sorry Mr. Farley is having a bad time," Jerry
went on, thinking the invalid's outbreak required
at least a passing reference. "You know down at
the store the boys still talk about him. Somebody's
always telling how he used to do things, and the
funny things he used to say. When I first struck
the plant, he used to scare me to death, sticking
his nose in the shipping-room without notice and
catching the boys larking. Once I had gone to the
mat with a plumber that was looking for a gas-
leak, and the boss came in and got us both by the
collar and threw us down the stairs like a pair of
old shoes. I thought I was a goner for sure when he

sent for me to come to the office that night and asked me who started the trouble. I told him the plumber said whenever he found gas-leaks in job-bing houses he always reckoned somebody was get-ting ready to collect the insurance. Uncle Tim — that's what the boys call him — asked me if I'd hit him hard, and I told him I guess he'd have consid-erable business with the dentist, all right. Just for that he raised my wages a dollar a week! Say, can you beat it!"

He snapped his fingers and shook his head im-patiently.

"Is n't that rank — just after Cecil lectured me all the way up here about cutting out slang! I promised him solemnly before we started that I would n't say *say;* and here I've already done it! How do you learn to talk like white folks, anyhow? I suppose you got to be born to it; it must be like swimming or rowing a boat, that you learn once and always catch the stroke right."

"Oh, I should n't worry about that," replied Nan consolingly. "I use a good deal of slang myself; and at school my English teacher said it was n't such a sin if we used it as though we were quoting — we girls held up two fingers — so!"

"That sounds reasonable, all right; I must tell my noble knight about that. It seems sometimes as though I just could n't get a ball over the plate — there I go again! And Cecil warned me specially against talking like a bleacher hoodlum when we got here."

"Oh, that's not worth bothering about. I'm so glad to see you that I could cry for joy. If you had n't come when you did, I don't know what might have happened."

He had been trying to direct the talk into other channels, and her remark puzzled him. That this wholly charming, delightful Nan could have given her benefactor cause for the objurgations he had heard poured out upon her was unbelievable. Still, it was rather pleasant than otherwise to find that she was human, capable of tears, and it was not less than flattering that she should invite his sympathy.

"Well," he began cautiously, "I guess we all have our troubles. Life ain't such an easy game. You think you're sailing along all right, and suddenly something goes wrong and you've got to climb out and study astronomy through the bottom of the machine. Why," he continued expansively, finding that he had her attention, "when I first went on the road I used to get hot when I struck some mutt who pulled lower prices on me or said he was over-stocked. But you don't sell any goods by getting mad. I picked up one of these 'Keep Smiling' cards somewhere, and when I got blue I used to take a sneaking look at it and put on a grin and tell the stony-hearted merchant the funniest story I could think of and prove that our figures f.o.b.

Peanutville were cheaper, when you figured in the freight, than Chicago or Cincinnati prices. I've made a study of freight tariffs; I can tell you the freight on white elephants all the way from Siam to Keokuk and back to Bangkok. I've heard the old boys down at the store talk about Farley till I know all his curves. Farley's all right; there's nothing the matter with Uncle Tim; only — you don't want to shift gears on him too quick. You've got to do it gentle-like."

Nan smiled forlornly, but Amidon was glad that he could evoke any sort of smile from her.

"It was all my fault," she said. And then with a frankness that surprised her she added: "I had deceived him about something and he caught me at it. He gave me a big blowing-up, and I deserved it."

"Well, I wouldn't say *that;* but, of course, playing the game straight was always a big card with him. I guess Cecil will smooth him down."

She was surprised to find herself talking to him so freely; his eagerness to take her mind away from the unpleasant episode with Farley gave her a comforting sense of his native kindliness. Her heart warmed with liking for him as she reappraised his good looks, his well-scrubbed appearance of a boy turned out for his first party by a doting mother; his general air of wholesomeness and good humor. He had known hard knocks, she did not question, but the bruises were well hidden. With all his slanginess and volubility there was a certain high-mindedness about him to which, in her hunger for sympathy, she gave fullest value.

He was afraid of her further confidences; afraid that she would disclose something she would regret later, and this he foresaw might embarrass their subsequent relations. She had been humiliated by Farley's abuse, and it was not fair, he argued, to take advantage of her present state of mind by allowing her to tell more of the trouble. But he was not able at once to change the current of her thoughts.

"You know," she said, sitting up straight and folding her hands on her knees, " I've been thinking a lot of things since I saw you out there by the river — about old times, and wondering whether it was good or bad luck that took me away from Belleville and brought me up here. I'd have been better off if I'd stayed there. I'd probably have been washing dishes in the Belleville hotel if the Farleys had n't picked me up, a dirty little beggar, and tried to make something decent out of me! I'm saying that to you because you know all about me. You've made your own way, and you're a lot happier than I am, and you're not under obligations to anybody; and here I am trying to climb a ladder my feet were n't made for!"

"Cut all that out!" he expostulated. "Just because Uncle Tim's been a little fretful, you need n't think everything's gone to the bow-wows. And as for staying in Belleville, why, the thought of it gives me shivers! There ain't any use talking about that."

Her face expressed relief at the vigor with which he sprang to her defense, and he plunged ahead.

"Say, speaking of dining-room girls, there was a girl at that Belleville hotel that was some girl for sure. She was fruit to the passing eye, and a mutt carrying samples for a confectionery house called her Gladys one day, her real name being Sarah, and asked her how she'd like going to the movies with him after she got the dishes washed; and she landed one order of poached cold-storage eggs on his bosom the neatest you ever saw. Some men never learn how to size up character, and any fool could 'a' told that that girl was n't open to a jolly from a sweet-goods peddler who'd never passed that way before. Sarah's mother owns the hotel, and Sarah only helps in the dining-room Saturday nights to let the regular crockery-smasher off to punch the ivories for the Methodist choir practice. I was sitting next that chap and he thought he'd show me what a winner he was. I'm not justifying Sarah's conduct, and about a half-portion of the golden side of that order caught me on the ear. I merely mention it to show you that you had better not think much of the life of the dining-room girl, which ain't all the handbills make out."

"I hope," remarked Nan, "that she did n't break the plate!"

"No more," he came back promptly, "than you could break a ten-dollar bill at a charity fair. That's another thing I learned from Cecil. He got me to take a stroll with him through a charity bazaar last winter — just to protect him from the snares of the huntress, he said. He started in with ten tens and had to borrow five I was hiding from my creditors before we got back to the door. And all we carried out of the place was a pink party-bag Cecil handed a tramp we found freezing to death outside and hoping a little charity would ooze through the windows."

"I was at the fancy-work counter at the fair," said Nan, "and I remember that Mr. Eaton bought something. I did n't see you, though."

"I noticed that you did n't; I was plumb scared you might! There I go again! *Plumb scared!* Oh, Cecil, if you had heard me then! "

He was wondering just how he happened to be sitting in a parlor on a fashionable street, talking to the only girl he had ever known whose name figured in the society columns, quite as jauntily as he talked with any of the stenographers or salesgirls he knew. He was confident that parlor conversation among the favored of heaven was not of the sort he had, in his own phrase, been "handing out." This thought gave him pause. He shook his cuffs from under the sleeves of his blue serge coat with a gesture he had caught from Eaton, and felt nervously of the knot of his four-in-hand.

THE PROOF OF THE PUDDING

Nan was asking herself whether the fact that a young fellow of Amidon's deficiencies could interest and amuse her was n't pretty substantial proof that he was the kind of young man the gods had designed for her companions. A year ago she would have resented his appearance in the house; to-night she had a feeling that his right to be there was as sound as her own. A different fling of the dice, and it might have been he whom the Farleys rescued from poverty and obscurity.

In spite of his absurdities, she was conscious of definite manly qualities in him. Several times she caught him scrutinizing her sharply, as though something about her puzzled him and gave him concern. His manners were very good — thanks, perhaps, to his adored Eaton; and she liked his clean, fresh look and good humor. After her talk with Eaton on the golf links, she had wondered whether the lawyer was n't making a butt of him; but she dismissed this now as unjust to Eaton, and as appraising Amidon's intelligence at too low a figure. During this reverie he waited patiently for her to speak, imagining that her mind was still upon her troubles, and when the silence became prolonged he rallied for a fresh attack.

"If you'd rather read," he remarked, "we'll hang up the silence sign the way they have it in the library reading-room and I'll say prayers till Cecil comes down."

"Oh, pardon me!" she laughed contritely. "You

see I am treating you as an old friend. Why don't
you go on and talk. You've had ever so many interesting adventures, and I need to be amused.
Please don't think I'm always like this; I hope
you'll see me some time when I'm not in the
dumps."

"I should be afraid to," he retorted boldly; and
then feeling that Eaton would have spurned such
banality, ejaculated: "Oh, rot! Let me scratch that
out and say something decent. Just for instance,"
— and his face sobered, — "I think you're nice!
You were perfectly grand to me that day down on
the river. I told Cecil about that, and I could see
it made a hit with him; it set me up with him —
that a girl like you would be polite to a scrub
like me."

"Don't be foolish," she said. "I'm not proud of
myself: I'm a failure, a pretty sad fizzle, at that."

She ignored his rapid phrases of protest and
asked him how much time he spent in town.

"Well, I'm likely to spend a good deal, from now
on. The boss has been shaking things up again, and
he called me in by telephone yesterday and changed
my job. That's the way with him; he won't show
up sometimes for six weeks, and then he gets down
early some morning and scares everybody to death.

"I thought I was settled on the road for the rest
of my life, and now he's made a job for me to help
the credit man — who does n't want me — and
take country customers out to lunch. A new job

made just for my benefit. And all because of a necktie Cecil gave me. The boss saw me sporting it one day and asked me where I got it. I had to make a show-down, and he thought I was kidding him. You see Cecil's about the last man he'd ever think of giving me presents. If I'd laid that necktie on any other living human being, it would n't have cut a bit of ice; but when I said, as fresh as paint, 'John Cecil Eaton picked that up in New York for me,' he laughed right out loud. 'What's the joke?' I asked him; and he says, 'Oh, Eaton never gave me any haberdashery, and I've known him all my life.' And like the silly young zebra I am, I came back with, 'Well, maybe that's the reason!' You'd have thought he'd fire me for that; but it seemed to sort o' make us better acquainted. He's the prince, all right!"

She had been trying, more or less honestly, to put Copeland out of her mind. Her knowledge of him as a business man had been the haziest; one never thought of Billy Copeland as a person preoccupied with business. She was startled when Amidon asked abruptly: —

"Of course, you know the boss?"

It was possible that Amidon had heard the gossip that connected her name with his employer's, and she answered carelessly: —

"Oh, yes; I know Mr. Copeland."

"I guess everybody knows William B.," said Amidon. "He's got the pep — unadulterated cay-

enne; he is n't one of these corpses that are holding
the town back. He's a live wire, all right."

Then, realizing that he had ventured upon thin
ice in mentioning Copeland, he came back to shore
at once.

"Cecil said that this being my first call, about
thirty minutes would do for me, so I guess it's time
for me to skid. He must be handing out a pretty
good line of talk on the upper deck."

She begged him not to leave her alone, saying
that Farley lived by rules fixed by his doctor and
that the nurse was likely to interrupt the call at
any minute. As he stood uncertain whether to go
or wait for Eaton, they heard the lawyer saying
good-bye, and in a moment he came down.

Nan looked at him quickly, but was able to read
nothing in his impassive face.

"I hope you two have been getting better acquainted," Eaton remarked. "Mr. Farley and I
have had a splendid talk; I never found him more
amusing. One of the most interesting men I ever
knew! What have you been talking about? The
silence down here has been ominously painful!"

"Mr. Amidon has been telling me of the egg-
throwing habits of the waitresses in my native town.
Life here in the city is nothing to what it is down
on the river. He's almost made me homesick!"

"My dear Amidon," said Eaton severely, "have
you been telling that story — in a private house?
I thought when I brought you here you'd be on

your good behavior. I'm sorry, Nan; I apologize for him. Of course, he must n't come back; I'll see to it that he does n't."

"Don't be cruel!" laughed Nan. "We got on beautifully!"

They heard Farley's groans and mutterings as the nurse put him to bed, and it seemed necessary to refer to him again before the men left.

"You won't mind, Nan," said Eaton, "if I say that Mr. Farley told me the cause of your little difficulty; I know the whole story. I think he probably won't mention it to you again. I asked him not to. Just go on as though nothing had happened. It was unfortunate, of course; but I've persuaded him that your conduct is pardonable — really quite admirable from your standpoint. If anything further arises in regard to it, I wish you'd communicate with me, immediately."

Ignoring her murmurs of gratitude, he turned to Jerry.

"Amidon, at this point we shake hands and move rapidly up the street. And, Nan, you need n't be troubled because Mr. Amidon heard the last echoes of your difficulty. He's perfectly safe, — discreet, wise, — though you'd never guess it. You may safely assume that he heard nothing. We must have some golf, you and I. My game's coming up!"

She went with them to the street door, where Amidon, in executing a final bow, nearly fell backward down the steps.

CHAPTER VIII

MRS. COPELAND'S GOOD FORTUNE

Now that they had the car, Farley insisted that Nan should go to market. His wife, like all the thrifty housewives of the capital, had always gone to market, and he thought the discipline would be good for Nan. He liked to accompany her and watch the crowd while she was doing her errands.

One Saturday, as Nan returned to the machine, with the chauffeur following with the basket, she found Fanny Copeland seated in the car beside Farley.

"Look here, Nan; I've picked up a surprise for you! We're goin' to take Mrs. Copeland home to lunch."

"I don't know whether you are or not," said Mrs. Copeland. "This is my busiest day and I've got to catch the twelve-o'clock interurban for the farm."

"Don't worry about that; we'll send you home all right," said Farley.

"Then I'm not going to have anything to say about it at all!" laughed Mrs. Copeland. "All right; if my cows die of thirst, I'll send you the bill."

"You do that, and it will be paid," Farley assented cheerfully.

THE PROOF OF THE PUDDING

"But I've got to stop at the bank a moment —"

"I suppose," said Nan, "you want to get rid of the money I just paid at your stand for two yellow-legged chickens — you can see the legs sticking out of the basket."

Mrs. Copeland had failed to act upon Nan's invitation to call upon her — a delinquency to which she referred now.

"I really meant to come, but I've been unusually busy. I carry on just enough general farming to be a nuisance; and dairying requires eternal vigilance."

"That's because you've got a standard," said Farley, with his blunt praise. "You've got the best dairy in Indiana. The state inspectors have put it strong."

"Oh," said Mrs. Copeland lightly, "they gave me a better report than I deserve just for being a poor, lone woman!"

Farley's admiration for Mrs. Copeland was perfectly transparent. It was Fanny's efficiency, her general competence, Nan reflected, quite as much as her good looks and cheerfulness, that attracted her foster-father. Several times lately he had quoted what Bill Harrington, the banker, had said of her — that she was the best business man in town. And there was also Farley's contempt for Copeland, which clearly accentuated his liking for Billy's former wife.

At the bank door Farley remembered that he had a check to cash and asked Nan to attend to it for him. As Mrs. Copeland and Nan mounted the bank steps together, they ran into Billy Copeland emerging in deep preoccupation. The juxtaposition of the two women plainly startled him. He took off his hat, mumbled something, and stood staring after them. Then his gaze fell upon Farley, bending forward in the touring-car and watching him with his small, sharp eyes. He instantly put on his hat and crossed the walk.

"Good-morning, Mr. Farley," he said cordially, offering his hand. "I'm glad to see you out again."

"Oh, I'm not dead yet," growled Farley. "I've decided to hang on till spring anyhow."

His tone did not encourage conversation. His face was twisted into a disagreeable smile that Copeland remembered of old, and there was a hard, ironic glitter in the gray eyes. Farley had witnessed the meeting on the bank steps with relish, and was glad of this opportunity to prolong his enjoyment of his former associate's discomfiture.

"I'm sure you'll see many more springs, Mr. Farley. That's a good machine you've got there. The fact that you've taken up motoring has given a real boost to the auto business. The agents are saying that if you've got in line there's no reason for anybody to hold back."

The old man grunted.

"I had to have air; I knew all the time that was what I needed; these damned doctors only keep people in bed so they can bulldoze 'em easier."

THE PROOF OF THE PUDDING

Copeland was attempting to be friendly, but Farley was in no humor to meet his advances.

"That last payment on the sale of my stock is due September first. I won't renew it," he said sharply.

"I had n't asked for an extension," Copeland replied coldly.

"All right, then; that will be the end of *that*."

Farley's tone implied that there might be other matters between them that this final payment would still leave open.

Copeland's ready promise that the twenty-five thousand would be paid irritated Farley, who saw one excuse for his animosity vanishing. He leaned forward and pointed his finger at Copeland, who was backing away, anxious to be gone before his former wife reappeared.

"You're ruinin' the house! You're lettin' it go to hell — the business your father and I made the best jobbin' house in this State! You're a drunkard and a gambler, but, damn your fool soul, there's one thing you can't do — you can't marry that little girl o' mine! If you've got that up your sleeve, be sure there's no money goes with her for you to squander! Remember that!"

It was the busiest hour of the day and the street was thronged. Pedestrians turned and stared curiously. Copeland raged inwardly at his stupidity in giving Farley a chance to abuse him publicly.

"You're very unjust to me," he said hotly.

"I've known Nan ever since she was a child and never had any but a friendly feeling for her. I have n't seen her for weeks. Now that I know how you feel toward me, I have no intention of seeing her."

"I guess you won't see her!" Farley snorted. "Not unless you mean to make her pay for it!"

Mrs. Copeland and Nan appeared at the bank entrance at this moment and witnessed the end of the colloquy. Copeland lifted his hat to Farley and walked rapidly away without glancing at them.

Farley became cheerful immediately, as he usually did after an explosion. This opportunity for laying the lash across Billy Copeland's shoulders had afforded him a welcome diversion; and the fact that Copeland had seen his former wife in Nan's company tickled his sardonic humor. He made no reference to Copeland, but began speaking of a new office building farther down the street. It was apparent that neither Nan nor Fanny shared his joy in the encounter and they attacked the architecture of the new building to hide their discomfort.

Nan appeared the more self-conscious. She was thinking of Billy. He had turned away from the machine with a crestfallen air which told her quite plainly that Farley had been giving him a piece of his mind. And Nan resented this; Farley had no right to abuse Billy on her account.

When they reached the house she took Fanny

upstairs. If the glimpse of Copeland on the bank steps had troubled Mrs. Copeland she made no sign. Her deft touches with the comb and brush, as she glanced in the mirror, her despairing comments upon the state of her complexion, which, she averred, the summer suns had ruined; her enthusiasm over Nan's silk waist, which was just the thing she had sought without avail in all the shops in town, — all served to stamp her as wholly human.

"But clothes! I hardly have time to think of them; they're an enormous bother. And I wear the shoes of a peasant woman when I come to town, for I have to cut across the fields when I leave the interurban and I can't do that in pumps! You see —"

The shoes really were very neat ones, though a trifle heavy for indoors. Nan instantly brought her shiniest pumps, dropped upon the floor and substituted them for Fanny's walking shoes. It flashed through her mind that Fanny Copeland inspired just such acts.

"You have the slim foot of the aristocrat," observed Fanny. And then with a wistful smile she leaned toward the girl and asked, "Do you mind if I call you Nan?"

Nan was touched by the tone and manner of her request. Of course there was no objection!

"I always knew I should like you," said Fanny. "Of course, I have n't seen much of you lately, but

MRS. COPELAND'S GOOD FORTUNE

I hear of you from a very ardent admirer: John Eaton talks of you eloquently, and to interest John Eaton is a real achievement! I'm afraid I bore him to death!"

"I can't believe it; he never lets himself be bored; but like everybody else, I'm never quite sure I understand him."

"Oh, I tell him that's one of his poses — baffling people. He surrounds himself with mystery, but pretends that he does n't. If he were a gossip he'd be horrible, for he knows everything about everybody — and knows it first!"

"He's the kindest of mortals," Nan observed. "He's always doing nice things for people, but he has to do them in his own peculiar way."

"Oh, John has the spirit of the true philanthropist; his right hand never knows, you know —"

"He's a puzzle to the people he's kindest to, sometimes, I imagine," said Nan.

She laughed as she thought of Amidon, and Fanny appealed for illumination as to what amused her.

"Oh, I was thinking of his protégé — a young man named Amidon. He and I were kids together, back in my prehistoric days. He never had any advantages — if you can say that of a boy who's born with a keen wit and a sense of humor. He does something at the Copeland-Farley store — went in as errand boy before papa left. They had him on the road for a while, but he's in the office now. Mr. Eaton has taken a great shine to him and

Jerry imitates him killingly. That fine abstracted air of Mr. Eaton's he's got nearly perfect; and he does the mysterious pretty well, too. But he's most delicious when he forgets to Eatonize himself and is just natural. He's quite short — which makes him all the funnier — and he wears tall, white-wing collars à *la* Eaton."

"Tell me more!" said Fanny. "How old is the paragon?"

"About twenty-five, I should say, figuring with my own age as a basis. He looked like a big boy to me in my river days. Mr. Eaton has undertaken his social and mental rehabilitation and the effects are amazing. They came to the house together to call, and I've rarely been more entertained than by Jerry while his good angel was upstairs talking to papa. He's trying to avoid any show of emotion just like his noble example, but once in a while he forgets himself and grins deliciously. After a round of high-brow talk, he drops into reminiscence and tells the most killing stories of the odd characters he's met in his travels with the sample-case. It can't be possible that Mr. Eaton has n't introduced him to you?"

"He has n't, and I'm going to complain about it bitterly," said Mrs. Copeland, amused by Nan's enthusiasm.

"You should, for Jerry is a nice boy, and very wise and kind."

"The only one of his benefactions he ever confided to me was the case of a girl — the daughter of an old friend who had fallen on evil times. He wanted to send her to college, and I became the visible instrument, so he need n't appear in the matter himself. The girl graduated last year and, like a fraud, I ! ad to go down to Vassar and pose as her good angel. She's a great success and is to teach somewhere, I think. But — I should n't be telling you this!"

"Oh, it's quite safe! I value his friendship too much to do anything to displease him."

"Well, things like that ought to be told," remarked Fanny reflectively; "particularly when some people think John Eaton cold and selfish."

Luncheon interrupted these confidences. Farley had not been to the dining-room for several months and he made much of the occasion.

"This is a celebration for me, too," said Fanny. "I've just had a piece of good fortune. Nobody knows of it yet; you're the first people I've told! You know I have n't many friends to confide in. An aunt of mine has just died and left me some money. In fact, there's a great deal of it; I'm richer than I ever expected to be."

"Good! Good!" Farley ejaculated, interested and pleased.

"It's fine," said Nan; "and it's nice of you to tell us about it."

Nan was afraid that Farley would demand the amount of the legacy, but evidently Fanny knew he would be curious as to all the details, and she went on to explain that it was her mother's sister, the last of the family, who had died recently in Ohio and left her all her property.

"I have visited her every year or two since I was a child and knew her very well, but I never had any idea she meant to do this. It will take some time to settle it up, but there's as much as two hundred thousand dollars in sight — maybe fifty more. She was a dear old woman; I'm so ashamed of myself that I was n't kinder to her, but she was difficult to handle — had n't left home for years, though she used to write to me two or three times a year. So there! That's why I'm running into the bank these days, to ask Mr. Harrington about investments."

"If you take his advice," said Farley emphatically, "you'll never lose any of that money!"

"Then what's to become of the farm?" asked Nan.

"Oh, I shall run it just the same. I'd rather lose that legacy than give it up. An unattached woman like me must have something to amuse herself with."

"That's a lot o' money; a whole lot o' money," said Farley; "and I'm mighty glad you've got it."

Nan saw a gleam in his eye and a covert smile playing about his lips. He chuckled softly.

"Two hundred; two hundred fifty; that's a whole lot o' money; and you don't want to let any of these sharks around here get it away from you; they'll be after you all right. But I guess you'll know how to handle 'em," he added with satisfaction.

When Fanny was ready to go he called for his car and he and Nan drove home with her.

That night, after the nurse had put him to bed, Nan heard an unusual sound from his room. She crossed the hall and stood in the doorway a moment. He was muttering to himself and chuckling.

"Picked up two hundred and fifty thousand dollars, just like findin' it! Turned her out; got rid of her! Well, that's a hell of a joke on you, Billy Copeland!"

CHAPTER IX

A NARROW ESCAPE

On a rainy evening in mid-September, a salesman for an Eastern chemical firm invited Amidon to join him in a game of billiards at the Whitcomb House. As Russell Kirby was one of the stars of the traveling fraternity, Jerry was greatly honored by this attention. Moreover, when he hung up his coat in the billiard room and rolled up the sleeves of his silk shirt, the traveler's arms proved to be thoroughly tanned — and this impressed Jerry as indicating that Kirby indulged in the aristocratic game of golf and did not allow the cares of business to interfere with his lawful amusements. Kirby played very good billiards, and did not twist his cigar into the corner of his mouth when he made his shots, as most of Jerry's friends did.

"The lid's on a little looser in your town than it was last winter," remarked the envied one, sipping a ricky. "I suppose by following our noses we could strike a pretty stiff game without going out into the wet."

"Oh, there's always more or less poker around here," replied Jerry, unwilling to appear ignorant of the moral conditions of his own city.

He chalked his cue and watched Kirby achieve a difficult shot. Billiards afforded Jerry a fine exercise for his philosophic temper, steady hand, and calculating eye. He had developed a high degree of proficiency with the cue in the Criterion Billiard Parlors. It was a grief to him that in trying to live up to Eaton he had felt called upon to desert the Criterion, where the admiration of lesser lights had been dear to his soul.

"Big Rodney Sykes is here," Kirby remarked carelessly. "They chased him out of Chicago that last time they had a moral upheaval."

Jerry was chagrined that he knew nothing of Big Rodney Sykes, presumably a gambler of established reputation. To be a high-salaried traveler, with a flexible expense account, was to be in touch with the inner life of all great cities. Jerry's envy deepened; it availed nothing that he could beat this sophisticated being at billiards.

"Rather tough about that boss of yours," Kirby continued. "It's fellows of his size that Big Rodney goes after. A gentleman's game and no stopping payment of checks the next morning."

"Oh, the boss is no squab; I guess he's sat in with as keen sharps as Sykes and got out with carfare home," replied Jerry.

"Of course; but on a hot night like this many a good man feels the need of a little relaxation. It just happened" — he prolonged the deliberation of his aim to intensify Jerry's curiosity — "happened I saw Copeland wandering toward Sykes's room as I was coming down."

THE PROOF OF THE PUDDING

"I guess the boss knows a thing or two," replied Jerry easily, in a tone that implied unlimited confidence in Copeland.

He was consumed with indignation that Kirby should be able to tell him anything about Copeland. It had been done, too, with a neatness of insinuation that was galling.

"Well, I guess," persisted Kirby, "you miss old Uncle Tim at the store. I used to have many a jolly row with Uncle Tim; he was one man it never paid to fool with; but he was all right — just about as clean-cut and straight a man as I ever fought discounts with. Uncle Tim was a merchant," he ended impressively as he bent over the table.

In calling Farley a merchant with this air of finality he implied very clearly that William B. Copeland was something quite different, and Jerry resented this imputation as a slur upon his house. Much as he admired Kirby's clothes and metropolitan ways, he hated him cordially for thus speaking of Copeland, who was one of Kirby's important customers. Mere defeat was no adequate punishment for Kirby; Jerry proceeded to make a "run" that attracted the admiring attention of players at neighboring tables and precluded further discussion of Copeland.

At midnight Kirby said he had had all the billiards he wanted and invited Jerry to his room.

"I always like to tell people about their own

126

town and I'll show you where they're piling up the chips," he remarked.

His room was opposite the elevator on the seventh floor, and having unlocked his door he piloted Jerry round a corner and indicated three rooms which he said were given over to gambling.

"If you give the right number of taps that first door will open," said Kirby, "but as an old friend I warn you to keep out."

As they were turning away a telephone tinkled faintly in one of the rooms and they heard voices raised excitedly, accompanied by the bang of overturned furniture.

"They've got a tip the cops are coming or there's a fight," said Kirby. "Here's where we fade!"

He led the way quickly back to his room, dragged Jerry in, and shut the door.

While the sounds of hasty flight continued, the elevator discharged half a dozen men and they heard the hotel manager protesting to the police that it was an outrage; that the rooms they were raiding had been taken by strangers, and that if there was anything wrong he wasn't responsible.

A few minutes later the return of the prisoners to the elevator announced the success of the raid. Several of them were protesting loudly against riding to the police station in a patrol wagon; others were taking the whole matter as a joke. Above the confusion Copeland's voice rose drunkenly in denunciation of his arrest.

THE PROOF OF THE PUDDING

Kirby, anxious not to be identified even remotely with the sinners who had been caught in their transgressions, had taken off his coat and was lighting a cigar.

"Try one of these, Amidon. We'd better sit tight until the cops get out of the building. Nice town this! Gambling in respectable hotels. No doubt all those fellows are leading citizens, including —"

At this instant the electric lights were extinguished. The darkness continued and Jerry opened the door and stuck his head out. Half the prisoners had been sent down and the remainder were waiting for the elevator to return. They growled dismally and somebody said it was a good chance to give the cops the slip.

One of the policemen struck a match and held it up to light the entrance to the car. Jerry's eyes ran quickly over the group facing the shaft, but he recognized none of the men. As the match died out a prolonged, weary sigh near at hand caused him to start. Some one was leaning against the wall close beside him. He reached out, caught the man by the arm, drew him into the room and softly closed the door.

Kirby demanded to know what Amidon had done, and during the whispered explanation the globes began to brighten. Jerry jumped for the switch and snapped off the lights. He climbed on a chair and surveyed the hall through the transom. The last officer was stepping into the elevator, and

some one demanded to know what had become of
Billy Copeland.

"Oh, he went down in the first load," replied
another voice.

Then the door clanged and the hall was quiet.

"Turn on the lights," commanded Kirby.

Copeland sat on the bed, staring at them foolishly.

"Wherenell am I?" he asked blinking. "Thiss
jail or somebody's parlor?"

"Your nerve, young man," Kirby remarked to
Jerry, "leaves nothing to be desired. I suppose
it did n't occur to you that this is my room?"

"Oh, that will be all right. If the cops ain't back
here in ten minutes, they'll probably think he's
skipped; and they won't waste time looking for
him; they know they can pick him up to-morrow,
easy enough."

"Zhat you, Kirby, good old boy; right off Broad-
way! Kind of you, 'm sure. Good boy, Amidon;
would n't let your boss get hauled off in patrol wagon.
Raise wages for that; 'preciate it; mos' grateful!"

"All right; but please stop talking," Jerry admonished. "We'll all get pinched if the cops find
out you're here."

"Los' five thous; five thou-sand dollars; hons'
to God I did!"

Copeland's face was aflame from drink and the
heat, and unable to comprehend what had happened to him he tumbled over on the bed. Kirby

eyed him contemptuously and turned upon Amidon angrily.

"This is a nice mess of cats! Would you mind telling me what you're going to do with our fallen brother? Please remember that reputation's my only asset, and if I get arrested my house might not pass it off as a little joke!"

"Oh, cheer up and be a good sport! I know the boys at the desk downstairs and I'm going to tell 'em you've cleared out to make way for an old comrade of the Army of the Potomac. I'll have you moved, and then I'll put the boss to bed."

"Anything to please you," said Kirby ironically, as Copeland began to snore. "Your boss is lying on my coat and I hope you'll have the decency to pay for pressing it!" . . .

At ten the next morning Amidon called at the Whitcomb and found Copeland half dressed. He had telephoned to his house for toilet articles and clean linen and presented the fresh and chastened appearance with which he always emerged from his sprees.

"I thought I'd drop in," said Jerry, seating himself in the window.

"Been to the store?" asked Copeland from before the mirror where he was sticking a gold safety pin through the ends of a silk collar.

"Yes; I took a look in."

"Any genial policeman lying in wait for me?"

"Nothing doing! Everything's all fixed."

A NARROW ESCAPE

"Fixed? How fixed?"

"Oh, I know the way around the pump at the police court, and I had a bum lawyer who hangs out there make the right sign to the judge. You owe me forty-seven dollars — that includes ten for the lawyer."

"Cheap at the price," remarked Copeland. He had taken a check book from the table and was frowningly inspecting the last stub.

"I did n't come to collect," said Jerry. "Any old time will do."

"How did the rest of the boys come out?" asked Copeland, throwing the book down impatiently.

"Oh, the big sneeze from Chicago got a heavy soaking. The judge took it out on him for the rest of you. Would n't do, of course, to send prominent business men to the work-house. All fined under assumed names."

"Rather expensive evening for me. Much obliged to you just the same for saving me a ride in the wagon."

"Oh, that was easy," said Jerry. "By the way, I guess we'd better slip my lawyer friend another ten. He dug this up for you — no questions, no fuss; all on the dead quiet."

He drew from his trousers pocket a crumpled bit of paper and handed it to Copeland.

Jerry was not without his sense of the dramatic. He rolled a cigarette and watched Copeland out of the corner of his eye.

"See here, Jerry," said Copeland quickly, "I don't know about this. If I gave that check, and I know I did, I've got to stand by it. It's not square—"

"Oh, I would n't burst out crying about that!" remarked Jerry easily. "Five thousand is some money, and the Chicago shark was glad enough to have the check disappear from the police safe. You were stewed when you wrote the check; and besides, it was a crooked game. Forget it; that's all!" He stretched himself and yawned. "Can I do anything for you?"

"It seems to me," said Copeland, "that you've done about enough for me for one day,— kept me out of jail and then saved me five thousand dollars!"

"We do what we can," replied Jerry. "Keep us posted and when in doubt make the high sign. You'd better keep mum about the check. The deputy prosecutor's a friend of mine and I don't want to get him into trouble."

"It makes me feel a little better about that check to know that it was n't good when I gave it," remarked Copeland dryly. "I've only got about a hundred in bank according to my stubs."

"I was just thinking," said Jerry, playing with the curtain cord, "as I came down from the police court, that five thousand per night swells the overhead considerable. This is n't a kick; I just mention it."

Copeland paused in the act of drawing on his

coat to bestow a searching glance upon his employee. He shook himself into the coat and rested his hand on the brass bedpost.

"What's the odds?" he asked harshly. "I'm undoubtedly going to hell and a thousand or two, here and there —"

"Why are you going?" asked Jerry, tying a loop in the curtain cord.

Copeland was not prepared for this; he did n't at once correlate Amidon's question with his own remark that had inspired it.

"Oh, the devil!" he ejaculated impatiently; and then he smiled ruefully as he realized that there was a certain appositeness in his rejoinder.

The relations of employer and employee had been modified by the incidents of the night and morning. Copeland imagined that he was something of a hero to his employees, and that Jerry probably viewed the night's escapade as one of the privileges enjoyed by the more favored social class. Possibly in his own way Amidon was guilty of reprehensible dissipations and therefore disposed to be tolerant of other men's shortcomings. At any rate, the young fellow had got him out of a bad scrape, and he meant to do something for him to show his gratitude.

"Well, a man's got to let loose occasionally," he said, as he began collecting his toilet acticles.

"I suppose he has," Amidon admitted without enthusiasm.

THE PROOF OF THE PUDDING

"I guess I ought to cut out these midnight parties and get down to business," said Copeland, as though recent history called for some such declaration of his intentions.

"Well, it's up to you," Jerry replied. "You can let 'er slide if you want to."

"You mean that the house is sliding already?" Copeland asked.

"It's almost worse than a slide, if you want to know. But I did n't come here to talk about that. There's plenty of others can tell you more about the business than I can."

"But they don't," said Copeland, frowning; "I suppose — I suppose maybe they're afraid to."

"I guess that's right, too," Jerry affirmed.

"Well, you're in a position to learn what's going on. I want to push you ahead. I hope you understand that."

"Oh, you treat me all right," said Jerry, but in a tone that Copeland did n't find cheering.

"I mean to treat everybody right at the store," declared Copeland virtuously. "If any of the boys have a kick I want them to come straight to me with it."

Jerry laid his hand on the door ready for flight and regarded Copeland soberly.

"The only kick's on you, if you can bear to hear it. Everybody around the place knows you're not on the job; every drayman in the district knows you're out with a paintbrush every night, and the

solid men around town are saying it's only a matter of time till you go broke. And the men down
at the store are sore about it; it means that one of
these mornings there'll be a new shift and they're
likely to be out of a job. Some of them have been
there a long time, and they don't like to see the
old business breaking down. And some of them, I
guess, sort o' like you and hate to see you slipping
over the edge."

During this speech Copeland stood with his
cigarette-case half opened in his hand, looking
hard at the top button on Amidon's coat.

"Well," he said, thrusting a cigarette into his
mouth and tilting it upwards with his lips while he
felt for a match, "go on and hand me the rest of it."

"I guess that's about all from me," replied Jerry,
"except if you want to bounce me right now, go
ahead, only — let's don't have any hard feeling."

Copeland made no reply, and Jerry went out
and closed the door. Then in a moment he opened
it, saw Copeland staring out across the roofs in
deep preoccupation, and remarked, deferentially:—

"I'll carry your bag down, sir. Shall I order a
taxi?"

"Never mind," said Copeland, with affected
carelessness; "I'll attend to it. I'm going to the
store."

CHAPTER X

THE AMBITIONS OF MR. AMIDON

No other branch of commerce is as fascinating as the wholesale drug business. A drug stock embraces ten thousand small items, and the remote fastnesses of the earth are raked to supply its necessities. The warehouses are redolent of countless scents that pique a healthy curiosity; poppy and mandragora and all the drowsy sirups of the world are enlisted in its catalogue. How superior to the handling of the grosser commodities of the wholesale grocery line! How infinitely more delightful than distributing clanging hardware or scattering broadcast the unresponsive units of the dry-goods trade!

Such, at least, were Jerry Amidon's opinions. Jerry knew his way around the store — literally. He could find the asafœtida without sniffing his way to it. He had acquired a working knowledge of the pharmacopœia, and under Eaton's guidance he purchased a Latin grammar and a dictionary, over which he labored diligently in the midnight hours. His curiosity was insatiable; he wanted to know things!

"Assistant to the President" was the title bestowed upon him by his fellow employees. By imperceptible degrees he had grown into a confidential relationship with Copeland that puzzled the whole establishment. The latest shifts had been unusually productive of friction, and Amidon had found his new position under the credit man wholly uncomfortable. Having asserted his authority, Copeland gave no heed to the results. The credit man was an old employee, very jealous of his prerogatives, and he had told Jerry in blunt terms that he had nothing for him to do. The auditor thereupon pounced upon him and set him to work checking invoices.

Jerry wrote a good hand and proved apt, and as a result of this contact with the office he absorbed a vast amount of information pertaining to the business to which, strictly speaking, he was not entitled. Copeland, seeing him perched on a stool in the counting-room, asked him what he was doing there, and when Jerry replied that he was just helping out for a day or two, Copeland remarked ironically that he guessed he'd better stay there; that he'd been thinking for some time that fresh blood was needed in that department.

No one else entered Copeland's office with so much assurance. If Jerry had n't been so amiable, so willing to help any one who called for his assistance, he would have been cordially hated; but Jerry was a likable fellow. He prided himself on keeping cheerful on blue Mondays when everybody else about the place was in the doldrums.

THE PROOF OF THE PUDDING

The auditor sent him to the bank frequently, and he experienced a pleasurable sensation in walking briskly across the lobby of the Western National. He knew many of the clerks he saw immured in the cages; some of them were members of the Little Ripple Club, and he made a point of finding out just what they did, and incidentally the amount of their salaries, which seemed disgracefully inadequate; he was doing quite as well himself. He liked to linger in the bank lobby and talk to people. He had hit on the happy expedient of speaking to men whether he knew them or not; he argued that in time they would ask who he was, which was a surer way of impressing himself upon them than through formal introductions.

Ambition stirred in the bosom of Jeremiah A. Amidon. He lavished his admiration upon the "big" men of the "street" — in the main they were hard workers, and he was pretty well persuaded of the virtue and reward of industry.

Nearly all the leading manufacturers and merchants were stockholders in banks. The fact that Copeland enjoyed no such distinction troubled Jerry. He studied the stock-list, hoping to see something some day that he could buy.

The local stock exchange consisted of three gentlemen calling themselves brokers. Whenever they met by chance on the steps of the Western National or in a trolley going home, the exchange was in session. The "list" must be kept active, and when there were no transfers the brokers could trade a few shares with one another to establish a price. These agitations of the local bourse would be duly reported on the market page of the newspapers — all but the number of shares changing hands! "A better tone prevailing"; "brisk demand for tractions"; "lively trading in industrials" would soberly greet the eye of students of local financial conditions.

Foreman, one of the brokers, who had been haunting the store for several days looking for Copeland, accosted Jerry in the bank one afternoon.

"Your boss does n't sit on his job much," Foreman remarked. "I'm getting tired chasing him."

"He's off motoring with Kinney — they're looking for a place to start another cement mill. Why don't you call for me when you honor the house?"

"Oh, my business with Copeland is too trifling to trouble you about," the broker remarked ironically. "You have n't any money, have you?"

Jerry bent his ear to catch the jingle of coin inside the cages.

"Oh, if you want to borrow, Copeland-Farley ain't a pawnshop."

"I guess C-F does n't *lend* much; it's the biggest borrower on the street," said Foreman.

"Every big jobber is a heavy borrower. It's a part of the game," Jerry replied. Foreman's anxiety to find Copeland had piqued his curiosity. "Of course, if your business with the boss can wait —"

"It's a trifling matter, that will probably annoy him when I mention it. I've got twenty shares of Copeland-Farley for sale. I thought he might want to pick 'em up."

"Must be a mistake," replied Jerry indifferently; "there's never any of our stock for sale."

"No; I suppose you've got most of it yourself downstairs in the safety vault!"

"Come through and pour the dope!" said Jerry, grinning cheerfully.

"Well, I've got 'em all right. An old party named Reynolds up at Fort Wayne had twenty shares and his executors wrote me that Copeland ought to have a chance to buy 'em. I've worn myself out trying to find your boss. I don't know who'd buy if he did n't. The things you hear about your house are a little bit scary: trade falling off; head of the company drinking, gambling, monkeying with out- ' side things, like Kinney cement —"

"Well, well!" Jerry chirruped; "you're just chuck full of sad tidings."

"Of course, you know it all; but maybe you don't know that Corbin & Eichberg are cutting into your business. There will be an involuntary consolidation one of these days and Copeland-Farley will be painted off the sign."

"You're the best little booster I've heard sing this week! What'll you take for the stock?"

"Par."

"Sold! Bring your papers here to-morrow at two and I'll give you the money."

Jerry had heard some one say that it was what you can do without money that proves your mettle in business. He had one thousand dollars, that represented the savings of his lifetime. The second thousand necessary to complete the purchase he borrowed of Eaton — who made the advance not without much questioning.

"Very careless on Copeland's part, but to be expected of a man who takes only a fitful interest in his business. You have about one thousand dollars! All right; I'll lend you what you need to buy the stock. But keep this to yourself; don't turn in the old certificate for a new one — not at present. Wait and see what happens. Copeland needs discipline, and he will probably get it. Kinney and Copeland seeing much of each other?"

"Well, they're off on a business trip together."

"I mean social affairs. They haven't been driving peaceful citizens away from the Country Club by their cork-popping quite so much, have they? I thought not; that's good. The general reform wave may hit them yet."

"On the dead, I think Copeland's trying to cut out the early morning parties," said Jerry earnestly. "He's taken a brace."

"If he doesn't want to die in the poorhouse at the early age of fifty, he'd better!" Eaton brushed an imaginary speck off his cuff as he asked, "How much did your boss give you of the five thousand you got back for him out of that poker game?"

Amidon fidgeted and colored deeply.

"Just another of these fairy stories!"

"Your attempt to feign ignorance is laudable, Amidon. But my information is exact. Rather neat, particularly lifting him right out of the patrol wagon, so to speak. And recovering the check; creditable to your tact — highly so!"

Jerry grinned.

"Oh, it was dead easy! You see, after helping the gang lick you in the primaries last May, they could n't go back on me."

"If you turned your influence to nobler use, this would be a very different world! Let us go back to that Corrigan matter — you remember?" asked Eaton, filling his pipe. "You probably noticed that the gentleman who was arrested for murder down there was duly convicted. His lawyer did n't do him much good. No wonder! I never saw a case more miserably handled — stupid beyond words."

"You was n't down there!" exclaimed Jerry, sitting up straight.

"*Were*, not *was*, Amidon! I should think you 'd know I'd been in the wilderness from my emaciated appearance. Believe I did say I was going to Pittsburg, but I took the wrong train. Met some nice chaps while I was down there, — one or two friends of yours, road agents, pirates, commercial travelers, drummers, — I beg your pardon!"

Jerry was moved to despair. He would never be able to surround himself with the mystery or practice the secrecy that he found so fascinating in Eaton. He had not imagined that the lawyer would bother himself further about Corrigan. He had read of the conviction without emotion, but it would never have occurred to him that a man so busy as Eaton or so devoted to the comforts of life would spend three days in Belleville merely to watch the trial of a man in whom he had only the remotest interest.

"They soaked him for manslaughter. I guess he got off easy!"

"He did, indeed," replied Eaton. "When did you see Nan last?"

"I've been there once since you took me, and the old man sent down word he wanted to see me. He was feeling good and lit into me about the store. Wanted to know about everything. Some of the fellows Copeland has kicked out have been up crying on Farley's doorstep and he asked me how the boss came to let them go. He sent Nan out of the room so he could cuss better. He's sure some cusser!"

"Amidon!" Eaton beat his knuckles on the desk sharply, "remember you are speaking English!"

"You'd better give me up," moaned Jerry, crestfallen.

THE PROOF OF THE PUDDING

"You are doing well. With patience and care you will improve the quality of your diction. No reference to the Corrigan matter, I suppose, — either by Farley or Nan?"

"Not a word. It was the night I read about the end of the trial, but nothing was said about it."

"She need n't have worried," Eaton remarked. "She was a very foolish little girl to have drawn her money out of the bank to hand over to a crooked lawyer."

"I suppose you coaxed the money back —"

"Certainly not! It might have been amusing to gather Harlowe in for blackmail; but you can see that it would have involved no end of newspaper notoriety; most disagreeable. I had the best opportunities for observing that fellow in his conduct of the case; in fact, I had a letter to the judge and he asked me to sit with him on the bench. There's little in the life or public services of Jason E. Harlowe that I don't know." He lifted his eyes to the solid wall of file-boxes. "H-66 is filled with data. Jason E. Harlowe," he repeated musingly. "If I should die to-night, kindly direct my executor to observe that box particularly."

"I've heard of him; he ran for the legislature last year and got licked."

"By two hundred and sixteen votes," added Eaton.

"What's your guess about that thousand bucks? Corrigan must have put Harlowe up to it."

THE AMBITIONS OF MR. AMIDON

"He did not," replied Eaton, peering for a moment into the bowl of his pipe. "It was Mr. Harlowe's idea — strictly so. And I'm ready for him in case he shows his hand again. Farley has some relations down that way, a couple of cousins at Lawrenceburg. Do you follow me? Harlowe may have something bigger up his sleeve. He ranges the whole Indiana shore of the Ohio; business mostly criminal. The more I've thought of that thousand-dollar episode, the less I've liked it. I take a good deal of interest in Nan, you know. She's a little brash and needs a helping hand occasionally. Not that I'm called upon to stand *in loco parentis*, but there's something mighty appealing in her. For fear you may misunderstand me, I assure you that I am not in love with her, or in danger of being; but her position is difficult and made the more so by her impulsive, warm-hearted nature. And it has told against her a little that the Farleys were never quite admitted to the inner circle here. This is a peculiar town, you know, Amidon, and there's a good deal of caste feeling — deplorable but true! You and I are sturdy democrats and above such prejudices, but there are a few people amongst us who never forget what you may call their position. Unfortunate, but it's here and to be reckoned with."

"Well, I guess Nan's as good as any of them," said Amidon doggedly.

"She is! But it's the elemental strain in her that

145

makes her interesting. She's of the race that believes in fairies; we have to take that into account."

Amidon nodded soberly. He had seen nothing in
Nan to support this proposition that she believed
in fairies, but the idea pleased him.

Eaton's way of speaking of women was another
thing that impressed Jerry. It was always with
profound respect, and this was unfamiliar enough
in Jerry's previous existence; but combined with
this reverential attitude was a chivalrous anxiety
to serve or protect them. The girls Jerry had
known, or the ones he particularly admired, were
those endowed with a special genius for taking
care of themselves.

"Nan," Eaton was saying, "needs plenty of air.
She has suffered from claustrophobia in her life
with the Farleys. Oh, yes; claustrophobia —"

He paused to explain the meaning of the word,
which Jerry scribbled on an envelope that he might
remember it and use it somewhere when opportunity offered.

"I'm glad Farley talked to you. You will find
that he will ask to see you again, but be careful
what you say to him about the store. He'll be
anxious to worm information out of you, but he's
the sort to distrust you if you seemed anxious to
talk against the house or the head of it, much as he
may dislike him."

"I guess that's right," said Jerry. "He asked
about the customers on the route I worked last

year and seemed to know them all — even to the number of children in the family."

"You've been back once since we called together? Anybody else around — any signs that Nan is receiving social attentions?"

"I did n't see any. She 'd been reading 'Huck Finn' to the old gent when I dropped in."

"Isolated life; not wholesome. A girl like that needs to have people about her."

"Well," Jerry ejaculated, "she does n't need a scrub like me! I felt ashamed of myself for going; and had to walk around the block about seven times before I got my nerve up to go in. It's awful, going into a house like that, and waiting for the coon to go off to see whether the folks want to see you or not."

"The trepidation you indicate is creditable to you, Amidon. Your social instincts are crude but sound. Should you say, as a student of mankind and an observer of life, that Nan is pining away with a broken heart?"

"Well, hardly; she was a lot cheerfuler than she was that first time, when you went with me."

"Thanks for the compliment! Of course, you get on better without me. 'T was always thus! Well, that first time was hardly a fair example of my effect upon womankind. The air was surcharged with electricity; Nan had made a trifling error of judgment and had been brought promptly to book. I 've always rather admired people who follow their impulses; it's my disposition to examine my own under the microscope. Don't check yourself too much: I find your spontaneity refreshing, particularly now that your verbs and nouns are more nearly in agreement. You say Copeland and Kinney are off motoring, to look at a new factory?" He lifted his eyes to one of the fileboxes absently. "I wish they'd wait till we get rid of that suit over Kinney's patents before they spread out. The case ought to be decided soon and there are times —"

He rose quickly, walked to the shelves and drew down a volume in which he instantly became absorbed. Then he went back to his desk and refilled his pipe deliberately.

"I think," he remarked, "that we shall win the case; but you never can tell. By the way, what is your impartial judgment of the merits of Corbin & Eichberg — rather wide-awake fellows, are n't they?"

As Jerry began to express scorn by a contemptuous curl of the lip and an outward gesture of his stiffened palm, Eaton reprimanded him sharply.

"Speak judicially; no bluster; none of this whang about their handling inferior goods. The fact is they are almost offensively prosperous and carry more traveling men after ten years' business than Copeland-Farley with thirty years behind them."

"Well," Jerry replied meekly, "I guess they are cutting in a little; Eichberg had made a lot of money before he went into drugs and they've got more capital than C-F."

"That increases the danger of the competition. Eichberg is a pretty solid citizen. For example, he's a director in the Western National."

"I guess that won't help him sell any drugs," said Amidon, who resented this indirect praise of Corbin & Eichberg.

"Not directly; no." And Eaton dropped the subject with a finality Jerry felt bound to accept.

Foreman had intimated that in due course Copeland-Farley would be absorbed by Corbin & Eichberg; possibly the same calamity was foreshadowed in Eaton's speculations.

Before he returned to his boarding-house Jerry strolled into the jobbing district and stood for some time on the sidewalk opposite Copeland-Farley's store. His twenty shares of stock gave him an exalted sense of proprietorship. He was making progress; he was a stockholder in a corporation. But it was a corporation that was undoubtedly going to the bad.

It was quite true that Corbin & Eichberg were making heavy inroads upon Copeland-Farley trade. They were broadening the field of their operations and developing territory beyond the farthest limits to which Copeland-Farley had extended local drug jobbing. It was not a debatable matter that if Copeland persisted in his evil courses the business would go by the board.

THE PROOF OF THE PUDDING

Copeland had n't been brought up to work; that was his trouble, Jerry philosophized. And yet Copeland was doing better. As Jerry thought of him his attitude became paternal. He grinned as he became conscious of his dreams of attempting — he, Jeremiah Amidon — to pull Billy Copeland back from the pit for which he seemed destined, and save the house of Copeland-Farley from ruin.

He crossed the street, found the private watchman sitting in the open door half asleep, roused him, and gave him a cigar he had purchased for the purpose.

Then he walked away whistling cheerfully and beating the walk with his stick.

CHAPTER XI

CANOEING

LIFE began to move more briskly for Nan. She was not aware that certain invitations that reached her were due to a few words carefully spoken in safe quarters by Eaton.

One of the first large functions of the dawning season was a tea given by Mrs. Harrington for a visitor. Mrs. Harrington not only asked Nan to assist, but she extended the invitation personally in the Farley parlor, much to Nan's astonishment.

One or two young gentlemen who had paid Nan attentions when she first came home from school looked her up again. John Cecil Eaton was highly regarded by the younger men he met at the University Club, and was not without influence. A reference to Nan as an unusual person; some saying of hers, quoted carelessly at the round table, was instrumental in directing attention anew to her as a girl worth knowing. If any one said, "How's her affair with Copeland going?" Eaton would retort, icily, that it was n't going; that there never had been anything in it but shameless gossip.

Jerry now reserved his Thursday evenings for Nan: not for any particular reason except that Eaton had taken him to the Farleys on a Thursday and from sentimental considerations he consecrated the day to repetitions of the visit. Nan was immensely kind to him; it was incredible that a girl so separated from him by immeasurable distances should be so cordial, so responsive to his overtures of friendship. Once she sent him a note — the frankest, friendliest imaginable note — to say that on a particular Thursday evening she could not see him. His disappointment was as nothing when weighed against his joy that she recognized his claim upon that particular evening and took the trouble to explain that the nurse would be out and that she would be too busy with Farley to see him. He replied with flowers — which brought him another note.

He had laid before her all his plans for self-improvement and her encouragement was even more stimulating than Eaton's. She fell at times into a maternal attitude toward him, scolding and lecturing him, and he was meek under her criticism.

Nan felt more at home with him than with any other young man who called on her. With some of these, whose mothers and sisters had been treating her coldly, she felt herself to be playing a part — trying to assume a dignity that was not naturally hers in order that they might give a good account of her at home. With Jerry she could be herself without dissimulation. When it came to mothers, he remembered her mother perfectly and she remembered his. In a sense she and Jerry were allies,

engaged in accommodating themselves to a somewhat questioning if not hostile atmosphere. In all
her acquaintance he was the one person who could
make the necessary allowances for her, who was
able to give her full credit for her good intentions.

On his seventh call he summoned courage to
ask her to join him on a Saturday afternoon excursion on the river.

"The foliage is unusually beautiful this year,"
he suggested with his air of quoting, "and it'll be
too cold for canoeing pretty soon."

"I'm afraid —" Nan began.

"I knew you'd say that; but you're as safe in
my boat as in your own rocking-chair."

"I wasn't going to say that," laughed Nan. "I
was going to say that I was afraid you wouldn't
enjoy the foliage so much if I were along."

He saw that she was laughing at him. Nan and
Eaton were the only persons whose mirth he suffered without resentment.

"I'll have to ask papa about it; or maybe you'll
ask him."

"I've already asked him."

"When did you ask him?"

"About ten minutes ago, just before I came downstairs. I told him two good stories and then shot
it in quick. He said he thought it would do you
good!"

"I like your nerve! Why didn't you ask me
first?"

THE PROOF OF THE PUDDING

"Because it was much more proper for me to open negotiations with the man higher up. I hope you appreciate my delicacy," he added, in Eaton's familiar, half-mocking tone, which he had caught perfectly.

"You're so thoughtful I suppose you've also arranged for a chaperone?"

"The canoe," he replied, "is more comfortable for two."

"Two have been in it rather often, I suppose."

"Yes; but that was last summer. I've seen everything different this season. I practiced casting on a day in June and met with an experience that has changed the whole current of my life."

"I hope it changed your luck with the rod! You got snagged on everything that would hold a hook, but I must say that you bore your troubles in a sweet spirit."

"I learned that early in the game. Even if you refused my invitation I'd try to bear up under it."

"I think I'll decline, then, just to see how you take it."

"Well, it's only polite to say it would be a blow. I have a pocketful of strychnine and it might be unpleasant to have me die on the doorstep."

"I could stand that probably better than the neighbors could. You'd better try a poison that's warranted not to kill on the premises."

Jerry tortured himself with speculations as to whether he should hire a taxi to transport them to the Little Ripple Club, but finally decided against it as an unwarranted extravagance, calculated to arouse suspicion in the mind of Farley. However, when he reached the house at two o'clock on Saturday, Nan announced that the nurse was taking her place as Farley's companion for his regular drive and that they would carry them to the club. This arrangement caused his breast to swell.

"That will give my credit a big boost; you'll see a lot of the boys drop dead when we roll up with Uncle Tim."

Farley alighted to inspect the clubhouse and the fleet of canoes that bobbed at the landing. It was a great day for Jerry.

"There's something nice about a river," said Nan, as Jerry sent his maroon-colored craft far out into the stream. "Ever since I came away I've missed the old river at Belleville."

This was one of the things he liked about Nan. She referred often to her childhood, and it even seemed that she spoke of it with a certain wistfulness.

"The last girl I had out here," Jerry said as he plied his blade, "was Katie McCarthy, who works in the County Treasurer's office — mighty responsible job. I used to know Katie when she stenogged at four per for a punk lawyer, but I knew she was better than that, so I pulled a few wires and got her into the court-house. Katie could be cashier in a bank — she's that smart! No; not much to look at. I studied Katie's case a good deal, and she'd never make any headway in offices where they'd rather have a yellow-haired girl who overdresses the part and is always slipping out for a retouch with the chamois. It's hard to find a job for girls like Katie; their only chance is some place where they've got to have a girl with brains. These perfumed office darlings, that's just got to go to vaudeville every Monday night so they can talk about it the rest of the week, never get anywhere."

"My heart warms to Katie. I wonder," murmured Nan lazily, as Jerry neatly negotiated a shallow passage between two sandbars, "if I had to do it — I wonder how much I could earn a week."

"Oh, I guess you'd make good all right. You've got brains and I've never caught you touching up your complexion."

"Which isn't any sign I don't," she laughed. "I've all the necessary articles right here in my sweater pocket."

"Well, somebody has to use the talcum; we handle it in carload lots. It's one of the Copeland-Farley specialties I used to brag about easiest when I bore the weighty sample-case down the line. It was a good stunt to ask the druggist to introduce me to some of the girls that's always loafing round the soda-counter in country-town drug stores, and I'd hand 'em out a box and ask 'em to try it on right there. It cheered up the druggist and the girls would help me pull a bigger order than I'd get on my own hook. A party like that on a sleepy afternoon in a pill-shop would lift the sky-line considerable."

"Well, if you saw me in a drug store wrestling with a chocolate sundae and had your sample-case open and were trying to coax an order out of a druggist, just how would you approach me?"

"I would n't!" he responded readily. "I'd get your number on the quiet and walk past your house when your mother was sitting on the porch all alone, darning socks, and I'd beg her pardon and say that, having heard that her daughter was the most beautiful girl in town, Copeland-Farley had sent me all the way from the capital to ask her please to accept, with the house's compliments, a gross of our Faultless Talcum. If mother did n't ask me to supper, it would be a sign that I had n't put it over."

"But if father appeared with a shotgun —"

"I'd tell him it was the closed season for drummers, and invite him down to the hotel for a game of billiards."

"You think you always have the answer, don't you?" she taunted.

"I don't think it; I've got to know it!"

"Well, I have n't seen you miss fire yet. My trouble is," she deliberated, touching the water lightly with her hand, "that I don't have the answer most of the time."

"I've noticed it sometimes," replied Jerry, looking at her quickly.

It was unseasonably warm, and he drove the canoe on to a sandy shore in the shade of the bank. He had confessed to himself that at times, even in their juvenile badgering, Nan baffled him. From the beginning of their acquaintance he had noted abrupt changes of mood that puzzled him. Occasionally, in the midst of the aimless banter in which they engaged, she would cease to respond and a far-away look would come into her violet eyes. One of these moods was upon her now.

"Do you remember the shanty-boat people down along the river? I used to think it would be fun to live like that. I still feel that way sometimes."

"Oh," he answered indulgently, "I guess everybody has a spell of that now and then, when you just want to sort of loaf along, and fish a little when you're hungry, and trust to luck for a handout at some back door when you're too lazy to bait the hook. That feeling gets hold of me lots of times; but I shake it off pretty soon. You don't get anywhere loafing; the people that get along have got to hustle. Cecil says we can't just mark time in this world. We either go ahead or slide back."

"Well, I'm a slider — if you can slide without ever getting up very far!"

"Look here," he said, drawing in the paddle and fixing his eyes upon her intently, "you said something like that the first night Cecil took me up to see you, and you've got a touch of it again; but it's the wrong talk. I'm going to hand it to you straight, because I guess I've got more nerve than anybody else you know: you have n't got a kick coming, and you want to cut all that talk. Uncle Tim gets cross sometimes, but you don't want to worry about that too much. He used to be meaner than fleas at the store sometimes, but the boys never worried about it. He's all sound inside, and if he riles you the best thing to do is to forget it. You can't please him all the time, but you can most of the time, and it's up to you to do it. Now, tell me to jump in the river if you want to, but it was in my system and I had to get it out."

"Oh, I know I ought to be grateful; but I'm wrong some way."

"You're all right," he declared. "Your trouble is you don't have enough to do. You ought to get interested in something — something that would keep you busy and whistling all the time."

"I *don't* have enough to do; I know that." she assented.

"Well, you ought to go in good and strong for something; that's the only ticket. Let's get out and climb the bank and walk awhile."

She had lost her bearings on the river, but when they had clambered to the top of the bank she found that they were near the Kinneys'. The road was a much-frequented highway, and she was sorry now that they had left the canoe; but Jerry, leading the way along a rough path that clung close to the river, continued to philosophize, wholly unconscious of the neighborhood's associations for Nan.

Where the margin between the river and the road widened they sat on a log while Jerry amplified his views of life, with discreet applications to Nan's case as he understood it. He was a cheery and hopeful soul, and in the light of her knowledge of him she marveled at his clear understanding of things. He confided to her that he meant to get on; he wanted to be somebody. She was wholly sympathetic and told him that he had already done a great deal; he had done a lot better than she had; and it counted for more because no one had helped him.

As they passed the Kinneys' on their way back to the canoe, a roadster whizzed out of the gate and turned toward town. They both recognized Copeland. As he passed, his eyes fell upon them carelessly; then he glanced back and slowed down.

"Now we're in for it!" said Nan uncomfortably.

"I guess I'm the one that's in for it," returned Jerry ruefully.

Copeland left his car at the roadside and walked rapidly toward them. He nodded affably to Jerry and extended his hand eagerly to Nan.

"This is great good luck! Grace is at home; why did n't you come in?"

"Oh, Mr. Amidon is showing me the river; we

just left the canoe to come up for a view from the bank."

"Why not come back to Kinneys'; I want to see you; and this is a fine chance to have a talk."

Jerry walked away and began throwing pebbles into the river.

"I can't do that. And I can't talk to you here. Papa drove me out and he's likely to come back this way."

"You seem to be pretty chummy with that clerk of mine," Copeland remarked.

"I am; it began about sixteen years ago," she answered, with a laugh. "We rose from the same ash-dump."

He frowned, not comprehending. She was about to turn away when he began speaking rapidly: —

"You've got to hear me, Nan! I have n't bothered you for a long time; you 've treated me pretty shabbily after all there 's been between us; but you can square all that now. I 'm in the deepest kind of trouble. Farley deliberately planned to ruin me and he's about done it! I 've paid him off, but I had to pledge half my stock in the store with the Western National to raise the money, and now my notes are due there and they're going to pinch me. Eichberg is a director in the bank and he means to buy in that stock — you can see the game. Corbin & Eichberg are scheming to wipe me out and combine the two houses. And Farley's put them up to it!"

His face twisted nervously as he talked. He was

thinner than when she saw him last, but he bore no
marks of hard living. His story was plausible; Farley had told her a month ago that he had got his
money out of Copeland, but it had n't occurred to
her that the loan might have been paid with money
borrowed elsewhere.

"Of course, you won't lose the business, Billy.
It would n't be square to treat you that way."

"Square! I tell you it was all framed up, and I 've
reason to know that Farley stands in with them.
It's a fine revenge he's taking on me for daring to
love you!"

She shook her head and drew further away from
him.

"Now, Billy, none of that! That's all over."

"No; it is n't over! You know it is n't, Nan! I 've
missed you; it cut me deep when you dropped me.
You let Farley tell you I was all bad and going to
the dogs and you did n't even give me a chance to
defend myself. I tell you I 've suffered hell's tor-
ments since I saw you last. But now I want you to
tell me you do care. Please, dear —"

His voice broke plaintively. She shook her head.

"Of course we were good friends, Billy; but you
knew we had to quit. It was wrong all the time —
you knew that as well as I do."

"I don't see what was wrong about it! It can't
be wrong for a man to love a woman as I love you!
If you had n't cared, it would be a different story,
but you did, Nan! And you 're not the girl I know

you to be if you've changed in these few weeks. I've got a big fight on and I want you to stand by me. Kinney's in all kinds of trouble with the cement business. If he goes down, I'm ruined. But even at that you can help me make a new start. It will mean everything to have your love and help."

He saw that his appeal had touched her. She was silent a moment.

"This won't do, Billy; I can't stand here talking to you; but I'm sorry for your troubles. I can't believe you're right about papa trying to injure you; he's too fond of the old business for that. But we were good pals — you and I. I'll try to think of some way to help."

He caught her hands roughly.

"I need you; you know I love you! Farley's told you I want to marry you for his money; but you can't tell anything about him. Very likely he'll cut you out, anyhow; he's likely to do that very thing."

She lifted her head and defiance shone for an instant in her eyes.

"I'll let you hear from me within a week; I must have time — But keep up your spirits, Billy!"

The distant honking of a motor caused her to turn away quickly. Amidon had settled himself halfway down the bank and she called to him and began the descent. . . .

If Jerry had expressed his feelings he would have said that Copeland's appearance had given him a hard jar. It was annoying, just when you have reached the highest aim of your life, to have your feet knocked from under you. To have your boss spoil your afternoon with the prettiest girl in town was not only disagreeable, but it roused countless apprehensions.

For the afternoon *was* spoiled. Nan's efforts to act as though nothing had happened were badly simulated, and finding that she lapsed frequently into long reveries, Jerry paddled doggedly back to the clubhouse.

CHAPTER XII

LAST WILLS AND TESTAMENTS

FROM the beginning of his infirmities Farley's experiments in will-writing had taxed the patience of Thurston, his lawyer. Within two years he had made a dozen wills, and he kept them for comparison in a secret drawer of Mrs. Farley's old sewing-table in his room. He penciled cryptic marks on the various envelopes for ease of identification, and he was influenced often by the most trivial circumstances in his revisions. If Nan irritated him, he cut down her legacy; when things went happily, he increased it. He was importuned to make bequests to great numbers of institutions, by men and women he knew well, and his attitude toward these changed frequently. There was hardly a phase of the laws of descent that Thurston had not explained to him.

A few days after her river excursion, the colored man-of-all-work handed Nan an envelope that had dropped from Farley's dressing-gown as it hung on a clothes-line in the backyard for its periodical sunning. The envelope was unsealed. In the upper left-hand corner was the name and address of Thurston and in the center were four small crosses in pencil. Nan thrust it into a bureau drawer,

intending to restore it to the dressing-gown pocket
when she could do so without attracting Farley's
attention.

Her eyes fell upon it that night as she was pre-
paring for bed. She laid it on her dressing-table
and studied the queer little crosses as she brushed
her hair.

Copeland had complained of Farley's hardness,
and if Billy had told the truth about the plight to
which he had been reduced by Farley's refusal to
renew the last notes for the purchase money, the
complaint was just. She crouched on a low stool
before the table and gazed into the reflection of
her eyes.

She played idly with the envelope, resisting an
impulse to open it for a glance at the paper that
crinkled in her fingers. She had been very "good"
lately, and to pry into affairs that Farley had sedulously kept from her was repugnant to her better
nature. . . . Farley's abuse of her on the day of the
luncheon, and his rage over her payment of the
thousand dollars for the defense of her brother
came back to her vividly. He had threatened to
make it impossible for Billy to profit by marrying
her. . . . She had a right to know what provision
Farley meant to make for her. If in the end he intended to throw her upon her own resources or to
provide for her in ways that curtailed her liberty,
there was every reason why she should prepare to
meet the situation.

LAST WILLS AND TESTAMENTS

The paper slipped from the envelope and she pressed it open.

I, Timothy Farley, being of sound mind, —

She had never seen a will before, and the unfamiliar phraseology fascinated her.

... in trust for my daughter, Nancy Corrigan Farley, for a period of twenty years from my decease, or until the death of said Nancy Corrigan Farley, should said death occur prior to the expiration of said twenty years, the sum of one hundred thousand dollars. The income from said sum shall be paid to the said Nancy Corrigan Farley on the first day of each calendar month. . . .

Two hundred thousand dollars he gave outright to the Boys' Club Association; fifty thousand to the Children's Hospital; and ten thousand each to five other charitable organizations. . . .

One hundred thousand dollars in trust! An income of five or six thousand — less than half the cost of maintaining the Farley establishment, exclusive of her personal allowance for clothes! And this was Farley's idea of providing for her. She had always heard that the act of adoption conferred all the rights inherent in a child of the blood; it was inconceivable that Farley would deal in so miserly a fashion with his own daughter.

THE PROOF OF THE PUDDING

The will was dated June 17, a week after the row over Copeland. She had heard that Farley's property approximated a million, and on that basis she was to pay dearly for that day at the Country Club!

The trusteeship, — in itself an insult, an advertisement of Farley's lack of confidence in her, — was to continue for what might be all the years of her life, restricting her freedom, fastening hateful bonds upon her. In case she married and died leaving children, the trusteeship was continued until they attained their majority. A paltry hundred thousand, and Farley's lean hand clutched even that!

Two hundred thousand for the Boys' Club — just twice what he gave her — and without restrictions! The Farleys' love for her was now reduced to exact figures. Her foster-father meant to humiliate her in the eyes of the world by a niggardly bequest. And he had been protesting his love for her and permitting her to sacrifice herself for him!

The revelations of the will reinforced Copeland's arraignment of Farley as a harsh and vindictive man, who drove hard bargains and delighted in vengeance.

She lay awake for hours, torturing herself into the belief that she was the most abused of beings. Then her better nature asserted itself. She reviewed the generosity and kindness of her foster-parents, who had given her a place in the world to which she felt, humbly, that she was not entitled. A hundred thousand dollars was more money than she had any right to expect; and the trusteeship was only a part of Farley's kindness — a device for safeguarding and protecting her.

Then she flew to the other extreme. He had brought her up as his own child, encouraging a belief that she would inherit his whole fortune, and now he was cutting her off with something like a tenth and contemptuously bidding her beg for alms at the door of a trust company!

She stared into the dark until the light crept through her blinds. Then she slept until the nurse called her at eight.

"Mr. Farley's waiting for you to have breakfast with him; how soon can you be ready?"

"Isn't he so well?" Nan asked quickly.

"Nothing unusual; but he seemed tired after his ride yesterday and had a bad night."

Nan, sitting up in bed, thrust her hand under her pillow and touched the will guiltily.

"I suppose," she said, as the nurse crossed to the windows and threw up the shades, "that he may have a relapse at any time. The doctor prepared me for that. Please order breakfast sent up and tell papa I'll be ready in five minutes."

In her broodings of the night she had dramatized herself as confronting him in all manner of situations, but she was reluctant to face him now. She jumped out of bed, fortified herself for the day with a cold shower, and presented herself to him in a flowered kimono as the maid was laying the cloth on the stand by his bed.

"Well, Nan," he said wearily, "I hope you had a better night than I did."

"Oh, I don't need much sleep," she answered. "Edison says we all sleep too much, anyhow."

"That's a fool idea. The doctor's got to give me the dope again if I have another such night. I guess there was n't anything I did n't think of. Lyin' awake is about as near hell as I care to go."

The querulousness manifest in the worst period of his illness had returned. He grumbled at the nurse's arrangement of his pillows and asked for a tray in bed, saying he did n't feel equal to sitting at the table.

"You sit there where I can look at you, Nan."

She was aglow from her bath and showed no trace of her sleepless night. It was pathetically evident that her presence brought him pleasure and relief. He had been very happy of late, accepting fully her assurance that everything was over between her and Copeland. Her recent social activities and the fact that some of the "nice people" were showing a renewed interest in her added to his satisfaction. He bade her talk as he nibbled his toast and sipped his milk.

"I read the newspaper an hour ago clear through the births and deaths and did n't see anything very cheerful. You been followin' that Reid will case up at Cleveland? I guess you don't read the papers much. You never did; but you ought to keep posted. Well, that's a mighty interestin' case. I guess the lawyers are goin' to get all the money. I knew old Reid, and he was as sane a man as ever lived. There ain't much use in a man tryin' to make a will when they're sure to tear it to pieces."

Nan looked at him quickly. It was possible that he had missed the will and was speaking of wills in general as a prelude to pouncing upon her with a question as to whether she had seen it. But he was not in a belligerent humor. He went on to explain the legal points involved in the Reid case.

"If a lot o' rascally lawyers get hold o' my property, I won't just turn over in my grave; I'll keep revolvin'! Reid tried to fix things so his children would n't squander his money. His daughters married fools and he wanted to try and protect 'em. And just for that they've had the will set aside on the ground that Reid was crazy."

Nan acquiesced in his view of this as an outrage. And she really believed that it was, as Farley spoke of it.

"I sometimes wonder whether it ain't better just to let things go," he continued. "I been over this will business with Thurston a thousand times, and I'm never sure he knows what he's talkin' about. Wills made by the best lawyers in the country seem to break down; there ain't nothin' sure about it."

THE PROOF OF THE PUDDING

"Well, I would n't worry about that, papa. Mr. Thurston ought to know about those things if anybody does."

Ordinarily he would have combated this, as he combated most emphatic statements; but his willingness to let it pass unchallenged convinced her that there had been a sharp change for the worse in his condition.

It was the way of her contradictory nature to be moved to pity for him in his weakness, and a wave of tenderness swept her. After all, if he wished to cut her off with a hundred thousand dollars and give the rest to charity he had a right to do it.

She took the tray from the bed, smoothed the covers and passed her cool hand over his hot forehead.

"Please, papa," she said, "don't bother about business to-day. Miss Rankin says it's only a cold, but she 'll have to report it to the doctor. I 'm going to telephone him to drop in this morning."

He demurred, but not with his usual venomous tirade against the whole breed of doctors.

"All right, Nan," he said, clinging to her hand. "And I wish you'd tell Thurston to come in this afternoon. I want to talk to him about some matters."

"Well, we'll see the doctor first, papa. We can have Mr. Thurston in any time."

She knelt impulsively beside the bed.

LAST WILLS AND TESTAMENTS

"I want you to know, papa, about wills and things like that, that I don't want you to bother about me. I hope we're going to live on together for long, long years. And anything you mean to do for me is all right."

She hardly knew herself as she said this. It was an involuntary utterance; something she could not have imagined herself saying a few hours earlier as she lay in bed hating him for his meanness.

"Well, dear, I want to do the right thing by you. It's worried me a lot, tryin' to decide the best way. I don't want to leave any trouble behind me for you to settle. And I don't want to do anything that'll make you think hard o' me. I want to be sure you never come to want: that's what's worried me. I want you to be happy and comfortable, little girl."

"I know you do, papa," she replied. "But don't bother about those things now."

The nurse came in to take his temperature. Nan went to her room for the will and, feigning to be straightening some of the things in his closet, she thrust the paper into the dressing-gown pocket.

An hour later the Kinney's chauffeur left a note from Grace: —

Come out this afternoon at any hour you can. Telephone me where to meet you downtown and I'll bring you out in the car. I need n't explain why, but after Saturday you'll understand.

THE PROOF OF THE PUDDING

The doctor found nothing alarming in Farley's condition, but ordered him to remain in bed for a few days. He said he must have sleep and prescribed an opiate.

At three o'clock Nan left the house.

CHAPTER XIII

A KINNEY LARK AND ITS CONSEQUENCES

"It's certainly good to see you again!" Mrs. Kinney exclaimed as Nan met her by arrangement at a confectioner's. "How much time are you going to give me?"

"Oh, I have n't any," laughed Nan. "I've run away. Papa is n't so well to-day and could n't take his drive as usual, so I'm truanting—and very naughty. I must be back in the house before five."

"Well, when I got your message I telephoned Billy to come to the house and he'll be there as soon as we are. He's been in the depths for weeks. You know you had got a mighty strong hold on dear old Billy, and when you dropped him it hurt. And we've all missed you!"

The Kinneys and their friends had missed her; they had missed her dash, her antics — the Nan she had resolved to be no more. But it was pleasant to be in Mrs. Kinney's company again. She was a simple, friendly soul who liked clothes and a good time; her capacity for enjoying anything serious was wholly negligible.

"I knew, of course, that Billy was back of your invitation. I saw him Saturday — quite accidentally, and he was bluer than indigo."

THE PROOF OF THE PUDDING

"He spent Sunday with us and told us all about
meeting you. He was perfectly furious because you
were out skylarking with one of his clerks! But he
got to laughing about it, — told us some funny
stories about your new suitor, — Jerry, is that the
name?"

"Mr. Jeremiah Amidon, please," laughed Nan.
"It was killing that Billy should find me out canoeing with him. Jerry and I were kids together, and
he's grown to be a great consolation to me."

"He must be a consolation to Billy, too; he says
the youngster's trying to reform him!" Grace
suddenly clasped Nan's hand. "You ought to take
charge of Billy! He's awfully in love with you,
Nan. He's going to urge you to marry him—at
once. That's why —"

"No! No! I'll never do it," cried Nan des-
pairingly.

It was another of her mistakes, this yielding to
Copeland's demand for an interview that could
have but one purpose. She was thoroughly angry
at herself, half angry at Mrs. Kinney for acting as
Copeland's intermediary.

Copeland was pacing the veranda smoking a
cigarette when they reached the house.

"It's mighty nice of you to come, Nan," he
said.

"I've heard, Billy, that the haughty John Eaton's
rather attentive to the late Mrs. Copeland," said
Grace, when they had gathered about the tea-

table. "She was among those present at a little dinner he gave at the University Club the other night in honor of that English novelist who's visiting here."

"You're bitter because he left you out," said Copeland indifferently.

"Oh, my bitterness won't hurt Fanny. I suppose you've heard that she's come into a nice bunch of money — something like a quarter of a million!"

Copeland's surprise was evident.

"That sounds like a fairy story; but I hope it's true."

"I know it's true," said Nan quietly. "Mrs. Copeland told me herself."

Mrs. Kinney had risen to leave them and Copeland had crossed the room to open the door for her. They were arrested by Nan's surprising confirmation of this report that Mrs. Copeland had come into an unexpected inheritance. Nan vouchsafed nothing more; and at a glance from Copeland Grace left them.

"I did n't know you and Fanny were seeing each other these days," he remarked as he sat down beside her. "Something new, is n't it?"

"Well, papa always admired her and he took me out to see her a little while ago, and then that day you saw her with us at the bank he insisted on taking her home for luncheon. She told us then about the money."

Copeland smiled grimly.

"Of course, you know what it means—Farley's sudden affection for Fanny?"

"Oh, he used to see a good deal of her, did n't he, when you were first married?"

"Mrs. Farley and Fanny exchanged a few calls and we were there for dinner once, while you were still away at school. But this is different; he's throwing you with her for a purpose, as you ought to see. It does credit to the old man's cunning. He thinks that if you become good friends with Fanny, he can be sure you've dropped me."

"Rubbish! Papa has always liked her; he likes the kind of woman who can run a farm and make money out of it; he thinks she's a good example for me!"

"Don't let him fool you about that!" he said petulantly. "He's an old Shylock and he's about taken the last ounce out of me. Paying him that last twenty-five thousand has put me in a bad hole. And it's pure vengeance. If he was n't afraid you were going to marry me, he would never have driven me so hard. He thinks if he can ruin me financially you'll quit me for good. It was understood when I bought him out that he'd be easy about the payments. There's a frame-up between him and Corbin & Eichberg to force me out of business. And he's been calling some of the old employees up to see him, and encouraging Amidon to trot up there so he can worm things out of him. I don't think he gets anything out of Jerry," he added, taking warning of a resentful gleam in Nan's eyes. "I think the boy's loyal to me; in fact" — he grinned ruefully — "he's full of an ambition to make a man of me! But you must see that it's all a game to draw you away from me. Farley's not the sort of man to waste time on a youngster like Amidon for nothing, and this throwing you in Fanny's way is about as smooth a piece of work as I ever knew him to do."

"You're exaggerating, Billy; and as far as Jerry is concerned, papa likes him; he always takes an interest in poor boys. And the fact that Jerry came from down there on the river where he had his own early struggles probably makes him a little more sympathetic with him."

"The old gentleman's sympathies," said Copeland, bending forward and meeting her gaze with a significant look, "are likely to cost you a whole lot of money, Nan."

"Just how do you make that out, Billy?"

"All the hospitals and charitable concerns in town have been working on Farley to do something for them in his will, and I heard yesterday that he's promised to do something big for the Boys' Club people. You've probably seen Trumbull at the house a good deal — he's the kind of fellow who'd make an impression on Farley. I got this from Kinney. He gave them some money last year and they put him on the board of directors. They're all counting on something handsome from the old man. I assume he has n't told you anything about it; it would n't be like him to! He means to die and let you find out just what his affection for you comes down to in dollars."

"Well, he has a right to do what he likes with his money," Nan replied slowly, repeating the phrase with which she had sought to console herself since the will fell into her hands. "I suppose he thinks he's done enough for me."

The phrases of the will danced before her eyes: Copeland's intimations squared with the facts as she knew them to be; she had seen tangible proof of their accuracy.

"We have to admit that he's been kind to you, but he has n't any right to bring you up as his daughter and then cut you off. You stand in law as his own child, and if he should die without making a will, you'd inherit everything."

"Well, the law has n't made me his own child," said Nan bitterly.

Seeing her resentment, and feeling that he was gaining ground, he proceeded cautiously.

"I suppose he's likely to have a sudden call one of these days?"

"Yes; or he may live several years, so the doctor told me. But I don't want to think of that. And I don't like to think of what he may do or not do for me," she added earnestly.

"Of course you don't!" he assented. "But he has n't any right to stand between you and your happiness. If he had the right feeling about you, he'd want to see you married and settled before he dies. I suppose he's never told you what he meant to do for you?"

"No. But he's told me what he would n't do if I married you; he laid that down in the plainest English!"

"I don't doubt it; but no man has a right to do any such thing. Just why he hates me so I don't understand. It ought n't to be a crime to love you, Nan."

His hand touched hers, then clasped it tightly.

"I don't see why we should be talking of these things at all," he went on. "I love you; and I believe that deep down in your heart you love me. You're not going to say you don't, Nan?"

"You know I've always liked you a lot, Billy," she answered evasively.

"Before Farley got the idea that I wanted to marry you for his money and abused me and made you unhappy, you cared; you can't deny that. And I don't believe his hatred of me really made any difference."

It was the wiser course not to abuse Farley. He felt that he was winning her to a yielding mood, and his hopes rose.

She withdrew her hand suddenly and bent her eyes upon him with disconcerting intentness.

"Please tell me, Billy, the real truth about your trouble with Fanny?"

THE PROOF OF THE PUDDING

The abruptness of her question startled him. The color deepened in his face and he blinked under her searching gaze. She had never before spoken of his trouble with his former wife.

"That," he said rallying quickly, "is all over and done. It has n't anything to do with you and me."

"Yes, Billy; I think it has! If you're really serious in wanting to marry me, I think I ought to know about that."

"I don't see how you could doubt my seriousness; you've been the one serious thing in my whole life!"

"But Fanny —" she persisted, gently touching his hands that were loosely clasped on his knee.

"Oh, the trouble was that we were never suited to each other. She's quiet, domestic — a country-town girl, and never fitted into things here. She wanted to sit at home every evening and sew and expected me to wait around for her to drop a spool so I could get excitement out of scrambling for it. And she did n't like my friends, or doing the things I like. Her idea of having a gay time was to go to the state fair once a year and look at live stock! I think she hated me toward the end."

"But that other story about her — about another man; she does n't look like that sort of woman, Billy."

He shrugged his shoulders impatiently.

"That was n't in the case at all. The divorce was given for incompatibility. Whatever else there may have been did n't figure. I made it as easy for her as possible, of course. And I've no doubt she was as glad to quit as I was!"

"But you did n't think — you did n't honestly believe —"

"Well, I thought she was interested in Manning; and we had some trouble about that. He used to come here a good deal. He was an old friend of mine and his business brought him to town pretty often for a couple of years. He's a fellow of quiet tastes — just her sort — and I hoped when I got out of the way she'd marry him. I want you to be satisfied about everything, Nan. I tell you everything's over between Fanny and me."

She rose and took a turn across the room, paused at the window, glanced out upon the lawn and the strip of woodland beyond. He became impatient as the minutes passed. Then she faced him suddenly.

"It's no use, Billy," she said.

He was eagerly protesting when Mrs. Kinney appeared at the door.

"What are you two looking so glum about? You need cheering up and I've got a fine surprise for you!"

"I must go," said Nan, relieved at the interruption.

"Not much, you're not! Bob has just telephoned that the Burleys of Chicago are in town and they're coming out for dinner. And I've telephoned

the Liggets and the Martins and George Pickard
and Edith Saxby and the Andrews. It will be like
old times to have the old crowd together once
more!"

"Of course, Nan will stay! She's been making
me miserable lately and that will help her square
herself," said Copeland.

"I must go, really," Nan reiterated, suspecting
that the party had been arranged in advance.

"Please don't!" cried Copeland. "You can telephone home that you've been delayed — you can
arrange it someway."

"When I went downtown on an errand! I don't
see it!"

"Dinner's at six; the Burleys have to go into
town early," said Mrs. Kinney.

"Oh, let her go!" exclaimed Copeland. "Our
Nan isn't the good sport she used to be, and she
doesn't love any of us any more. She's gone back
on all her old friends."

"Oh, no, she hasn't. I never knew her to take
a dare! I don't believe she's going to do it now."

Nan surveyed them defiantly and looked at her
watch.

She felt that she had finally dismissed Billy, and
her last word to him had left her elated. It might
be worth while to wait, at any hazard, to ease his
discomfiture, and to show the Kinneys and their
friends that she had not cut them; and, moreover,
she was unwilling to have them know how greatly

her old freedom was curtailed. The time had passed quickly and she could not reach home before seven even if she left immediately. Miss Rankin had covered up her absences before and might do so again.

"Let me telephone and I'll see how things are going."

The nurse's report was reassuring. Farley, who had rested badly for several nights, was sleeping. He might not waken for an hour — perhaps not for several hours. Miss Rankin volunteered to explain Nan's absence if he should call for her.

"All right, Grace, you may a lay a plate for me!" she announced cheerfully. "But I must be on my way right after dinner. You understand that!"

"It's great to see you on the good old cocktail route again, Nan!" declared Pickard. "We heard you'd taken the veil!"

The cocktails were passed before they went to the table; there were quarts for everybody, Grace assured them. The men had already fortified themselves downtown against any lack of an appetizer at the house. Mocking exclamations of surprise and alarm followed Nan's rejection of her glass.

"That's not fair, Nan!" they chorused, gathering about her. "You used to swallow six without blinking an eye."

"She's joined the crape-hangers for sure! I did n't think it of our Nan!" mourned Pickard.

THE PROOF OF THE PUDDING

"Oh, anything to stop your crying!" Nan took the glass Kinney had been holding for her. "There! I hope you're satisfied. It's silly to make so much fuss about a mere cocktail. No, thanks; not another! There's no point in taking the same dare twice!"

At the table the talk at once became animated. Nan had been away from them so long that she had half forgotten their range of interests. Burley's expensive new machine, in which he had motored down from Chicago; "shows" they had seen; a business scheme — biggest thing afoot, Burley threw in parenthetically, with a promise to tell Kinney more about it later; George Pickard's attentions to the soubrette in a musical comedy, and references to flirtations which the married men present had been engaging in — these things were flung upon the table to be pecked at and dismissed.

"You people are the only real sports in this dismal swamp of a town! I don't know how you live here among so many dead ones!" said Burley.

Kinney declared that he intended to move to New York as soon as he got rid of his patent suits; he was tired of living in a one-horse town. This suggested a discussion of the merits of New York hotels — a subject which the Kinneys everywhere west of Manhattan Island find endlessly exciting.

When champagne was served, Burley rose with elaborate dignity and invited the other men to join in a toast to the ladies; they were the best girls in America; he defied anybody to gainsay him. He wished they might all travel about together all the time hitting only the high places; and he extended a general invitation to the company to meet him at Palm Beach the next winter for what he promised should be a grand time.

"He'd make it Japan if he'd only had a few more drinks," his wife remarked to Nan.

By the time salad was served George Pickard thought it well to justify his reputation as a "cut-up." His father, a successful lawyer, had left him a comfortable fortune which George was rapidly distributing. George had rebelled against the tame social life of the town in which he was born; he was bored by respectability, and found the freedom of the Kinneys' establishment wholly to his liking. He went to the living-room for the victrola and wheeled it in, playing the newest tango, to a point just behind Nan's chair.

"Got to have music; got the habit and can't eat without music!"

This was accepted as a joke until Copeland protested that he could n't stand the noise and began struggling with Pickard, who bitterly resented his effort to push the machine out of the room. The music was hushed presently and Pickard resumed his seat with the understanding that he might play all he pleased after dinner.

"And we'll have a dance — I have n't danced a

step in ages!" cried Nan, entering into the spirit of the occasion.

She had always excused their vulgarity on the ground that they were at least cheerful, and that probably they were just as good as the people who frowned upon them. Their admiration was evident from the frequency with which they invited her opinion on the questions under discussion; and it was a relief to escape from the invalid air of home and from what she had convinced herself was Farley's hostility.

Several times her fingers touched the stem of her wineglass, only to be withdrawn quickly. Copeland, sitting beside her, noticed her indecision and drew the glass toward her.

"Just one, for old times' sake, Nan?"

"All right, Billy!"

She emptied her glass, and then, turning to Copeland, laid her fingers lightly across the rim.

"That's all; not another drop!" she said in a low tone.

He laughed and held up his glass for inspection; he had barely touched his lips to it.

"I had only one cocktail and I have n't taken any of this stuff," he said with a glance that invited approval. "I can do it; you see I can do it! I can do anything for you, Nan!"

The furtive touch of his hand seemed to establish an understanding between them that they were spectators, not participants in the revel.

A KINNEY LARK AND ITS CONSEQUENCES

"I know you can, and you must, Billy."

The noise and confusion increased. Edith Saxby had begun to cry — Nan remembered that Edith usually cried when she was tipsy. She was bewailing the loss of her salted almonds which she charged Andrews with appropriating. Andrews thereupon went to the sideboard and brought the serving-dish of almonds and poured the contents upon the girl's head.

Pickard leaned across the table to wipe away her tears with his napkin. In attempting this feat he upset the wineglasses of his immediate neighbors, causing a wild scamper to escape the resulting deluge. Liggett and Burley retaliated by pushing him upon the table, where he crowned himself with the floral centerpiece. Boisterous expressions of delight greeted this masterstroke.

"This is getting too rotten!" shouted Copeland.

He seized Pickard and dragged him from the table amid general protests.

"Biggest joke of all," cried Kinney, pointing at Copeland, "that Billy's sober. Everybody else drunk, but Billy sober's a judge!"

Mrs. Liggett, a stout blonde, shrilly resenting this as an imputation upon her character, attempted to retaliate by slapping Kinney, who began running round the table to escape her. This continued with the others cheering them on until she tripped and fell headlong amid screams of consternation from the women and roars of delight from the men.

THE PROOF OF THE PUDDING

"This is what I call a real ball!" declared Burley.

After Mrs. Liggett had been carried to a divan in the hall to recuperate, they decided that the possibilities of the table had been exhausted and returned to the living-room where the victrola was again set going.

Nan, lingering in the hall, found Andrews beside her.

"Always meant to tell you I loved you, Nan; now's a good time," he blurted. "No girl like you, Nancy!"

His wife appeared suddenly at the door and screamed at him to behave himself, while the others laughed loudly.

"Rules all suspended to-night; nobody going to be jealous!" cried Burley encouragingly.

"Got to kiss me, Nan," Andrews resumed; "kiss everybody else but you never —"

She pushed him away in disgust. Kinney entertainments, viewed soberly, clearly lacked the zest she had found in them when exhilarated. She looked at her watch. She must leave immediately. Copeland beckoned to her and she turned to him with relief.

"It's half-past eight, Nan; how soon must you go?"

"At once; I should n't have stayed in the first place."

"Well, I'll be glad enough to shake this bunch! Get your things and I'll go for the car."

A KINNEY LARK AND ITS CONSEQUENCES

He had been a very different Billy to-night. It was clear that he meant to be kind and considerate. The butler passed them bearing a jingling tray to answer a demand for high-balls from the living-room. Billy was the only sober man in the company, and she gave him full credit for his abstemiousness. They were calling her insistently to come and do some of the "stunts" that she had always contributed to their parties.

She walked to the open door and laughed at them mockingly.

"I'm all in, dead tired! Billy's going to take me home!"

The sight of them, flushed, rumpled, maudlin, increased her desire to escape as quickly as possible. She bade them good-night amid their loud reproaches, went for her hat and coat, and was soon in Copeland's white roadster spinning toward town.

"Well, Nan, this is fine. We can go on with our talk now."

"But we finished that, Billy. We can't go back to it again!"

"Oh, yes, we can; there's only one way to end it! That sort of thing" — he jerked his head toward the Kinneys' — "isn't for you and me. I've cut it out; passed it up for good. I'm going to live straight and try to get back all I've lost: I know everybody's down on me — waiting to see me take the count. But with you everything will be different. You know that; you understand it, Nan!"

Nan's thoughts were sober ones. She did like Billy; his good conduct at the party was encouraging; he could be a man if he would. He was a boy — a big, foolish boy, kind of heart, and generous, with a substratum of real character. The actual difference in years did not matter greatly; he was as slim and trim as a youngster just out of college. From the beginning of their acquaintance they had got on amazingly well together. And he loved her; she was honestly convinced of this. Like many young girls she had found the adoration of an older man flattering. A Farley had been cruelly unjust to her; there was always that justification. Even after she had given him her solemn assurances that she would not marry Billy, he had deliberately planned to give the bulk of his fortune to charity.

After the scenes at the Kinneys' she found infinite relief and comfort in the rush of the cool night air, and in the bright shield of stars above. Billy was the only person in all the world who cared, who understood! In her anxiety to be just, she gave to his good conduct during the evening an exaggerated importance and assured herself that there was a manliness in him that she had never appreciated.

"Dear old Billy!" she said softly, and laid her hand lightly on his arm.

"Oh, Nan!"

With a happy laugh he brought the machine to an abrupt stop.

"Dear little girl! Dear little Nan!" he murmured, his arms clasping her. "You belong to me now; nobody's ever going to take you away from me. I love you; you're dearer to me than all the world; and I'm so happy and proud!"

They talked for a time in subdued tones of the future. Yes; she had made the great decision. It seemed, now that she had given her word, that it had been inevitable from the beginning. There would be no more uncertainty, no more unhappiness. His arms were a happy refuge. No one had ever been as kind to her as he had been. She no longer questioned his good faith, or doubted his love.

"Oh, Billy, we must hurry! I'm in for a bad time, if I'm caught."

When she reached the house the nurse let her in. Farley had wakened once and asked for her, Miss Rankin said, but he had been satisfied with an explanation that Nan had gone early to bed.

CHAPTER XIV

BILLS PAYABLE

At six o'clock every morning Mr. Jeremiah Amidon's alarm-clock sent him trotting down the hall of his boarding-house to the bathroom for an immersion in cold water. When he had carefully dressed himself, he pulled weights for ten minutes, and thus refreshed and strengthened was able to wring a smile from the saddest boarder at the breakfast table.

He now opened the office mail. No one knew who had conferred this responsibility upon him; all that any one knew about the matter was that Jerry got down first and had the job done usually by eight o'clock. He did it well; there was no denying that. It was the only way, he told Copeland, that you could keep track of the business. He assumed also the task of replying to complaints of protesting customers, and carried the replies to Copeland to sign. The errors, omissions, and delays complained of became, under Jerry's hand, a matter of chagrin and personal grief to the head of the house. These literary performances were in a key of cheerful raillery, made possible by his knowledge of the domestic affairs or social habits of the kicking customer. Where there was real ground for

complaint and the patron was a valued one, Jerry
telegraphed an apology. Copeland demurred at
this.

"What if that fellow does get a damaged ship-
ment occasionally?" said Copeland, frowning over
one of these messages; "he's one of the slowest
customers on our list. It would n't be any great
calamity if we lost him."

"He's slow all right," Jerry admitted, "but he's
dead sure; and he has an old uncle who owns about
a section of the fattest bottom land on the Wabash.
When the old gent dies, Sam's going to put up a
building for himself and build a drug store that
will be more beautiful than Solomon in full evening
dress."

"These old uncles never die," observed Copeland dryly, handing back the telegram.

"Sam's will. He's mostly paralyzed now and it
won't be long till we get an order for a new stock.
Sam was in town last week and talked over the
fittings for his new store. You'll find seven dollars
in my expense account that covers victuals and
drink I threw into Samuel; but I paid for the tickets
to the Creole Queens Burlesque out of my own pocket
so's to bring down my average."

"All right; let 'er go," laughed Copeland.

No one else in the establishment ever joked with
Copeland. His father had been a melancholy dys-
peptic; and the tradition of Farley's bad temper
and profanity still caused the old employees to

walk softly. Copeland found Jerry's freshness and cheek diverting. Jerry, by imperceptible degrees, was infusing snap into the organization. And Copeland knew that the house needed snap.

"About telegrams: I guess we do more telegraphing than any house on the street!" Jerry informed him. "You can send a jolly by lightning anywhere in Indiana for a quarter; and nothing tickles one of these country fellows like getting a telegram."

"You've got to consider the dignity of the house just a little bit; try to remember that."

"Our game," replied Jerry confidently, "is to hold the business we've got and get more. The old system's played out. This is n't the only house that feels it," he added consolingly. "Everybody's got to rustle these days. We're conservative, of course, and deliver the goods straight every time, but we must keep shooting pep into the organization."

Jerry had gone to the private office with one of his sugar letters, as he called his propitiatory masterpieces, on the day after Copeland's meeting with Nan at the Kinneys'.

"By the way, Jerry," said Copeland, as Amidon turned to go, "what's this joke you've put over in the Bigger Business Club? I did n't tell anybody I wanted to be president. I was never in the clubrooms but once and that was to look at that billiard table I gave the boys."

Jerry ran his finger round the inside of his collar and blinked innocently.

BILLS PAYABLE

"It was just an uprising of the people, Mr. Copeland. The boys had to have you. You got two hundred votes, and Sears, of the Thornwood Furniture Company, was the next man with only sixty-two."

"You did that, you young scoundrel," said Copeland good humoredly, "and I suppose you gave 'The News' my picture to print in their account of the hotly contested election!"

"No, sir; I only told the reporter where I thought he would find one."

The Bigger Business Club was an organization of clerks and traveling men, that offered luncheon and billiards and trade journals in a suite of rooms in the Board of Trade Building. It took itself very seriously, and was highly resolved to exercise its best endeavors in widening the city's markets. Incidentally the luncheon served at thirty cents was the cheapest in town, and every other Saturday night during the winter there was a smoker where such subjects as "Selling Propositions," "The Square Deal" and "Efficiency" were debated.

"Well, now that you've wished it on me, what am I going to do about it?"

"Your election scores one for the house and, of course, you're going to take the job. The directors meet once a month, and you'll have to attend some of the meetings; and you ought to turn out at a few of the smokers, anyhow. It will help the boys a lot to have you show an interest."

THE PROOF OF THE PUDDING

Copeland's face became serious. He swung round in his chair and stared at the wall for a moment.

"You think I might do those young fellows some good, do you?" he demanded bitterly. "Well, you seem to have a better opinion of me than most people. I'm much obliged to you, Jerry. If you're going up there for lunch to-day I'll go along."

Copeland had ceased to be amused by Jerry's personal devotion; there was something the least bit pathetic in it. If any one else had taken the trouble to make him president of a club of clerks and drummers he would have scorned it, — but no one else would have taken the trouble! He was satisfied of that.

Copeland was at last thoroughly sobered by his financial situation. For two years the drug business had been losing steadily. Farley's strong hand was missed; in spite of his animosity toward Farley, Copeland realized that his father's old partner had been the real genius of the business.

His original subscription of fifty thousand dollars for Kinney's cement stock had been increased from time to time in response to the importunities of the sanguine and pushing Kinney until he now had three hundred thousand dollars invested. The bank had declined to accept his cement stock as collateral for the loan he was obliged to ask to take up Farley's notes and had insisted that he put up Copeland-Farley stock, a demand with which he had reluctantly complied.

One hundred thousand dollars of paper in the Western National matured on the 1st of November, only five days distant. Copeland was pondering a formidable list of maturing obligations that afternoon when Eaton appeared at the door of his private office. Copeland had never had any business with Eaton. Though Eaton was defending Kinney's patents, Copeland had never attended any of their conferences and the lawyer's attenuated figure and serious countenance gave him a distinct shock.

It was possible, if not likely, that Farley had got wind of Nan's interview with him and had sent the lawyer with a warning that Nan must be let alone. Eaton would be a likely choice for such an errand — likelier than Thurston. Copeland had always found Eaton's gravity disconcerting; and to-day the lawyer seemed unusually sedate.

"Hope I have n't chosen an unfortunate hour for my visit? I don't have much business down this way and I'm never sure when you men on the street are busy."

"Glad to see you at any time," Copeland replied with a cordiality he did not feel.

"We don't seem to meet very often," remarked Eaton. "I used to see you at the University Club in old times, but you've been cutting us out lately."

"I don't get there very often. The Hamilton is nearer the store and it's a little more convenient place to meet anybody you want to see."

"I shall have to quit the University myself if

the members don't stop napping in the library after luncheon," remarked Eaton musingly. "Rather a dim room, you remember? Only a few afternoons ago a fellow was sprawled out on a divan sleeping sweetly and I sat down on him — very annoying. The idea of gorging yourself so in the middle of the day that you've got to sleep it off is depressing. I suppose we can be undisturbed here for a few minutes?"

"Yes; we're all right here," Copeland assented with misgivings. He thrust the list of accounts payable into a drawer, and waited for Eaton to unfold himself.

"I come on a delicate matter, Copeland; business that is rather out of my line."

"I hoped you'd come to tell me we'd got a decision in the cement case. It would cheer us a good deal to know that Kinney's patents have been sustained."

"I'm sorry we haven't got a decision yet. But I'm reasonably sure of success there. If I hadn't had faith in Kinney's patents I shouldn't have undertaken to defend them. We ought to have a decision now very shortly; any day, in fact."

"Well, Kinney isn't worrying; he's been going ahead just as though his rights were founded on rock."

"I think they are. It might have been better policy not to extend the business until we had clearance papers from the highest court, but Kinney thought he ought to push on while the going's good. He's an ambitious fellow, and the stuff he makes is in demand; but you know more about that than I do."

"To be frank about it, I'd be glad to clear out of it," said Copeland. "But I can't desert him while his patents are in question — the stock's unsalable now, of course."

"There was a time when we might have compromised those suits on fairly good terms; but I advised Kinney against it. The responsibility of making the fight is mine. And," Eaton added with one of his rare smiles, "I shall owe you all an apology if I get whipped."

Copeland shrugged his shoulders. His uncertainty as to the nature of Eaton's errand caused him to fidget nervously.

"As I said before," Eaton resumed, "my purpose in coming to see you is wholly out of my line. In fact, I shan't be surprised if you call it sheer impudence; but I wish to assure you that I come in the best spirit in the world. I hope you will understand that."

Copeland was confident now that Eaton brought some message from Farley. There was no other imaginable explanation of the visit. He was thinking hard, and to gain time he opened his top drawer and extended a box of cigars.

"No, thanks," said Eaton, staring absently at the cigars. "To repeat, Copeland, my errand isn't an agreeable one, and I apologize for my presumption in undertaking it."

Copeland chose a cigar carefully and slammed the drawer on the box. Perhaps Farley had chosen Eaton as a proper person to marry Nan; she liked him; Eaton had always had an unaccountable fascination for women. He became impatient for the lawyer to continue; but Eaton had never been more maddeningly deliberate.

"May I assume, for a moment, Copeland, that you have obligations outstanding that cause you, we will say, temporary embarrassment? Just a moment, please!" Copeland had moved forward suddenly in his chair with resentment burning hot in his face. "The assumption may be unwarranted," Eaton continued; "if so, I apologize."

Copeland thrust his cigar into his mouth and bit it savagely. Farley had undoubtedly taken over the maturing notes at the Western National and had sent Eaton to taunt him with the change of ownership. Eaton removed his eyeglasses and polished them with the whitest of handkerchiefs. His eyes, unobscured by the thick lenses, told Copeland nothing.

"I may have misled you into thinking that my errand is purely social. I shall touch upon business; but I am not personally concerned in it in any way whatever. You might naturally conclude that I represent some corporation, bank, or trust company. I assure you that I do not. It may occur to you that Mr. Farley sent me, but he has not mentioned you to me in this, or in any other connection remotely bearing upon my errand. You may possibly suspect that some one near you — some one in your office, for example — has been telling tales out of school. I will say explicitly that young Amidon, while a friend of mine, and a boy I particularly like, has given me no hint — not even the remotest idea — of any such state of things. I hope you are satisfied on those points?"

Many persons at different times in John Cecil Eaton's life, enraged by his cool, unruffled demeanor, had been moved to tell him to go to the devil; but no one had ever done so. Copeland did not do so now, though he was strongly impelled to violent speech.

"I will go the length of saying that you are in considerable danger right now," Eaton went on as Copeland continued to watch him impassively. "If the Western National should foreclose on your stock, you would be pretty nearly wiped out of this old concern, that was founded and conducted for years by your father and is still identified with his name. I am in a position to pay those notes and carry them — carry renewals until you can take them up. I will say frankly that I don't consider them a good investment, and I have said so to the person I represent; but to repeat again, I am not here as a lawyer or business man. My purpose is wholly friendly, and quite disinterested. I should

merely go to the bank and take up the notes —
thus destroying the hopes of certain gentlemen —
your competitors in business — who entertain the
cheerful idea of buying in your stock and putting
you out of business. That would be a calamity —
for you; and it would be deplorable to have an
old house like Copeland-Farley lose its identity."

Copeland was still silent. He had caught at one
motive for this visit after another, but Eaton had
disposed of all of them. Eaton's reputation as a
man of strict — of rather quixotic — honor did not
encourage the belief that he would deliberately lie.
But there was a trap concealed somewhere, Copeland reflected; he resolved not to be caught. If he
effected an immediate marriage with Nan, Farley
would, he believed, do something handsome for
her. He would storm and bluster in his usual way;
but he would hardly dare go the length of cutting
her off entirely. It was conceivable that he might
advance money to save Copeland-Farley from
catastrophe. There was a vein of sentiment in
Timothy Farley; brought face to face with the idea
of having the business he had done so much to
establish eliminated, it was wholly possible that he
would come down handsomely if Nan were introduced into the situation as a factor.

Copeland was irritated by Eaton's cocksure
manner — a manner well calculated to cause irri-
tation. Men did not make such offers from purely
philanthropic motives. Eaton, moreover, was no

friend of his; they hardly spoke the same language. Nan, he still suspected, was somehow the object and aim of these overtures. His mind worked quickly. He meant to marry Nan at once, within a few days if his plans succeeded, and he was not to be frustrated by any scheme for placing himself at the mercy of a new and concealed creditor.

"I'm much obliged to you, Eaton," he answered steadily; "but I'm not quite all in yet. I can't imagine where you got that idea. If I didn't know you were a gentleman I should be pretty hot. Things have been a little tight with me, I confess; but that's largely due to cutting down my capital in the drug business to back up what I had invested with Kinney. I'm working out satisfactorily and don't need help; but I'm obliged to you just the same."

Eaton nodded reflectively; his face betrayed no surprise.

"It might be possible, of course, for me to buy those maturing notes without your knowledge or consent. But I thought it would look better—help your credit, in other words — if you took them up yourself. You can see that."

Copeland had already thought of this; the idea did not add to his comfort. The mystery that enveloped Eaton enraged him; business was not done in this way. If anybody wanted to put one hundred thousand dollars into the drug house, there were

direct businesslike ways of suggesting it. He
tipped himself back in his chair and pointed the
unlighted cigar he had been fumbling at a calendar
that hung on the wall over his desk.

"My paper in the Western National is n't due
for five days: I dare them to sell it — to you or
anybody else! As you know perfectly well, it would
be bad banking ethics for a bank to sell the paper
of an old customer. It is n't done! I've about
made up my mind to quit the Western, anyhow.
Those fellows over there think they've got the right
to sweat every customer they've got. They're not
bankers; they've got the souls of pawnbrokers and
ought to be making loans on household goods at
forty per cent a month."

"That," replied Eaton calmly, "has nothing to
do with the matter in hand. I understand that you
decline my offer, which is to take up the Western's
notes."

"You're right, mighty right! You would n't
accept such an offer yourself, Eaton. If I were to
come to you with a mysterious offer to advance
you money, you'd turn me out of your office."

"Very likely," Eaton assented. "And I don't
undertake to defend the idea; I confess that it's
indefensible. As I understand you, you've passed
on the matter finally."

"I have," replied Copeland sharply.

Eaton rose. He bent his gaze with an absent air
upon the calendar, as though surprised to find it

there. Then, seeming to recall that he had finished his errand, he walked to the door.

"Thank you very much, Copeland," he said; and passed out.

Jerry Amidon paused in the act of shaking hands with a country customer to stare at the departing figure, but Eaton stalked austerely into the street quite unmindful of him.

CHAPTER XV

FATE AND BILLY COPELAND

WHEN Nan left Copeland the night of the Kinney party she promised to call him the next day. As telephoning from home was hazardous, she made an excuse for going downtown and called from a department store. Copeland was not in, and she repeated her call several times without reaching him. Copeland, if she had known it, was in the directors' room at the Western National, discussing his affairs with the president.

She had a superstitious awe of petty frustrations of her plans and hopes. The Celt in her was alert for signs and miraculous interventions. It occurred to her that perhaps the angels of light or darkness were bent upon interfering; the idea kindled her imagination.

In the street she ran into Fanny Copeland. To meet Billy's former wife, just when she was trying to perfect plans for marrying Billy, was altogether dismaying.

"You dear child, I'm so glad to see you!" cried Fanny, taking both Nan's hands. "I was just wondering whether I had time to run up to the house. How is Mr. Farley?"

"Papa has n't been quite so well," Nan answered;

"but it's only a slight cold. I had to come down-town on an errand," she explained.

She experienced once more a feeling of self-con-sciousness, of unreality, in meeting Fanny face to face: within a day or two she might be another Mrs. Copeland! And yet Billy had once loved this woman, undeniably; and she had loved him — she might, for all Nan knew, still love him. She envied the little woman her equanimity, her poise, her good cheer. If she were only like that, instead of the wobbly weather-vane she knew herself to be! Why had n't she a firm grip on life instead of a succession of fatuous clutches at nothing! Nan wished, as she had wished a thousand times, that troublesome problems would not rise up to vex her.

The Farley chauffeur had run his machine to the sidewalk to pick her up.

"I hope your father will be better soon," said Fanny. "Give him my love, won't you?"

Nan's eyes followed her as the car got under way.

When she reached home she met a special delivery messenger at the door. Her heart jumped; it was a note from Billy, who had risked sending her a message that might very easily have fallen under her foster-father's eye. She thrust it into her pocket unopened and ran upstairs.

"Well, you're back again, are you?" Farley said harshly.

"Yes, papa; I had an errand I could n't put off."

"It's always been a mystery to me," he grumbled, "what women find to trot downtown for so much."

"Pins!" she replied lightly. "We always need little things. I met Mrs. Copeland — looking for pins, too; so you see I'm not the only one."

"You saw *her*, did you?" he asked with a show of eagerness.

"Yes; I met her as I was coming out of Sterling's. She was just starting home."

"I'd been hoping she'd stop in to see me, but she's a busy woman."

"She has a lot to do, of course. If you'd like to see her I'll telephone her to come in for luncheon to-morrow."

He appeared to be pondering this and his hands opened and shut several times before he answered.

"No; never mind. She's busy and it really does n't matter." He stared vacantly at the ceiling for a moment. "I guess that's all fixed now," he added musingly, apparently forgetting her.

She was anxious to be off to her room to read Billy's note; but she lingered, curious as to what further he might have to say about Fanny.

"You like that woman, don't you, Nan? You and she get on — you have n't found any traces of ill-feeling toward you?"

His small gray eyes were bent upon her with an odd expression of mingled hostility and kindness.

"Of course I like her, papa; and I believe she

likes me. There's no reason why she should n't like me!"

"No reason!" he caught her up contemptuously.

She knew that he was thinking of Billy. His face twitched as a wave of anger seized him.

"That man is a scoundrel!" he blurted. "If he had n't been he'd never have treated that woman as he did!"

"It does n't seem to worry her much!" she flashed back at him. "I don't know a happier woman anywhere!"

She realized instantly that the remark was unfortunate. He pointed a shaking finger at her.

"That woman," he said, pronouncing the words with ominous deliberation, "ought to get down on her knees every night and thank God that she's rid of him! That great bully, that worthless loafer! But I'll show him a few things! If that blackguard thinks he can put anything over on me he'll find that I'm smarter than he thinks I am! You remember that!"

"You must be quiet, Mr. Farley," admonished Miss Rankin, who had been standing by the window; "the doctor said you were n't to excite yourself."

"I'm not excited," he flared. "Doctors and lawyers make a nice mess of this world. They don't any of 'em know anything!"

He gave himself an impatient twitch and several documents slipped from under his pillow. He clutched them nervously and thrust them back.

THE PROOF OF THE PUDDING

Nan was jubilant for a moment in the knowledge that she knew what those documents contained — devices for humiliating her after he was gone. If only he knew how little she cared! He thought of nothing but his money and means of keeping it from her.

"Go away; I want to think," he said gruffly.

Nan was grateful for this dismissal, and a moment later had softly closed her door and was eagerly reading Copeland's message. It covered three letter-sheets and the daring of its contents caused her heart to beat wildly.

What he proposed was immediate marriage. There was to be a military wedding that night at the church in the next block. Nan, he assumed, would attend. At the end of the ceremony she had merely to pass out of the church and his machine would be waiting around the corner. She could pack a suit-case, ostensibly filled with articles for the cleaner's, and he would have a messenger call for it. They would run up to Lafayette, where he had a married cousin who would have a minister ready to marry them; then take a train for Chicago and return the next day and have it out with Farley.

Nan had never shared Copeland's faith in the idea that once they were married they might safely rely on Farley's forgiveness. Farley's passionate outbreaks at the mere mention of Copeland pretty effectually disposed of that hope. But that was not so important, for, in spite of Farley's unfavorable opinion of Copeland's business capacity and Billy's own complaint of hard times, she had an idea that Copeland was well off, if not rich. To outward appearances, the drug business was as flourishing now as in the days when Farley was still active in its affairs. It was the way of business men to "talk poor" even when they were most prosperous; this had, at least, always been Farley's way.

The gaunt figure in the room across the hall rose wraithlike before her, giving her pause. Yes, the Farleys had been kind to her; they had caught her away from the world's rough hand and had done all that it was in their power to do to make a decent, self-respecting woman of her. Her advantages had been equal to those enjoyed by most of the girls she knew. Many people — the town's "old stock," Farley's substantial neighbors — would see nothing romantic or amusing in her flight with Copeland. They would call her the basest ingrate; she could fancy them saying that blood will tell; that after all she was a nobody, a girl without background or antecedents, whom the Farleys had picked up, out of the kindness of their simple hearts, and that she had taken the first chance to slap them in the face.

Then she remembered the will that had given her the key to Farley's intentions. Possibly the new will, which Thurston had brought to the house that day, cut her expectations to an even lower figure. . . .

THE PROOF OF THE PUDDING

It pleased her to think that she was studying the matter dispassionately, arguing with herself both for and against Billy's plan. It was more honest to marry Copeland now and be done with it than to wait and marry him after Farley's death. This she found a particularly satisfying argument in favor of marrying him at once. Her histrionic sense responded to the suggestion of an elopement; it would be a great lark, besides bringing her deliverance from the iron hand of Farley. Yes; she would do it! Her pulses tingled as she visualized herself as the chief figure in an event that would stir the town. It was now four o'clock. Copeland had written that at five a messenger would call for her suit-case, and all she had to do was to step into his car when she came out of the church.

She was downstairs listening for the bell when the messenger rang. As she handed him the suit-case she felt herself already launched upon a great adventure. While she was at the door the afternoon paper arrived and she carried it up to Farley and read him the headlines.

She had her dinner with him in his room. There was a pathos in his lean frame, his deep-furrowed brow, in the restless, gnarled hands. She was not so happy over her plans as she had expected to be. She kept saying to herself that it was n't quite fair — not an honest return for all the kindnesses of her foster-parents — to run away and leave this broken old man. As she thought of it, every unkind

214

word he had said to her had been merited; she had lied to him, disobeyed him, and tricked him.

"What's the matter with your appetite, Nan?" he asked suddenly. "Seems to me you've looked a little peaked lately. Maybe you don't get enough exercise now we've got the machine."

"Oh, I'm perfectly well," she replied hastily.

"Well, you've been cooped up here all summer. You'd better take a trip this winter. We'll keep a lookout for somebody that's goin' South and get 'em to take you along."

"Oh, that isn't necessary, papa. I never felt better in my life."

"Isn't this the night for that Parish girl's wedding?" he asked later.

"Yes; I thought I'd go," she answered carelessly. "It's at the Congregational Church, and I can go alone."

"All right; you be sure to go. You never saw an army wedding? I guess 'most everybody will be there."

When he reminded her that it was time to dress she answered indifferently that she didn't care to go to the reception, and that the gown she had on would be perfectly suitable.

"I'll just watch the show from a back seat, papa; you can see a wedding better from the rear, anyhow."

"Well, don't hurry back on my account."

She had been afraid that he would raise some

objection to her going without an escort; but he
made no comment.

She ran her eyes over the things in her room —
photographs of girls she had known at boarding-
school, trifles for the toilet-table that had been
given her on birthdays and holidays. It was a
big comfortable room, the largest bedroom in the
house, with a window-seat that had been built
specially for her when she came home from school.
She glanced over the trinkets that littered the
mantel, and took from its leathern case a medal
she had won in school for excellence in recitations.
On the wall hung a photograph of herself as Rosalind, a part she had played in an out-of-doors pre-
sentation of "As You Like It." . . .

She must leave some explanation of her absence
— so she sat down at her desk and wrote: —

Dear Papa: —

Please don't be hard on me, but I've run away
to marry Mr. Copeland. We are going to Lafayette
to his cousin's and shall be married at her house
to-night. I hope you won't be hard on me; I shall
explain everything to you when I see you and I
think you will understand. We shall be back very
soon and I will let you know where I shall be.

She hesitated a moment and then closed with
"Your loving daughter, Nan." She thrust this
into an envelope, addressed it in a bold hand to

FATE AND BILLY COPELAND

Timothy Farley, Esq., and placed it under a small silver box on the mantel.

She stood a moment at the door, then closed it softly and went in to say good-night to Farley. He took the hand on which she had half-drawn her glove and held it while his eyes slowly surveyed her.

"I did n't know whether you'd wear a hat to an evening wedding. I never know about those things."

"Oh, this is such a foolish little thing, papa; you'd hardly call it a hat," she laughed.

"Well, don't let one of those army officers pick you up and carry you off. I want to hold on to you a little longer."

As she bent to kiss him tears sprang to her eyes. Face to face with it, there was nothing heroic, nothing romantic in abandoning the kindest friend she was ever likely to know, and in a fashion so shamelessly abrupt and cruel.

"Good-night, papa!" she cried bravely and tripped downstairs, humming to keep up her courage.

She absently took her latch-key from a bowl on the hall table and did not remember until she had thrust it into her glove as she went down the steps that she would have no use for it. It was the finest of autumn nights and many were walking to the church; there was a flutter of white raiment, and a festal gayety marked the street. She waited for those immediately in sight to pass before leaving the yard and then walked toward the church.

She eluded an officer resplendent in military dress who started toward her and stole into the nearest seat. The subdued happiness that seemed to thrill the atmosphere, the organist's preludings, the air of expectancy intensified her sense of detachment and remoteness.

The notes of the "Lohengrin" march roused her from her reverie and she craned her neck for a first sight of the attendants and the bride.

Just before the benediction she left, and was soon in the side street where Billy was to leave his car. She had expected him to be in readiness, but he had evidently waited for the end of the ceremony — which seemed absurd when they were so soon to have a wedding of their own! It was inconsiderate of him to keep her waiting. The street began to fill and she loitered, ill at ease, while the organ trumpeted joyfully.

Then she saw the familiar white roadster, with Billy in the chauffeur's seat, turning into the side street where several policemen were already directing the movements of the parked carriages and motors toward the church entrance. His overcoat was flung open and the light of the lamp at the intersecting streets smote upon his shirt bosom. It was ridiculous for him to have put on evening clothes and a silk hat when he had a long drive before him ! The policemen bawled to him not to interfere with the traffic. Ignoring their signals he drove his car forward. Nan watched with mounting anger the disturbance he was creating. The crowd that had assembled in the hope of catching a glimpse of the bride now found Copeland and his altercation with the police much more diverting. .

"Billy Copeland's drunk again," some one behind Nan remarked contemptuously.

The white car suddenly darted forward and crashed into a motor that was advancing in line toward the corner, causing a stampede among the waiting vehicles.

While the police were separating the two cars, Nan caught sight of Eaton, who seemed to be trying to persuade the policemen of Copeland's good intentions. Billy's voice was perfectly audible to the spectators as he demanded to be let alone.

"They have n't got any right to block this street; it's against the law to shut up a street that way!"

The policemen dragged him from the seat and a chauffeur from one of the waiting cars jumped in and backed the machine out of the way. Nan waited uncertainly to see what disposition the police were making of Billy; but having lifted the blockade they left him to his own devices. He had been drinking; that was the only imaginable explanation of his conduct, and her newly established confidence in him was gone. However, it would be best to wait and attempt to speak to him, as he might mingle in the crowd and make inquiries for her that would publish the fact that they had planned flight.

Suddenly she heard her name spoken, and turned to find Eaton beside her.

"Too bad about Copeland," he remarked in his usual careless fashion; "but one of those policemen promised to see that he went home."

She was bewildered by his sudden appearance. Eaton never missed anything; he would certainly make note of her gown and hat as not proper for occasions of highest ceremony. Nor was it likely that he had overlooked the two suitcases strapped to the rear of Billy's car.

"Looked for you all over the church, and had given you up," Eaton was saying. "You can't say no — simply got to have you! Stupid to be pulling off a wedding the night we're dedicating the new swimming-pool at the Wright Settlement House. Programme all shot to pieces, but Mamie Pembroke's going to sing and you've got to do a recitation. Favor to an old friend! They dumped the full responsibility on me at six o'clock — six, mind you!"

Nan bewildered, uncertain, suffered him to pilot her round the corner, wondering how much he knew, and trying to adjust herself to this new situation. A car that she recognized as the Pembrokes' stood at the curb.

"Oh, come right along, Nan; there's no use saying you won't!" cried Mamie Pembroke.

FATE AND BILLY COPELAND

The Pembrokes were among those who had dropped her after she became identified with the Kinneys, and her rage at Copeland was mitigated by their cordiality.

"Hello, Mamie! What on earth do you want with me!"

"Oh, it's a lark; one of this crazy Eaton man's ideas."

Nan knew that she had been recognized by many people, and that even if Copeland had not made a fool of himself the elopement was now out of the question. She felt giddy and leaned heavily on Eaton's arm as he helped her into the car.

"You were alone, were n't you, Nan?" Eaton asked as the machine started.

"Yes," she faltered, settling back into a seat beside Mrs. Pembroke.

"Then we'd better stop at your house so Mr. Farley wont be troubled about you."

As she had not meant to return at all, it seemed absurd to go back now to say that she was going to a settlement house entertainment and would be home in an hour or so. The telltale letter could hardly have been found yet and she must dispose of it immediately. The car whirled round to the Farleys' and Nan let herself in with her key.

Farley was awake, reading a magazine article on "The Ohio in the Civil War."

"Back already! Getting married does n't take long, does it? — not as long as getting out of it!"

THE PROOF OF THE PUDDING

"Oh, the wedding was stunning!" she cried breathlessly. "I never saw so much gold braid in my life. I'm going with the Pembrokes and Mr. Eaton down to dedicate a swimming-pool at the Wright Settlement House. I just stopped to tell you, so you would n't worry."

"Tom Pembroke going down there?" he growled. "I thought that tank was for poor boys. What's Eaton got to do with it?"

She explained that Eaton was substituting for the president of the Settlement House Association, who had been called from town, and that he had asked her to recite something.

"Well, 'The Ole Swimmin' Hole' will come in handy. I always like the way you do that. Run along now!"

She darted into her room and found the letter just as she had left it on the mantel. She tore it into strips and threw them into her beribboned waste-paper basket. Her revulsion of feeling was complete. It was like waking from a nightmare to find herself secure amid familiar surroundings. She turned to Farley's room again and impulsively bent and kissed him.

"Ain't you gone yet?" he demanded, with the gruffness that often concealed his pleasure.

"I'm off for sure this time," she called back. "Thanks for suggesting 'The Ole Swimmin' Hole' — that's just the thing!"

They found the hall packed with an impatient

crowd. Eaton led the way to the platform and opened the exercises without formality. The superintendent of the house dealt in statistics as to the service rendered by the Settlement. Mamie Pembroke sang "The Rosary" and responded to an encore.

Nan had not faced so large an audience since her appearance as Rosalind at school. She drew off her gloves before her name was announced, and as she stood up put aside her hat. At least half a dozen nationalities were represented in the auditorium; and she resolved to try first a sketch in which an Irishman, an Italian and a German debated in brisk dialogue the ownership of a sum of money. She had heard it done in vaudeville by a comedian of reputation and had mastered it for dinner-table uses. She had added to it, recast, and improved it, and she now gave it with all the spirit and nice differentiation of which she was capable. Eaton, who had heard her several times before, was surprised at her success; she had taken pains; and how often Eaton, in thinking of Nan, had wished she would take pains!

There was no ignoring the demand for more, and she gave another comic piece and added "The Ole Swimmin' Hole" for good measure. She received her applause graciously and sat down wondering at her own happiness. Mrs. Pembroke patted her hand; she heard somebody saying, "Yes, Farley's daughter, — adopted her when she was a child!"

THE PROOF OF THE PUDDING

Eaton was announcing the close of the programme. It was his pleasant office, he said, to deliver the natatorium that had been added to the
Settlement House into the keeping of the people of
the neighborhood.

"Many lives go to the making of a city like this.
Most of you know little of the men who have built
this city, but you profit by their care and labor as
much as though you and your fathers had been
born here. It is the hope of all of us who come
here to meet you and to help you, if we can, that
you may be builders yourselves, adding to the dignity and honor and prosperity of the community.

"Now, only one man besides myself knows who
gave the money for the building of the swimming-
pool. The other man is the donor himself. He is
one of the old merchants of this city, a man known
for his honesty and fair dealing. He told me not
to mention his name; and I'm not going to do it.
But I think that if some one who is very dear to
him — the person who is the dearest of all in the
world to him — should hand the keys to the superintendent, I should not be telling — and yet, you
would understand who this kind friend is."

He crossed the platform and handed Nan a bunch
of keys.

"I'm sure," he said, turning to the interested
spectators, "that you will be glad to know that the
keys to the bathhouse have come to you through
Miss Farley."

FATE AND BILLY COPELAND

Tears sprang to Nan's eyes as she rose and handed the keys to the superintendent amid cheers and applause. She was profoundly moved by the demonstration. They did not know — those simple foreign folk who lifted their faces in gratitude and admiration — that an hour earlier it had been in her heart to commit an act of grossest ingratitude against their benefactor. She turned away with infinite relief that the exercises were over, and followed the rest of the visitors to inspect the house. It was like Farley not to tell any one of his gift; and she felt like a fraud and a cheat to stand in his place, receiving praise that was intended for him.

On the way home she was very quiet. The many emotions of the day had so wearied her that she had no spirit to project herself into the future. And it seemed futile to attempt to forecast a day's events, when she had, apparently, so little control of her own destiny.

"Hope Mr. Farley won't abuse me for giving him away?" Eaton remarked, as he left her at the door. "But the temptation was too strong — could n't resist putting you into the picture. Your recitations made a big hit; and those people are real critics!"

She lay in the window-seat till daybreak, dreaming, staring at the stars.

CHAPTER XVI

AN ABRUPT ENDING

NAN sang as she dressed the next morning. The gods had ordained that she should n't marry Billy, and after her uncertainties on that point she was relieved to find that the higher powers had taken the troublesome business out of her hands. She was surprised at her light-hearted acceptance of the situation. She had n't married Billy and she sang in the joy of her freedom.

Just as she was ready to leave her room the maid brought up a special delivery letter from Copeland. It had been posted at six o'clock. She tore open the envelope and read frowningly: —

Dear Nan: —

Sorry about the row at the church last night. Never occurred to me that there'd be such a jam. I hung around the neighborhood as long as I could, hoping to find you. But it will be nicer, after all, to make the run by daylight. Telephone me where we can meet this morning, say at ten. I shall be at the office early and shall expect to hear from you by nine-thirty. For God's sake, don't fail me, Nan!

This was scawled in pencil on Hamilton Club paper. She propped it against her dressing-table mirror and stared at it wonderingly. It did not seem possible that she had ever contemplated running away with Billy. The remembrance of him as he sat in his car, quarreling with the police, with the eyes of a hundred people upon him, sickened her.

Either you love me, Nan, or you don't; you either have been fooling me all along or you mean to stand by me now and make me the happiest man alive. . . .

She smiled at Billy's efforts to be pathetic — a quizzical little smile. The paper smelt odiously of tobacco smoke. She tore the note to pieces and let them slip slowly from her hand into her wastebasket. No; she did not love Billy. Only a few hours earlier she had been ready to run away with him; but that was all over now. She was sorry for Billy, but she did not love him. How could she have ever been foolish enough to think she did! But why, she wondered, was she forever yielding to impulses from which a kind fate might not always protect her? "You little fool!" she ejaculated. A moment later she stood smiling in Farley's door.

"Nan, look here what they say about you in the paper!" he said, glancing at her over his spectacles. "I told Eaton not to blab about that swimmin'-tank business and here they've got us all in the paper!"

"Oh, if only you could have been there, papa!"

THE PROOF OF THE PUDDING

She saw that he was pleased. He bade her ring for the maid to bring up their breakfast; he wanted to know all about the exercises at the Settlement House.

"I guess you made a hit all right," he said proudly, after making her read the account aloud. "I never liked your sayin' pieces in public; but I guess if you can tickle a crowd like that I ain't got any right to kick."

The reporter had built his story around her; and had done full justice to her part in the surprise of the evening. Her recitations were praised extravagantly as worthy of a professional; "it is unfortunate," ran the article, "that Miss Farley's elocutionary talents are so rarely displayed in public."

It was compensation for much greater catastrophes than the loss of Billy Copeland to find Farley so pleased.

"It's kind o' nice to do things like that — to do things for people," Farley remarked wistfully, after subjecting Nan to a prolonged cross-examination. "I'm sorry now I didn't tell you about that swimmin' pool. You've got a mighty kind heart, Nan. I used to think I would n't make any will, but let what I've got go to you, and leave it to you to help some of these schemes for the poor. You know you've worried me sometimes — we won't talk about that any more; I guess it's all over now."

AN ABRUPT ENDING

The questioning look he bent upon her gave her conscience a twinge. If Billy had n't become embroiled with the police she would not be listening to Farley's praise!

"Yes, papa; it's all over," she replied softly, and bent down and kissed him.

When later she called Copeland on the telephone it was to laugh at their misadventure — it seemed safer to make light of it.

"Please forget all about it, Billy. It was n't my fault or yours either; it was all wrong any way. No —"

He was talking from his desk at the store and as he began to argue she dismissed him firmly.

"Please don't be cross, Billy. You ought to be as glad as I am that we did n't do it. No; never again! Cheer up; that's a nice boy!"

She hung up on his angry reply.

Nan spent all day at home virtuously addressing herself to household affairs, much to the surprise of the cook and maid.

Mamie Pembroke stopped to leave a huge bunch of chrysanthemums for Mr. Farley. He sent for her to come to his room and asked her all about the evening at the Settlement House. Mamie's appearance added to his happiness. He had been deeply grieved when Mamie and the Harrington girls dropped Nan; it was a good sign that they were beginning to evince a renewed interest in her. He attributed the change in their attitude to Nan's abandonment of Copeland and the Kinneys, never dreaming in his innocence of the quiet missionary work that Eaton had been doing with the cautious mothers of these young women.

"You'd better give Nan some work to do on some of your charity schemes, Mamie. She's been shut up here with me so much she hasn't got around with the rest of you girls as I want her to."

"Oh, don't think I do so much! Mamma does it for the whole family. I'm sure Nan does as much as any of the girls."

"Thanks for your kind words, Mamie; you know perfectly well they dropped me from the Kindergarten Board for cutting all the meetings. But I think we all ought to help in these things. It certainly opened my eyes to see that crowd down there last night; I had no idea the Settlement had grown so big."

"I wish you and Mamie would go down and look at the Boys' Club sometime. They've only got a tumble-down house, but they're talkin' of doin' something better. A poor boy has a mighty hard time. When I was a boy down on the Ohio —"

The story was a familiar one to Nan, and as he talked her thoughts reverted to the will in which his provisions for the Boys' Club had so angered her.

All day she marveled at her happiness, her newly-awakened unselfishness. In her gratitude for what she sincerely believed to have been a providential deliverance from Copeland she voluntarily gave the nurse the night off.

Her good cheer had communicated itself to Farley. The nurse was a nuisance, he said, and he would soon be well enough to dispense with her altogether. Over the supper they ate together in his room she exerted herself to amuse him and he proved unusually amiable. The afternoon paper's account of his gift of the swimming-pool revived this as a topic of conversation.

"I have n't done as much as I ought to for the poor and unlucky. I expect they've called me a pretty hard specimen; and I've turned down lots of these people that's always chasin' round with subscription papers. But I always had an idea I'd like to do something that would count. I'm sorry now I did n't give those Boys' Club folks a boost while I could see the money spent myself. I've tried makin' wills and ain't sure about any of 'em. I got a good mind to burn 'em all, Nan, and leave it up to you to give away what you think's right. Only I would n't want you to feel bound to do it. These things don't count for much unless you feel in your heart you want to do 'em."

She tried to divert his thoughts to other channels, but he persisted in discussing ways and means of helping the poor and unfortunate. She was surprised at his intimate knowledge of local philanthropic organizations; for a number of them he expressed the greatest contempt, as impractical and likely to do harm. Others he commended warmly and urged her to acquaint herself with their methods and needs.

"We ought to do those things ourselves, while we're alive. You can't tell what they'll do with your money after you're dead," he kept repeating.

She wondered whether he regretted now having made the will that had caused her so much anguish. Perhaps . . . But her resentment had vanished. His solicitude for friendless boys, based upon his own forlorn youth, impressed her deeply. It was out of the same spirit that he had lifted her from poverty — she had even greater cause for gratitude and generosity than he, and she said so in terms that touched him.

"You mustn't think of those things any more, papa," she said finally. "If you have a bad night, Miss Rankin will give me a scolding. I'm going to read you something."

"All right," he acquiesced. "To-morrow I'll talk to you some more about my will. It's worried me a whole lot; I want to do the right thing, Nan; I want you to know that."

"Of course I know that, papa; I'd be a mighty stupid girl if I did n't; so don't waste your strength arguing with me. You've been talking too much; what shall I read?"

"Don't read me any of this new-fangled stuff. Take down 'Huck Finn' and read that chapter

about the two crooks Huck meets on the river.
You ain't read me that lately."

He lay very quiet until she had finished the
chapter.

"Much obliged," he said absently. "You run
along now. I'll be all right."

In the hall she met the maid coming to announce
a caller.

Jerry, chastely attired in a new fall suit, greeted
her with the ambassadorial dignity that he assumed for social occasions, with apologies to J. C. E.
He could bow and shake hands like his idol and
mentor, and though his manner of speech was still
his own, he had greatly subdued its original vio-
lences. The area of collar and cuff that could be sustained on a salary lately increased to eighty dollars
a month might provoke smiles; but Jerry was not
troubled. By discreetly soliciting custom for a
tailor who made a twenty-five dollar suit which
only the most sophisticated sartorial critic could
distinguish from a sixty-dollar creation, he got his
clothes at a discount. While he had not yet acquired
a dress-suit or a silk hat, he boasted a dinner-coat
and a cutaway. He had dedicated the latter by
wearing it boldly to Christ Church, where he was
ushered to the third pew from the chancel and placed
beside a lady whose kneelings and risings he imitated sedulously. This was Eaton's church, and
while that gentleman was not present on that
particular morning, a tablet commemorating his

father's virtues (twenty years warden and vestry-
man) gave Jerry a thrill of pride and a sense
of perspective. His mother had been a Camp-
bellite, and a vested clergy and choir, sprung
upon him suddenly, had awed him to a mood of
humility.

"I'd been wondering as I came up what I'd do
if you were out: I could n't decide whether to jump
in the river or lie down in the middle of the street
and be killed by a large, fat auto. Nan," — he held
her hand and gazed into her face with tragic in-
tensity, — "Nan, you have saved my life!"

She met him promptly on his own ground.

"I should have worn mourning for you, Jerry;
you may be sure of that."

"The thought seems to give you pleasure. But
I like you best in blue — that suit you had on the
day we paddled up the river still haunts me."

"Oh, that was a last year's bird-nest. I have a
lot better clothes than that, but I don't wear them
to picnics."

"You'd be dazzling in anything; I'm dead sure
of that!"

He ran on in his usual key for some time, and
then rose abruptly and walked toward her.

"Are we quite alone?" he whispered tragically.

"We are," she replied, imitating his tone. "I
hope you don't mean to rob the house."

"No," he replied; "I did n't come to steal; I've
brought you a large beautiful present."

AN ABRUPT ENDING

This she assumed to be the preliminary to a joke of some kind.

"I left it behind that big rosebush in the yard and I'll bring it in—nobody likely to come—no?"

"No; the nurse is out and I just now heard the maid climbing the back stairs to her room."

A smothered "Oh!" greeted him as he reappeared bearing the suit-case she had entrusted to Copeland's messenger the day before. He placed it quietly by the door, a little shamefacedly, in spite of his efforts to pass the matter off lightly. Nan flushed, staring at him defiantly.

"I saw this down at the works and I just thought I'd bring it up. Maybe," he said reflectively, "it ain't yours; but I thought I'd take a chance."

"N. F." neatly printed on the end of the bag advertised its ownership to any observant eye.

"You and I are good friends, I hope," she said uneasily.

"Don't be silly, Nan; if we're not, what are we?"

This was not a question she cared to debate; the immediate matter was the narrowness of her escape from a marriage with Copeland and just what she should tell Jerry about it.

"If you know about — *that* —"

"I make it my business never to know anything! I don't want to know anything about that bag. So we'll just forget it."

Seeing that her eyes rested nervously on the

suitcase, he carried it into the hall out of range of any chance caller's eyes.

"Thank you," she said absently as he came back. He began speaking volubly of the delights of "Ivanhoe" which Eaton had lately given him to read.

"How many people know about — *that?*" she demanded, breaking in sharply upon his praise of Scott.

"Oh, the bag? Not a soul; I told you not to worry about that. I found it behind the door in his private office. Purely accidental — honest, it was! He was n't feeling well to-day," he added. "He hung around the store all morning looking pretty glum and did n't show up at all this afternoon. I went to the club and fished him out about six o'clock and took him home in a taxi. That's all."

Reduced to terms, Billy had characteristically celebrated the failure of the elopement by continuing the drunk he had begun the night before. Her good luck had not deserted her if no one but Jerry knew that her suit-case, packed for flight, had stood all day in Copeland's office. Jerry's intuitions were too keen for her to attempt dissimulation. It would be better to confess and assure herself of his secrecy.

"You don't need to worry about that little matter, Nan," Jerry continued reassuringly. "Nobody's going to know anything about it. Nobody *does* know anything about it —"

AN ABRUPT ENDING

"Mr. Eaton?" she suggested faintly.

"I have n't seen Cecil for two days. I've told you all there is to tell. I don't know any more and I don't want to know. Now, forget it! Only" — he deliberated a moment and then added brokenly — "only, for God's sake, don't ever try it again!"

It flashed upon her suddenly that the presence of her suit-case in Copeland's office was susceptible of grave misconstruction.

"I'm going to tell you the whole story, Jerry; I think I'll feel happier if I do."

"Well, you don't have to tell me anything; remember that!"

"Maybe not, Jerry. But I feel that having known me away back in the old times, you'll understand better than anybody else."

There was an appeal in this that filled his heart with pride. He was struck with humility that a girl like Nan should confide in him. He had not yet recovered from his surprise that she tolerated him at all.

"Please don't think I was going to do anything wrong, Jerry," she said pleadingly; "we were to have been married last night; it was n't — it was n't anything worse!" she faltered.

"Nan!" he gasped; "don't say things like *that!* I would n't think it — I had n't thought it of him! And you —!"

"Well, you might have thought it," she said,

237

with a despairing note; "but you did n't because you're my good friend and a gentleman."

He was so astounded by her unsparing self-condemnation that he almost missed this heart-warming praise. She hurried on with the story, tears filling her eyes. It was an undreamed-of thing that he should see his divinity weep. For the first time in his life he felt that he, too, was capable of tears. But he must restore her equanimity, and before she concluded he had decided to pass the whole thing off as a joke.

"Forget it, Nan! You never really meant to do it, anyhow. If Cecil had n't turned up, it's a safe bet you'd have weakened before you got into the boss's machine. It was a good joke — on the boss; that's all I see in it. Come on, now, and give a merry ha-ha. The only sad thing about it is that it put the boss on the blink all day. If he'd been a real sport he would n't have let you escape so easy; looks as though he was n't exactly crazy about it himself!"

"Oh, you think he was n't!" she flared.

"I thought I'd get a rise out of you with that! Take it from me, if I'd framed up a thing like that I'd 've pulled up large shade trees and upset tall buildings putting it over. But all you've got to do is to charge it up to profit and loss. Hereafter you'd better not make any engagements without seeing me," he concluded daringly.

"There may be something in that," she laughed.

"I'm glad I told you, Jerry. It helps a lot to tell your troubles to some one — and you don't think much worse of me?"

"Oh, too much sympathy would n't be good for you!" he said, looking at her fixedly. "Your trouble is, Nan, if you will take it from an old friend, that you've had too soft a time. You need a jar or two to make you watch the corners. So do I; so does everybody! When things come easy for me I get nervous. I've got to have something to fight; but I don't mean punching heads; not any more. Cecil says his great aim in life is to teach me to fight with my brains instead of my fists and feet. But it's hard work, considering the number of heads there are that need punching."

She was touched by his anxiety to serve her, to see her always in the best possible light. He was a comforting person, this Jerry. His philosophy was much sounder than her own; he was infinitely wiser. He had done much better with his life than she had with hers, and the advantages had been so immensely in her favor! There was no one else in the world, she reflected, to whom she could confide as in him. She marveled that she trusted him so implicitly — and he knew how little she merited trust! A sudden impulse carried her across the room to where he stood fingering a book.

"You are very good to me, Jerry!" she said with deep feeling.

Her hand touched his — a light, caressing stroke;

239

then she sprang away from him, abashed. The color mounted to his face, and he thrust the hand awkwardly into his pocket. The touch of her hand had thrilled him; a wave of tenderness swept him.

"I want to be good to you; I want to help you if I can," he said simply.

But he was afraid of Nan in tears, and there were tears in the eyes with which she now regarded him. She turned away, slipping her handkerchief from her sleeve. This would never do. He waited a moment, then began talking, as though nothing had happened, of old times on the river, of steamboat men and their ways, in the hope of restoring her tranquillity.

"I guess I had my share of fun down there; if I could be a kid again I'd want to be born right down there on the old Ohio. I remember once —"

A muffled crash in the room above sent her flying into the hall and upstairs.

"Papa!" she called, standing in the doorway of Farley's room and fumbling for the electric button.

As the ceiling lights flooded the room she called loudly to Jerry.

Farley lay on the floor in a crumpled heap. The crash that had accompanied his collapse had been due to the overturning of the electric table lamp, at which he had caught as he felt himself falling.

Jerry was already on his knees beside the prone figure.

AN ABRUPT ENDING

Nan snatched the receiver of the telephone from its bracket and called the regular physician; and then, remembering another doctor who lived just around the corner, she summoned him also. Amidon lifted Farley and placed him on the bed. While waiting for her numbers she told him where to find a restorative the doctor had provided for emergencies, and before she finished telephoning he had tried vainly to force a spoonful of the liquid between Farley's lips.

"It's no use," said Jerry, placing his hand over the stricken man's heart.

"No! No! It can't be possible!" Nan moaned. "He'd been so well to-day!"

In a few minutes both physicians were in the room. They made a hurried examination, asked a few questions, and said there was nothing to be done.

The indomitable spirit of Timothy Farley had escaped from its prison-house; what was mortal of him remained strangely white and still. Nan, kneeling beside the bed, wept softly. Her foster-mother had died after a brief illness and she had experienced no such shock as now numbed her. She had, after all, been closer to Farley than to his wife. Mrs. Farley, with all her gentleness and sweetness, had lacked the positive traits that made Timothy Farley an interesting, masterful character.

"There will be things to do," Amidon was saying

gently. "Do you mind if I tell Mr. Eaton? He'd want to know."

"No; I should like him to come," she replied.

Jerry went below with the physicians and called Eaton on the telephone in the lower hall.

Nan rose and began straightening the room. Farley had evidently drawn on his dressing-gown with a view to remaining up some time, and had walked to the quaint little table that had so long stood near the window. Nan saw now what had escaped her when she rushed into the room. The oblong top of the table had been so turned that it disclosed a compartment back of the trio of drawers in which Mrs. Farley had kept her sewing articles. Four long envelopes lay on the lid; two others had fallen to the floor and lay among the debris of the lamp. At a glance she saw that these were similar to the ones she had seen Farley hiding on several occasions, and the counterpart of the envelope containing the will she had read with so much concern. One of the envelopes was torn twice across, as though he had intended disposing of it finally. The others were intact.

She gathered them all together and thrust them back into the table; then ran her fingers along the underside of the lid until she found a tiny catch. Noting the position of this, she drew the top into place, satisfied herself that the spring had caught, and rose just as Jerry came back.

CHAPTER XVII

SHADOWS

NAN lay on her bed, fully dressed, on the evening of the day of the funeral, listening to the sounds of the street with an uncomfortable sense of strangeness and isolation. The faint tinkle of the bell roused her and the maid came up bearing Eaton's card. She had told the girl to excuse her to callers, but Eaton sent word that he wished particularly to see her. She appeared before him startlingly wan and white in her black gown.

"I knew you wanted to be alone, Nan, but there's a matter I must speak to you about, and I thought it best to do it at once. I shan't bother you long. I left a dinner at the Lawyers' Club to run up for a minute; in about an hour I shall be making a speech; so you need n't prepare for a long visit!"

"I'm glad you came. It's much harder than I thought it would be. I'm sorry I did n't keep Mrs. Copeland or one of the girls with me."

"Of course, you're bound to feel it. It came as a great shock to all of us. A man like your father can't pass out of the world without being missed — very deeply missed. He was a real person; a vivid personality. It has done me good to hear the fine things said of him; the crowd here at the serv-

243

ices showed that he had been held in very deep affection by all sorts of people."

There was a moment's silence. The tears had come into her eyes and he waited for her to control herself.

"I should n't be troubling you if I had n't felt that my business — if it can be called business — was urgent. I'm taking the liberty of an old friend — of yours and of Mr. Farley's."

"Oh, there can't be any question of liberty!" she protested. "You're always so thoughtful, so kind!"

"My purpose is in no sense professional," he continued. "Mr. Thurston was Mr. Farley's lawyer and he will no doubt confer with you at once on business matters. He's an excellent man; wholly trustworthy. No one stands higher at our bar."

"Yes; I know papa had every confidence in him," Nan replied, wondering what Eaton, who looked very distinguished in his evening clothes, could have to say to her.

"It's in relation to that little difficulty — an unfortunate but wholly pardonable mistake you made — you see I speak frankly — in reference to a man named Harlowe, a lawyer from the south part of the State, in regard to a demand he made on you some time ago. Mr. Farley explained about it — all that he knew."

Nan clenched her hands tightly and drew a deep breath. It was inconceivable that that specter could reappear to trouble her.

"Yes," she whispered faintly; "I remember. I was so grateful to you for your help that night. I don't know what would have happened if you had n't come just then. Papa was very bitter about what I did, and of course it was cowardly of me; and very stupid, not to have advised with some one."

"You did what seemed perfectly justifiable at the moment; Mr. Farley saw it that way afterward."

"He never spoke to me about it again; I have you to thank for that."

"No; it was Mr. Farley's aim to be just. Now, about this Harlowe: I don't want to alarm you, but I have found it best to be prepared for difficulties even where there's only a remote chance of having to confront them. I merely want you to know that if that man turns up again I'm ready for him. I have, in fact, accumulated a considerable amount of data that can be used against him if he makes another move. He's an unscrupulous blackguard, a disgrace to the profession."

"But that case against my brother is all over now. He could n't ask for more money?"

"Not in that particular way," Eaton replied slowly; "but having succeeded once in frightening money out of you, he might try it again. I suppose Mr. Farley never told you what I discovered — established with documentary proof that I have safely put away in my office — that the Corrigan this Harlowe pretended to represent was not in fact your brother."

He went on quickly, ignoring the astonishment and bewilderment written on her face.

"That man was no more your brother than he is mine — you need have no doubts about it. Harlowe's client went to the penitentiary — quite properly, no doubt. The poor fellow never knew how he had been used — never heard of that money! I take off my hat to Brother Harlowe — a shrewd scoundrel. It's because I respect his talents that I've taken so much pains to look him up! Possibly you won't hear from him at all; then again, you may. I've given some study to the peculiar moral nature of persons like Harlowe, and I won't deny that it would please me to have a chance at him — though, of course, Mr. Thurston would be quite as competent to deal with the case as I am. My aim would be to get rid of him quietly, perhaps by methods that would n't appeal to Mr. Thurston. Please listen to him carefully, if he should come to you. Concede nothing, but let him go as far as he will. That's all, I think. Pardon me if I look at my watch."

"It's very kind of you to warn me," she said, with feeling. "It's horrible to know there are people plotting against you in the dark. I was ashamed of myself for yielding as I did when that man came to me; I knew right away that I had made a mistake."

"Well, as our friend Mr. Amidon would remark, forget it! forget it! We all make mistakes. I wish I had never made a worse one than that little slip of yours," he added kindly.

She had always been amused by Eaton's oddities, his mysteriousness; but in this hour of dejection his sympathy and friendliness warmed her heart. She rose and stood before him, her hands clenched at her sides, and demanded passionately: —

"Why am I always doing the wrong thing? Why do I escape so often when I have every intention of doing what I know to be wrong? I suppose if I'd waited another day I should n't have sneaked my money out of the trust company and turned it over to that man! But I've had escapes I don't understand; something gets in the way and I don't — I *can't* — do things I fully mean to do! And I look back and shudder. Why is that — can you tell me?"

He lifted his arm with one of his familiar gestures and inspected his cuff-links absently.

"You're seeing things a little black now, that's all, Nan. When you gave up that money you thought it was the right thing to do. You saw the mistake yourself the moment after it was done. That's just our human frailty. It's our frailties that make life the grand fight it is!"

"That's not very consoling," she replied, with a rueful smile. "I suppose we never know how much we count in other people's lives. Oh, I don't mean that I do — except to do harm; I was thinking of you!"

His eyeglasses gleamed as he bent her a swift glance.

"I — I'd be very happy to think I'd been of use to somebody."

"Oh, you saved me once from going clear over the brink! You did n't know that, did you?" she cried earnestly.

"I most certainly did not!"

"If you don't know," she said gravely, "I shall never tell you. Are you really sure you don't know what I'm talking about?"

"My dear Nan, why do you ask me if I guess things — when facts are the consuming passion of my life! If I was ever of the slightest service to you it was unconscious good fortune on my part. And I hope there may be many such occasions! But, Nan," — he waited until he was quite sure of her attention, — "Nan, we can't rely too much on the man on shore in emergencies. He won't always reach us in time. We've got to mind the thin ice ourselves — skate away as soon as we hear it cracking! We can't trust to chance. Luck supports sound judgment — mainly. And we've got to fight our own battles."

"But if you're a worthless, wobbly person like me, what are you going to do?" she demanded.

"Cease wobbling! Good-night!" ·

SHADOWS

Eaton had not been gone more than five minutes when a light knock on the glass panel of the front door startled her. The clocks through the house had just struck ten and she had dismissed the maid for the night. The rap was repeated more loudly, and stealing to the door she drew back a corner of the curtain and peered out. Copeland stood in the entry, plainly revealed by the overhead light; his hand was lifted for another knock.

Her heart throbbed with fear and anger. Billy had no right to come at this hour in this furtive fashion — and on this day, of all days, to the house of the man who had so cordially hated him. She waited a moment hoping he would go away, but he began beating upon the glass.

This clearly would not do, and she drew back the bolt and opened the door a few inches.

"Please go away! You have no right to come here at this time of night!"

He seized the door as she was about to close it and forced his way past her.

"I've got to see you a minute — just a minute," he said eagerly. "It's a matter of importance or I should n't have come to-night. I thought it best not to wait. It's really a serious matter, Nan!"

"You have no right to come at all," she replied angrily. "What if the neighbors saw you! they know I'm alone. You know this won't do; please go, Billy!" she pleaded.

"I suppose," he said, walking toward the parlor,

249

"that it's all right for John Eaton to come when he pleases, but not for me."

"That was very different; he rang the bell and the maid let him in! And he came on a business matter. You can't stay, Billy; you understand that. You must go at once!"

"Well, I came earlier, but saw Eaton's silk hat bobbing in and I've been hanging around waiting for him to go. I didn't care to meet him here; and as far as business is concerned, maybe mine's just as important as his. You'll have to take my word for that."

His manner and tone were amiable. There clearly was nothing to be gained by debating the question of his right to be there, but she remained resolutely in the parlor door, trying to devise some means of getting rid of him.

"You'll have to be quick, then," she said, without relaxing her severity.

"Yes; I understand that, Nan," he agreed readily. "It's about the property — no — don't stop me!" he exclaimed as she cried out impatiently. "You have certain rights and it's the business of your friends to see that you get them. Another day and it will be too late."

"I'm to see Mr. Thurston to-morrow; everything's in his hands; you have nothing to do with it!"

He took a step toward her and his voice sank to a whisper.

"That's just it! Everything is not in his hands. That's what I want to tell you."

She stared at him blankly. His excited manner aroused her curiosity as to what he might have to say, but it was unlikely that he knew anything of importance about Farley's affairs.

"They're saying downtown that Farley was a crank about will-making; he made a lot of wills and kept them hid. Thurston's let that out himself. If you know this, we can drop that part of it."

She made no reply, and her silence encouraged him to go on.

"The fact is, as we all know," he began ingratiatingly, "that Farley was n't himself at all times. He probably made wills that he destroyed — or meant to destroy. It's wholly possible that he vented his wrath on you at times by cutting down what he meant to give you, and the next day he'd be sorry for it. That would be like him. In old times at the store he used to blow up with fury one minute and be as tame as a lamb the next. But there's no reason — there's not the slightest reason why you should suffer if he died leaving a will lying around that might rob you of your just inheritance — that did n't really express his normal attitude toward you. He never meant to be mean to you; I'm satisfied of that; but if there are some of those wills here in the house — you would have a right, considering his condition and all that — you would have a right — you see —"

THE PROOF OF THE PUDDING

He had been watching her narrowly for some sign of interest or encouragement, but finding neither he broke off without saying just what it might be right for her to do. However, while he waited a quick flutter of her lids indicated that she comprehended. Their eyes met in a long gaze. Her face grew white and her lips opened several times before any sound came from them. He had drawn closer, but he stepped back as he saw horror and repugnance clearly written in her face.

"You have no right to talk to me like this! It's too shameful, too terrible!" she gasped.

"Please, Nan, don't take it that way," he begged.

"How else can I take it! To think that you should believe me capable of that, Billy!"

"If I had n't known that he had treated you like a brute and that he always carried his vindictiveness to the limit, I should n't be here. I don't want to see you cut off with little or nothing when the whole estate ought to be yours — *will* be yours if you don't make a fool of yourself! He had no right to bring you up as his daughter and then leave you with nothing. Thurston is n't going to protect your interests; he merely did from time to time what Farley told him to do, and you won't get any help out of him. If there are different wills hidden about — you may know where he hid them — "

He threw out his arms with a gesture meant to demonstrate the ease with which matters might be taken into her own hands. In the sobering hours

252

that had followed Farley's death only his great
kindness and generosity had been in her thoughts.
The enormity of what Copeland proposed grew
upon her. She bestirred herself suddenly. She
must not let him think that she was tolerating his
suggestion for an instant.

"I'm sorry you thought that kind of thing
would appeal to me! That's your idea of me,
is it?"

"I'm appealing to your good sense, Nan; in a
few hours it will be too late, and if you know where
he kept his papers, you can easily look them over
and satisfy yourself as to just what he meant to do;
and then you can do as you like. His last will
would stand; maybe you don't know that; and if
it's in the house, why should n't you, at least, have
a look at it?"

"I would n't — I *could n't* do such a thing!"
she cried.

"If there should n't be any will at all," he resumed, with his eyes fixed upon her intently, "then
you would inherit everything! The adoption made
you his child in law; there would n't be any way
of escaping that. It's these wills that you've got
to fear — the whims, the sudden vindictive anger
of an old man who really meant to do the right
thing by you. Neither he nor his wife had any near
kin; there would be nobody to share with you in
case there proves to be no will at all!"

"You make it perfectly plain what it would be

possible for me to do!" she replied with quivering
lips. "That seems to be all you have to say—and
it's enough! I want you to leave this house, and
be quick about it!"

"But, Nan, you are taking this all wrong! It's
not as though you were robbing other people: you
certainly have a better right to the money than
anybody else. Suppose that in one of his mental
lapses he had willed the greater part of his fortune
to some silly charity; all the rest of your days you'd
be sorry you had n't done what you could to protect
yourself."

"Please go," she urged in a plaintive whisper,
"so I can forget that you've been here!"

"Of course I'll go," he assented. "If I had n't
felt that you looked to me at least as a friend, I
should n't have come. And if there's anything to be
done it must be done quickly — that's as plain as
daylight."

He advanced this in a crisp, businesslike tone,
as though there were nothing remarkable in his
suggestions. She was already wondering, as he
meant she should, whether, after all, there was
anything so enormous in the idea. Fear stole into
her heart; it would be unsafe to listen to anything
further lest he persuade her of the justice of his
plan. But he dropped the matter instantly, wisely
calculating that he had said enough.

"You know, Nan, that nobody is as interested
in your happiness as I am. If I did n't care so much

SHADOWS

— if I did n't hope that you cared, I should n't have come here to-night; I should n't have dared!"

She made no response, but stared at him with widely distended eyes. Her silence made him uneasy. Her black gown had strangely transformed her. She was not the Nan who had promised to marry him — who would now, but for his folly, be his wife. He walked to the door and then said in the low tone he had employed from the beginning, —

"There are other things I want to speak of, but I know this is not the time. I shall hope to see you again soon, and please try to think better of me, Nan!"

She remained where she had stood throughout the interview until she heard the iron gate click behind him.

She put out the lights and climbed the stairs slowly. The loneliness that had stifled her before Eaton's appearance had deepened. She passed through the silent upper hall and locked herself in her room, resolved not to leave it until the world woke to life again.

"No! No! No!" she moaned aloud to fortify her resolution. . . .

At one o'clock she was still awake, questioning, debating with herself, while strange shadow-shapes danced in the surrounding blackness.

CHAPTER XVIII

NAN AGAINST NAN

WAS Billy right, after all?

The question haunted her insistently. She lighted the lamp by her bed and tried to read, but the words were a confused jumble. She threw down her book impatiently. If only she had kept Fanny Copeland in the house or had given the papers hidden away in the old table to Eaton to carry away, she would have escaped this struggle.

Her thoughts were fixed upon Eaton for a time. He had enjoined her to take a firmer hold of herself. She readily imagined what his abhorrence would be of the evil thing Copeland had proposed. . . .

But, after all, Farley had meant to treat her generously, as Copeland had said, and if in some angry mood he had rewritten his will to reduce his provision for her, there was no reason why she should n't seize an opportunity to right a wrong he never really intended. . . .

She rose, drew on her kimono, snapped on all the lights and found that it was only half past one. She assured herself that she would not open the door of Farley's room; and yet, the thought kept recurring that no one would ever know if she read those wills and destroyed them. The fear that she might yield chilled her. She became frantic for something to do and set herself the task of putting the drawers of her desk in order. Some letters that Mrs. Farley had written her while she was at boarding-school caught her eye.

Yes, the Farleys had been kind, even foolishly indulgent. She read in her foster-mother's even, old-fashioned hand: —

Don't worry about your money, dear. I suppose when you go into town you see a lot of little things that it's nice for a girl to have. We want you to appear well before the other girls. I'm slipping a twenty-dollar bill into this letter just for odds and ends. Don't say anything to papa about it, as I would rather he did n't know I send you money.

A little later she turned up a letter of Farley's in which he had enclosed a fifty-dollar bill as an addition to her regular allowance. In a characteristic postscript he enjoined her not "to tell mamma. She thinks you have enough money and it might make her jealous!"

She closed the drawer, leaving it in worse confusion than before. Comforts and luxuries were dear to her. She had enjoyed hugely her years at boarding-school. To be set adrift with a small income while the greater part of Farley's money went to philanthropy — maybe Billy was right, after all! . . .

THE PROOF OF THE PUDDING

Two o'clock. She was in Farley's room, crouched in a low rocker with her arms flung across the table in which the papers were hidden. Her heart beat furiously, and her breath came in quick gasps. She had decided now to read the wills; it would do no harm to have a look at them. If everything was to be taken away from her, she might as well know the worst and prepare for it.

Her fingers sought the catch that released the spring; the top turned easily. The papers lay as she had left them the night Farley died. She folded the open ones and thrust them into their envelopes. She counted them deliberately; there were six, including the one that had fallen from the dressing-gown, which she identified by the crosses on the envelope. . . .

If there should be no will, Copeland had said, all the property would go to her as the only heir. There was a grate in the room with the fuel all ready for lighting. It would be a simple matter to destroy all the wills. She could explain the burnt-out fire to the maid by saying that the house had grown cold in the night and that she had gone into Farley's room to warm herself. She was surprised to find how readily explanations covering every point occurred to her. The very ease with which she thought of them appalled her. No doubt it was in this fashion that hardened criminals planned their defense. . . .

She struck a match and touched it to the paper

under the kindling. The fire blazed brightly. She
was really chilled and the warmth was grateful.
As she held her hands to the flames she surveyed
the trifles on the mantel and her gaze wandered
to a portrait of Mrs. Farley which had been done
from photographs by a local artist after her death.
The memory of her foster-mother's simple kindliness and gentleness gave her a pang. She turned
slowly until her eyes rested upon the bed in which
Farley had suffered so long. She went back to the
beginning and argued the whole matter over again.

As at other times, in moods of depression, she
thought of the squalor of her childhood; of her
father, Dan Corrigan, trapper, fisherman, loafer,
brutal drunkard. She gazed at her white, slim fingers and recalled her mother's swollen, red hands
as she had bent for hours every day over the wash-
tub. Her mother had been at least an honest woman,
who had addressed herself uncomplainingly to the
business of maintaining a home for her children.

All that the Farleys had done in changing her
environment to one of comfort and decency and
educating her in a fashionable school with the daughters of gentlefolk had not affected the blood in her.
She had not been worthy of their pity, their generosity, their confidence. Yet it had meant much to
these people in their childlessness to take her into
their hearts and give her their name. Farley's ideas
of honor had been the strictest; the newspapers
in their accounts of his career had laid stress on this.

And how he would hate an act such as she meditated, that would prove her low origin, stamp her as the daughter of a degenerate! . . .

Still, there was no reason why she should n't read the wills. She returned to the table, drew one of them out, played with it for a moment uncertainly, then thrust it back.

It was Nan against Nan through the dark watches of the night. If she yielded now she would never tread firm ground again. Once this trial was over, she would be a different woman — better or worse; and she must reach a decision unaided. She buried her face in her arms to shut out the light and wept bitterly in despair of her weakness. . . .

Four o'clock. A sparrow cheeped sleepily in the vines on the wall outside the window. Farley had liked the sparrows and refused to have them molested. They were "company," he said, and he used to keep crumbs of bread and cake for them. . . .

She lifted her head, and confidence stole into her heart. She had not done the evil thing; she had not even looked at the sheets of paper that recorded Farley's wavering, shifting faith in her.

"Why don't you do it? You are a coward; you are afraid!"

Her voice sank to a whisper as she kept repeating these taunts. Then she was silent for a time, sitting with arms folded, her eyes bent unseeingly upon the envelopes before her. There could be no happiness in store for her if she yielded. She saw

herself carrying through life the memory of a law·
less act dictated by selfishness and greed. Suddenly she rose and walked to the bed; and her voice
rang out with a note of triumph, there in the room
where Farley had died: —

"I have not done it; I will not do it!"

The sound of her voice alarmed her, and she
glanced nervously over her shoulder. Then she
laughed, struck by the thought that if Farley's
spirit lurked there expecting to see her yield, it
was a disappointed ghost!

"You silly little fool," he had often said to her
in his anger. Well, she was not so wicked as he
had believed; but she thought of him now without
bitterness.

Wings fluttered; the sparrows began a persistent
twitter.

Light was creeping in under the shades. She returned to the table, stared at it, frowning, drew
away quickly, ran to the door, and glanced back
breathlessly. She walked back slowly, turned the
papers over, peered into the drawer to make sure
that she had overlooked nothing.

She took up the wills that recorded Timothy Farley's doubts and uncertainties and wavering gener-
osities, dropped them into the little well in the table
and drew the top into place.

A feeling of exaltation possessed her as she heard
the click of the spring. This, perhaps, was the reward of righteousness. "We're all happier," the

simple-hearted Mrs. Farley used to say, "when we're good!"

She stood very still for a minute, stifling her last regret. Then she turned to the window and opened it, unfastened the shutters, and thrust her hands out into the gray light. A farmer's wagon, bound for market, passed slowly by, the driver asleep with a lighted lantern on the seat beside him.

She remained there for a quarter of an hour listening to the first tentative sounds of the new day. The newspaper carrier threw the morning paper against the door beneath the window, unconscious that she saw him. She closed the window, crept back to her room and threw herself exhausted on her bed. . . .

Outside Farley's windows the sparrows chirruped impatiently for crumbs from the hand that would feed them no more.

CHAPTER XIX

NOT ACCORDING TO LAW

NAN was reading the newspaper report of Eaton's speech over her coffee when at nine o'clock he called her on the telephone.

"Your speech sounds fine, though I don't understand all the jokes," she said. "But I'm sure you made a hit."

"Not so sure of it myself, Nan. But please listen to me carefully. Our friend from the southern part of the State is here. I have him marked at his hotel. He has probably come to see you. Let him say all he has on his mind, then report to me. You will probably hear from Thurston, too, during the day. He's trying a case this morning. But our brother from the South comes first. Don't let him frighten you; just listen and encourage him if necessary to show what he's up to this time."

"Very well," she replied, though the thought of facing Harlowe alone filled her with misgivings.

Mrs. Copeland was on the wire immediately afterward, to ask if she could be of any service. Then Thurston's clerk called her to make an appointment for three o'clock.

The night's vigil had left its marks upon her. She was nervously alert for the day's developments, but nothing could be worse than the long struggle against temptation. She had, she fancied, considered every possibility as to the future and she was prepared for anything that might befall her. She was happy in the thought that she faced the world with a clean conscience; never in her life had she been on so good terms with herself.

She was standing at the parlor window when at eleven a familiar figure entered the gate. Harlowe, tall, slightly stooped, advanced to the door. She called to the maid not to trouble to answer the ring and let the man in herself.

He began with formal condolences on what he called "her irreparable loss."

"Much as we may be prepared for the death of a loved one, it always comes with a shock. I sympathize with you very deeply, Miss Farley."

She murmured her thanks and bade him be seated. She wished she had asked Eaton to be present at the interview, which he had forecast with a prescience that justified all her faith in his unusual powers.

"I came as quickly as possible after hearing of Mr. Farley's death, in the hope of being of some service to you — of avoiding any difficulties that might possibly arise with reference to the settlement of Mr. Farley's affairs."

She nodded, and remembering Eaton's injunction, gave him strict attention.

"I hope," he went on, "that my handling of the

very distressing and delicate matter that brought me here last June won your confidence to such an extent —"

He paused, watching her narrowly for any sign of dissent.

"I appreciated that, Mr. Harlowe; it was very considerate of you to come to me as you did."

"I did n't report on that case further, feeling that it might embarrass you, assuming that the whole matter was strictly between ourselves."

"Quite so," she agreed.

"I was distressed that after all our interest, and your own generosity, we could not save your unfortunate brother. Still, it's something that we were able to secure what was a light sentence — taking everything into consideration. Only circumstantial evidence, to be sure, but it pointed very strongly to his guilt. You doubtless read the result in the papers?"

"Yes, I followed the case," she answered. "And I 'm sure you did the best you could."

His solemnity would have been amusing at any other time. He clearly had no idea that she had learned of his duplicity in taking money from her for the defense of a Corrigan who was in no manner related to her.

"I assume," he said, "that no steps have yet been taken to offer for probate any will Mr. Farley may have left. I had hoped to see you first; this accounts for my visit to-day. I thought it best to see you before going to Mr. Thurston. Mr. Joseph C. Thurston was, I believe, Mr. Farley's attorney?"

"Yes. He was one of papa's best friends and he had charge of his affairs as far back as I can remember."

"An excellent man. There's no better lawyer in the State," Harlowe responded heartily. "But I occasionally find it best to deal directly with a client. We lawyers, you know, are sometimes unwisely obstinate, and lead our clients into unnecessary trouble. As you are the person chiefly concerned in this matter, I came directly to you. I did this because in that former matter you were so quick to see the justice of my — er — request."

Her amazement at his effrontery almost equalled her curiosity as to what lay behind his deliberate approaches.

"It is generally known that Mr. Farley was a man of violent temper," he went on. "Some of his old friends on the river remember him well, and you may never have known — and I am sorry to be obliged to mention so unpleasant a fact — that his mother died insane. That is a matter of record, of course. The malady from which Mr. Farley suffered for many years is one that frequently affects the mind. No doubt living with him here, as you did, you noticed at times that he behaved oddly — did n't conduct himself quite normally?"

Remembering Eaton's instructions she acqui-

266

esced without offering any comment. His designs, she now assumed, were not personal to herself, but directed against Farley's estate.

"I represent two cousins of Mr. Farley's who live in my county. Very worthy men they are; you may have heard Mr. Farley speak of them."

"Yes; I knew about them. I sent them telegrams advising them of his death."

"That was very thoughtful on your part, Miss Farley, and they appreciate it. But by reason of their poverty they were unable to attend the funeral. They asked me to thank you for thinking of them. Several times during the past twenty years Mr. Farley had advanced them small sums of money — an indication of his kindly feeling toward them."

"I did n't know of that; but it was like papa."

"In case Mr. Farley left a will, it is my duty to inform you, that you may have time for reflection before taking up the matter with Mr. Thurston, that we are prepared to attack it on the ground of Mr. Farley's mental unsoundness. I assume, of course, that Mr. Farley made a handsome provision for you, but quite possibly he overlooked the natural expectations of his own kinsfolk."

She merely nodded, thinking it unnecessary to impart information while he continued to show his hand so openly.

"You have probably understood, Miss Farley, that in case your foster-father died intestate, that is to say, without leaving a will in proper form, you would, as his heir, be entitled to the whole of his property."

"Yes; I think I have heard that," she answered uneasily.

The cold-blooded fashion in which he had stated his purpose to contest the will on the ground of Farley's insanity had shocked her. Copeland had suggested the same thing, but it was a preposterous pretension that Timothy Farley's mind had been affected by his long illness. Even the assertion that his mother had been a victim of mental disorder, plausibly as he had stated it, would hardly stand against the fact that Farley's faculties to the very end had been unusually clear and alert.

"In case there should be no will," Harlowe continued, "your rights would rest, of course, upon your adoption. It would have to be proved that it was done in accordance with law. The statutes are specific as to the requirements. I'm sorry, very sorry indeed, my dear Miss Farley, that in your case the law was not strictly complied with."

"I don't know what you mean; I don't understand you!" she faltered.

"Please don't be alarmed," he went on, with a reassuring smile. "I'm sure that everything can be arranged satisfactorily; I am not here to threaten you — please remember that; I merely want you to understand my case."

"But my father never dreamed of anything of that kind," she gasped; "it's impossible — why, he

would never have made a mistake in so serious a
matter."

"Unfortunately, we are all liable to err, Miss
Farley," he answered, with a grotesque affectation
of benevolence. "And I regret to say that in this
case the error is undeniable. What Mr. Farley's intentions were is one thing; what was actually done
to make you his child in law is another. We need
not go into that. It is a legal question that Mr.
Thurston will understand readily; the more so,
perhaps," he added with faint irony, "because he
was not himself guilty of the error, not being Mr.
Farley's attorney at the time the adoption was
attempted."

The room swayed and she grasped the arms of
her chair to steady herself. The man's story was
plausible, and he spoke with an easy confidence.
All Farley's deliberation about the disposal of his
property would go for naught; her victory over the
temptation to destroy his wills had been futile!

"Please don't misunderstand me, Miss Farley,"
the man was saying. "My clients have no wish to
deprive you wholly of participation in the estate.
And we should deplore litigation. In coming to
you now, I merely wish to prepare you, so that you
may consider the case in all its aspects before taking
it up with your lawyer. No doubt a satisfactory
settlement can be arranged, without going into
court. I believe that is all. Henceforth I can't with
propriety deal directly with you, but must meet

your counsel. I assume, however, that he will not wholly ignore your natural wish to — er — arrange a settlement satisfactory to all parties." . . .

The door had hardly closed upon him before she was at the telephone calling Eaton, and in half an hour he was at the house. Harlowe's words had so bitten into her memory that she was able to repeat them almost *verbatim*. Eaton listened with his usual composure. It might have seemed from his manner that he was more interested in Nan herself than in her recital. She betrayed no excitement, but described the interview colorlessly as though speaking of matters that did not wholly concern her. When she concluded Eaton chuckled softly.

"You're taking it nobly," were his first words; "I'm proud of you! You see, I had expected something of the sort — prepared for it, in fact, right after this fellow got that thousand dollars out of you. He's crafty, shrewd, unscrupulous. But you have nothing to worry over. He came to you first and at the earliest possible moment in the hope of frightening you as he did before, hoping that you'd persuade Thurston to settle with him. As for Farley's incompetence to make a will, that's all rubbish! His mother suffered from senile dementia — no symptoms until she was nearly ninety. Every business man in town would laugh at the idea that Tim Farley wasn't sane. He was just a little bit saner than most men. His occasional fits of anger were only the expression of his vigorous personality; wholly characteristic; nothing in that for Harlowe to hang a case on.

"But this point about the adoption is more serious. When I was down there watching Harlowe defend the man he pretended to you — but to nobody else — was your brother, I looked up those adoption proceedings, out of sheer vulgar curiosity. The law provides that adoption proceedings shall be brought in the county where the child resides, and that the parents appear in court and consent. Your parents were dead, and Mr. Farley's petition was filed in this county after you had been a member of his household for fully two years.

"I seriously debated mentioning these points to Thurston, after my visit down there, but on reflection decided against it. Contrary to the common assumption the law is not an ass — not altogether! I can't imagine the courts countenancing an effort to set aside this adoption on so flimsy a pretext. Mr. Farley not only complied with the law to the best of his belief, but let the world in general understand that he looked on you as his child and heir."

"That's what every one believed, of course," Nan murmured.

"I dare say there's a will," Eaton continued. "Thurston may have to defend that — but you may rely on him. I have already made an appointment to meet him at luncheon to turn over to him all my data. I'll say to you in all sincerity that I don't see the slightest cause for uneasiness. If there's a valid will, that settles the adoption line of attack, though this man may go the length of trying to annul it on the insanity plea, merely to tie up the estate until you pay something to these cousins to get rid of him."

"There is a will; there are a number of them, I think," said Nan soberly.

"Mr. Farley told you about them — let you know what he was doing?"

"No; he never spoke of them, except in general terms. I used to see him hiding them; once one dropped out of his dressing-gown." She hesitated; then added quickly: "I read that one before putting it back. I know I should n't have done it, but I did — as I 've done a good many things these last two years I should n't!"

"Don't be so hard on yourself! It was quite natural for you to look at it."

"The night he died," she went on breathlessly, "he had been looking at a number of wills he kept hidden in mamma's old sewing-table. I put them back in the drawer. I suppose Mr. Thurston will ask for them when he comes."

"Yes; he should see all such papers. You must tell him everything you know that relates to them."

"I almost burnt them all up last night," she exclaimed in a strange, hard tone. "That one I read made me angry. I thought it niggardly and unjust. And — some one told me" — in her eagerness to make her confession complete she nearly blurted out Copeland's name — "that if there should be no will I'd inherit everything. And last night I fought that out. And it was a hard fight; it was horrible! But for once in my life I got a grip on myself. You may remember saying to me, 'Don't wobble.' Well, I wobbled till I was dizzy — but I wobbled right! And now that that's over, I believe — though I'm afraid to say it aloud — that I'm a different sort of a girl some way. I hope so; I mean to be very, very different."

"You poor, dear, little Nan," he said softly. "I'm proud of you — but not very much surprised!"

"But you see it does n't count, anyhow," she said, smiling, pleased and touched by his praise. "If there's a will, it's bad; if there is n't, I'm not to be considered!"

"Don't belittle your victory by measuring it against mere money. As for those purely business matters, they'll be attended to. You're not going to be thrown out on the world just yet."

"I should n't cry — not now — if it came to that! Now that I know what they mean, I think I rather like these little wars that go on inside of us. But I tell you it was good to see the daylight this morning and know I could pass a mirror and not be afraid of my own face!"

"It is rather nicer that way; much nicer," he said, with his rare smile. "I'm glad you told me this. I see that I don't need to worry about you any more."

"You have n't really been doing that?"

"At times, at times, my dear Nan," he said, looking at her quizzically, "you've brought me to the verge of insomnia!"

CHAPTER XX

THE COPELAND-FARLEY CELLAR

AT twelve o'clock on the night of Nan's prolonged struggle, Jerry, having walked to the station with a traveling man of his acquaintance, paused at the door of Copeland-Farley, hesitated a moment, and then let himself in. He whistled a warning to the watchman, as was his habit when making night visits to the establishment. Hearing no response, he assumed that the man was off on his rounds and would reach the lower floor shortly.

He opened his desk and busied himself with some memoranda he had made from the books that afternoon. There was no denying that the house was in a bad way; the one hundred thousand dollars of notes carried by the Western National matured the next day, and in addition to these obligations the Company was seriously behind in its merchandise accounts.

A quarter of an hour passed, and the watchman made no sign. Jerry closed his desk, walked back to the elevator-shaft, and shouted the man's name. From the dark recesses of the cellar came sounds as of some one running, followed by a stumble and fall. He called again, more loudly, but receiving no response, he ran to the stairway, flashed on the lights, and hurried down.

His suspicions were aroused at once by a heap of refuse, surmounted by half a dozen empty boxes, piled about the wooden framework of the elevator-shaft.

The room where oils, paints, ethers, acids and other highly inflammable or explosive stock was stored was shut off from the remainder of the cellar by an iron door that had been pushed open. As he darted in and turned on the lights, he heard some one stealthily moving in the farther end of the room.

Seizing a fire-extinguisher he bawled the watchman's name again and plunged in among the barrels. A trail of straw indicated that the same hand that had piled the combustibles against the shaft had carried similar materials into the dangerous precincts of the oil room. In a moment he came upon a barrel of benzine surrounded with kindling.

He decided against calling for help. No harm had yet been done, and it was best to capture the guilty person and deal with him quietly if possible. He kicked the litter away from the barrel and waited. In a moment a slight noise attracted his attention, and at the same instant a shadow vanished behind an upright cask. He waited for the shadow to reappear, advancing cautiously down the aisle with his eyes on the cask.

THE COPELAND-FARLEY CELLAR

"Come out o' that!" he called.

A foot scraped on the cement floor and definitely marked the cask as the incendiary's hiding-place. He jumped upon a barrel, leaped from it to the cask, and flung himself upon a man crouched behind it. They went down together with Jerry's hand clutching the captive's throat.

"Good God!" he gasped, as he found himself gazing into Copeland's eyes.

The breath had been knocked out of Billy and he lay still, panting hard. His right hand clenched a revolver.

"Give me that thing!"

Jerry wrenched it from Copeland's convulsive clutch, thrust it into his coat pocket, and stood erect.

"I'm very sorry, sir," he said.

"Damn' near shootin' you, Jerry," drawled Copeland, sitting up and passing his hand slowly across his face; "damn' near! Gimme your hand."

Jerry drew him to his feet. Copeland rested heavily on the cask and looked his employee over with a slow, bewildered stare.

"Might 'a' known I couldn't pull 'er off! Always some damn' fool like you buttin' into my blizness. 'S *my* blizness! Goin' do what I damn' please with *my* blizness. Burn whole damn' thing down 'f want to. I'm incenjy — what you call 'm? — incenjyary, — what you call 'm — pyromaniac. Go to jail and pen'tenshary firs' thing I know."

THE PROOF OF THE PUDDING

"Not this time," said Jerry sternly. "I'm going to take you home."

"Home? Whersh that?" asked Copeland, grinning foolishly.

"Well, I guess a Turkish bath would be better. Where's Galloway?"

"Gall'way's good fellow; reli'ble watchman. Wife's sick; sent him home with my comp'ments. Told 'im I'd take full reshponshibility."

"You didn't expect to collect the insurance on that story, did you? You must have a low opinion of the adjusters. I'll fire Galloway to-morrow for leaving you here in this shape."

"Not on yer life y' won't! Silly old man did n't know I wuz loaded. Came on me sud'ly — very sud'ly. Only had slix slocktails — no; thass wrong; thass all wrong. You know what I mean. Effect unusual — mos' unusual. Just a few small drinks at club. Guess I can't carry liquor's graceful-ly as I used to. Billy Copeland's no good any more. Want lie down. Good place on floor. Nice bed right here, Jerry. Lemme go t' sleep."

He grasped the edge of the cask more firmly and bent his head to look down at the heap of straw he had been planting round it when Amidon interrupted him.

"Not much I won't! But before we skip I've got to clean up this trash. Steady, now; come along!"

He seized Copeland's arm and forced him to the

stairway, where he left him huddled on the bottom step.

"No respec' for head of house; no respec' whatever," Copeland muttered.

Jerry bade him remain quiet, and began carrying the straw and boxes back to the packing-room. He swept the floor clean, and when he was satisfied that no telltale trace remained he got Copeland to the counting-room and telephoned for a taxi.

"Goin' to be busted to-morrow; clean smash. You made awful mistake, Jeremiah, in not lessing — no, not lesting me burn 'er up. Insurance'd help out consid'ble. Need new building, anyhow."

"I guess we don't need it that bad," remarked Jerry, rolling a cigarette. He called the police station and asked for the loan of an officer to do watchman duty for the remainder of the night; and this accomplished he considered his further duty to his befuddled employer.

Now that the calamity had been averted, his anger abated. Copeland's condition mitigated somewhat the hideousness of the crime he was about to commit. Only his desperate financial situation could have prompted him to attempt to fire the building. Jerry's silence and unusual gravity seemed to trouble Copeland.

"Guess you're dis'pointed in your boss, Jeremiah. Don' blame you. Drunken fool — damn' fool — incenjy-ary; no end bad lot."

THE PROOF OF THE PUDDING

"Put your hat on straight and forget it," remarked Jerry.

He telephoned to Gaylord, an athletic trainer who conducted a Turkish bath, and told him to prepare for a customer. He knew Gaylord well, and when they reached his place Jerry bade him stew the gin out of Copeland and be sure to have him ready for business in the morning. While Copeland was in the bath, Jerry tried all the apparatus in the gymnasium and relieved his feelings by putting on the gloves with Gaylord's assistant. After all the arts of the establishment had been exercised upon Copeland and he was disposed of for the night, Jerry went to bed. . . .

In the morning Gaylord put the finishing touches on his patient and turned him out as good as new. It had occurred to Amidon that Copeland might decide to avoid the store that day. He was relieved when he announced, after they had shared Gaylord's breakfast, that he would walk to the office with him.

"Guess I'll give the boys a jar by showing up early," he remarked.

It was a clear, bracing morning, and Copeland set a brisk pace. He was stubbornly silent and made no reference to the night's affair until they reached the heart of the city. Then he stopped suddenly and laid his hand on Jerry's arm.

"Jerry, I never meant to do that; for God's sake, don't believe I did!" he broke out hoarsely. "I was troubled about the business, and some other things had worried me lately. I took too many drinks — and I'd never meant to drink again! I would n't have tried that sober — I would n't have had the nerve!"

"It was the drink, of course," Jerry assented. "It's all over now. You'd better forget it; I'm going to!"

"I wish to God I could forget it!"

Copeland shrugged his shoulders impatiently, then drew himself erect and walked on more quickly. Jerry cheerfully changed the subject, and when they were near the store dived into an alley that led to the rear door of Copeland-Farley to avoid appearing before the clerks in Copeland's company.

Copeland remained in his room all morning, summoning the auditor from time to time to ask for various data. He called Jerry once and bade him make every effort to find Kinney by telephone. Kinney was in New York; had been there for a week. Copeland smiled sardonically at this news.

"All right. I knew he'd been away, but the fool said he'd be back to-day," he said spitefully. "That's all!"

At two o'clock he put a bundle of papers into his pocket and walked toward the Western National. The bookkeepers exchanged meaningful glances and Jerry imagined that even the truckmen loading freight appeared depressed. Copeland's desperation had been expressed vividly enough in his drunken attempt to burn the store. And now, if the Western National refused to extend his loans, Copeland-Farley might cease to exist. Jerry's usual nonchalance left him. He failed to seize a chance to "land" on a drummer from a New York perfumery house who was teasing him for the latest news of Main Street. . . .

At three o'clock Eaton called Jerry on the telephone.

"I want to see Copeland; please call me the minute he comes in," said the lawyer.

Shortly before four Copeland came back and walked directly to his office. There was another exchange of glances along the accountants' desks, where the clerks bent with affected diligence over their books.

The auditor was summoned again, carried a book into Copeland's room, and reappeared instantly. The air was tense. It was a source of relief to Jerry to hear Eaton's voice as he reported Copeland's return.

"Watch him," said the lawyer, with his usual calmness; "and don't let him leave the store."

As Jerry nervously watched the door for Eaton's appearance, Louis M. Eichberg, of Corbin & Eichberg, entered and asked for Copeland. The bookkeepers exchanged glances again and bent over their ledgers with renewed zeal. The door of the private office closed upon Eichberg. It snapped shut sharply — ominously, Jerry thought.

CHAPTER XXI

A SOLVENT HOUSE

"I've bought in your stock," Eichberg was saying to Copeland. "You put up fourteen hundred and eighty-five shares with the Western National and I've bought 'em in at private sale under your collateral agreement. As I understand it there are fifteen shares held by employees to qualify as directors. I guess there won't be any trouble about them, and we'll let 'em stand for the present."

"Those men paid for their stock and you have no right to touch it," said Copeland. "The stock in this company has an actual value of two hundred dollars a share —"

"Rubbish! Your capital's shrunk till you can't see it any more."

"Don't you believe it! The house was never as sound as it is to-day. I hope you don't think I'm going to stand by and let the Western sell me out on a small loan in this high-handed fashion! It's a frame-up, a conspiracy to clean me out. I've still got a majority of the stock, and I'll give you a run for your money before you get through with me!"

"Keep your temper, Copeland! I don't like doing this, but it's better for me to have the business than to let it peter out, the way it's doing.

I'll even say that after we consolidate I'll be glad to make a place for you in the house."

"Oh, you need n't trouble!" returned Copeland hotly. "You're not going to get rid of me so easy!"

"All right! Just how much stock do you think you've got?" asked Eichberg with a faint ironic smile.

"I've got fifteen hundred shares; the bank understood that when I refused their demand for a majority," Copeland replied, frowning over the stock-ledger.

"That shows how much you know about your own business! There's twenty shares out of your half that I've been trying to lay my hands on for two months. It was a deal Farley made the last year he was down here with a Fort Wayne jobber named Reynolds that he bought out after your father died. I know because we tried to buy up Reynolds ourselves, but old Uncle Tim went us one better. There was n't much to the business, but the good-will was worth something and Farley let Reynolds have twenty shares just to beat us out of the sale. Farley had sense! When Reynolds died his executor sold the stock to somebody here. Foreman handled it, but he won't tell me who he sold to. I know you did n't get it! Foreman says he spent a month last summer lookin' for you to give you a chance to buy the stock, but he could n't get hold of you. You were always off sportin' with Kinney!"

Copeland had forgotten about the Reynolds

shares. He mentally cursed Farley for not remind-
ing him of them; Farley had never dealt squarely
with him! Very likely he had personally told Eichberg and the Western National of the Reynolds
shares. It was galling to be obliged to learn from
Eichberg things he should have known himself. He
had flattered himself that in persuading the bank
to accept fourteen hundred and eighty-five shares
as collateral instead of the majority for which demand had been made at first, he had shown his
business sagacity; but evidently Eichberg had
known of the Reynolds shares all along.

"I don't intend that what's left of this business
shall go to the bad," said Eichberg. "Either you
come to terms, and let 'em know outside that
we've arranged a merger in a friendly way, or I'll
call up my lawyer and tell him to apply for a receiver."

Outside, the interested and anxious clerks and
stenographers, cold with excitement, watched their
associate, Mr. Jeremiah Amidon, who was inviting
the wrath of the gods by knocking upon Copeland's
door. When he entered in response to an angry
bellow, they expected to see him reappear instantly,
possibly at the end of William B. Copeland's foot.
To their chagrin Amidon remained in the private
office for some time; and they judged from the sudden quiet that followed his disappearance that he
was exerting a calming influence upon Copeland
and his visitor. . . .

THE PROOF OF THE PUDDING

"I beg your pardon," Jerry remarked while Copeland and Eichberg glared at him.

To Copeland the sight of Jerry was an unwelcome reminder of the previous night. His remorse over his effort to burn the store vanished; if it had n't been for this meddlesome cub he would n't now be entertaining Eichberg in his office!

"Well, what does the boy want?" demanded Eichberg, when Copeland found it impossible to express his wrath at Jerry's intrusion.

Eichberg knew Jerry perfectly well; everybody in the street knew Jerry! And it was the basest insult to refer to him as the boy.

"Excuse me, Mr. Eichberg! I just wanted to hand a memorandum to Mr. Copeland."

He drew from his pocket the certificate he had purchased from Foreman, and handed it to Copeland, who snatched it from him with an angry snarl.

"Where did you get this?" he asked faintly after a glance at the paper.

"Oh, it just blew in my way early in the fall. I never bothered to get a new certificate, but I'll turn it in right now."

He pulled out a fountain pen, removed the cap deliberately, and wrote his name in the blank space above the executor's endorsement. This done, he brushed an imaginary speck from his cuff, as he had seen Eaton do, and went out, closing the door softly.

"Well, here's the answer, Eichberg," said Copeland, with affected nonchalance; "here are those Reynolds shares."

"How did that damn' little fool get this?" demanded Eichberg, after a careful scrutiny of the certificate and endorsements.

"Oh, he's a useful little damn' fool! He's always picking up something," replied Copeland coolly.

"I suppose it was all set up," Eichberg sneered. "Why did n't you come right out and say you had that stock, and save my time? It's worth something if yours ain't! You'll either sell me that stock or I'll have the court throw you out. It's up to you!"

"I told you the truth about these shares," said Copeland, whose good humor was returning. "I'm ashamed to say I'd clean forgotten them; but you see stock never figured much in our corporation; it's always been a sort of family affair. I have no idea where Amidon got Reynolds's shares — that's straight! He's always doing something he is n't paid for. And you see it is n't quite so easy to clean me out. But I take off my hat to you; you're a business man!"

Hope had risen in him. In spite of his futile efforts to tide over the crisis there was still the remote chance that Kinney, who always seemed able to borrow all he wanted for his own purposes, might extend a helping hand. His change of manner had its effect on Eichberg.

THE PROOF OF THE PUDDING

"The stock does n't cut any ice," he fumed.
"I'm not goin' to have a hundred thousand dollars
in a concern that's losin' money like this one!
That statement you showed the bank was rotten!
You ain't got any credit; and you know mighty well
you can't go on here. You'll either come to terms
or I'll get a receiver to-morrow. That's all there
is of that!"

He clapped on his hat and turned to the door
just as it opened upon Eaton.

"I'll look in again in the morning, Copeland,"
said Eichberg in a loud tone. "You just think over
that matter, and I guess you'll see it my way."

"Never put off till to-morrow what you can do
to-day," remarked Eaton, projecting himself into
the office. "I'll close the door if you don't mind,
Copeland. And, Mr. Eichberg, please wait a
moment."

"If you're his lawyer, you don't want me here.
I've said all I've got to say to Copeland," Eichberg answered. But he waited, glowering at Eaton,
who removed his overcoat, placed it carefully on a
chair, and began drawing off his gloves.

"Mr. Eichberg, they told me a moment ago at
the Western National that certain stock held as
collateral for maturing Copeland-Farley notes had
been bought by you. Is that true?"

"That's correct! I guess it was all regular,"
Eichberg snapped.

"We'll come to that presently. You have now

in your possession through that purchase fourteen hundred and eighty-five shares of stock?"

"Right!" ejaculated Eichberg loudly.

Eaton raised his hand, glanced intently at the palm, and then, with one of his familiar tricks, bent his gaze directly upon Eichberg.

"Being a competitor of Copeland-Farley and a director of the bank, you have naturally — quite naturally — thought it would be a good investment to own a large block of the stock? And it undoubtedly occurred to you that a combination of Copeland-Farley with Corbin & Eichberg would be highly advantageous? In fact, you thought you had more stock than Copeland owns, and that you could come in here and discharge him like a drayman!"

"That's my business! You have n't explained yet how you come to be buttin' in here."

"Presently — presently!" replied Eaton soothingly.

His calm demeanor and refusal to lift his voice further infuriated Eichberg, who breathed hard for a moment, then pointed a stubby forefinger at the lawyer as his wrath found utterance.

"Copeland-Farley's ruined — busted! If you'll take a look at their last statement you'll see they can't pull out!"

"You anticipate me," replied Eaton gently. "The fact is I had meant to buy that stock myself, but the bank's haste to turn it over to you has spoiled that. I was annoyed — greatly annoyed — when I found awhile ago that the stock had been sold — sold, in violation of the stipulation — on the bank's usual form — that three days' grace were to be given to the debtor to release his collateral. I don't believe the Comptroller would like that. I shall consider seriously bringing it to his attention."

"What good would three days have done him?" cried Eichberg. "The sooner he's put out the better. His accounts payable are goin' to bring his general creditors down on him in a few days! Don't you suppose I know? Have n't they been telegraphin' me from all over the country for months askin' about this house?"

"And, of course," said Eaton softly, "you did all you could to protect your competitor — neighborly feeling, and that sort of thing. Well, it will be a great relief to you to know that those accounts will be paid to-morrow — just as soon as the exchange window of your piratical bank is opened. There's a hundred thousand dollars to the credit of Copeland-Farley over there right now. I know, because I went in a quarter of an hour ago and made the deposit. This house is solvent — absolutely solvent. Moreover, Copeland's stock in the Kinney Ivory Cement Company is now marketable. I take some pride in that fact myself — immodestly, I dare say, and yet — I am only human!"

He drew a telegram from his waistcoat pocket and handed it to Copeland.

A SOLVENT HOUSE

"That patent case was decided to-day — in favor of Kinney. Copeland, I congratulate you!"

Copeland read the message, and looked dully from Eaton to Eichberg. He was roused by Eichberg, who had no difficulty in expressing his emotions.

"You fool," he shouted, shaking his fist in Eaton's face. "If you're tellin' the truth, what you mean to do about my stock?"

Eaton was drawing on his gloves without haste. His face expressed the mildest surprise at Eichberg's perturbation.

"My dear Mr. Eichberg, you were in such a rush to buy the Western's collateral that I'm surprised that you should trouble me — a casual acquaintance — with such a question."

"It's a cheat; it's a swindle! If there's any law for this —"

He flung out of the office and tramped heavily to the front door, while the clerks, worn with the many agitations of the day, stared after him mutely.

"In the morning," Eaton was saying to Copeland, "I'll have fuller details of the decision, but there's no doubt about it — we've won on every point. Allow me to congratulate you!"

Copeland half rose to take his proffered hand; then with a groan he sank back and buried his face in his hands.

CHAPTER XXII

NULL AND VOID

"Those documents have a familiar look," remarked Thurston with a smile as Nan placed the packet of wills on the table beside him in the Farley parlor. "Mr. Farley was hard to please; I've learned a lot about will-writing just from studying the different schemes he proposed from time to time."

Nan described the manner in which she had found the wills on the night of Farley's death.

"He was evidently troubled about them and got out of bed to look them over. This one, that I found lying open on the table, is torn across as though he had begun to destroy it when the end came."

"Very likely that was his intention," Thurston replied. "I had just written a new will for him, but it was n't signed — not unless he executed it that same afternoon. Perhaps you know about that?"

"No one was here, I'm sure," said Nan, after a moment's consideration. "The nurse was off duty; she left for the evening at four o'clock, and I'm sure the servants were n't in his room. I carried up his dinner tray myself."

"It's hardly possible he had signed that last will.

I was always present on such occasions and I got the witnesses. When I called now and then with a couple of his friends, or telephoned for them, there was a will to be signed. You probably understood that."

He began opening the papers, glancing quickly at the last sheet of each will, and turning them face down on the table. The torn one he scrutinized more carefully, and returned to it for further examination when he had disposed of the others. Nan watched him nervously. He was a small, slight man of sixty, with a stiff gray mustache and a sharp, rasping voice. It would not have been easy to deceive Thurston if she had destroyed the wills; she could never have gone through with it!

She felt that she had touched with her finger-tips the far horizons and knew at last something of the meaning of life. She had subjected herself to pitiless self-analysis and stood convicted in her own conscience of vanity, selfishness, and hardness. The recollection of her gay adventures with the Kinneys and her affair with Copeland had become a hideous nightmare. Not only was she ashamed of her dallying with Billy, but she accused herself of having exerted a baneful influence upon him. In all likelihood he would never have sunk so low as to propose the destruction of Farley's will but for his infatuation for her.

Farley's death had in itself exercised a chastening effect upon her. She was conscious of trying to see herself with his eyes and fortify herself with something of the stern righteousness that made him, in the retrospect, a noble and inspiring figure. The upturned faces at the Settlement haunted her; there was a work for her to do in the world if only she could lay her hands upon it! In this new mood the life of ease which money would secure weighed little against self-dependence and service. Money had ceased to be an important integer in her calculations.

Having concluded his examination of the papers, the lawyer lifted his head with an impatient jerk, then sighed, and began smoothing the open sheets into a neat pile.

"Those wills are worthless, Miss Farley, — not one of them can be probated. The testator's signatures and the names of the witnesses have been scratched out!"

In proof of his statement he extended one of the wills, pointing to the heavy cross-crosses at the bottom of the sheet.

"You have no idea when he did this — you were n't present, I suppose?"

"No; he used to do his writing at the table where he hid the wills. He occasionally wrote a letter or a check there; but I never saw him open the table. I never knew of that inner compartment till the night he died."

"Oh, I know that table very well; he had shown me the hidden drawer and explained how to open it. But this is most unfortunate, deplorable! I kept in touch with his doctor about his condition and feared something like this might happen. And he dreaded it himself — was afraid he might die some time without leaving just the will he had determined to make. I account for all the wills I wrote for him but the last. The last time I was here I brought a new will, which I don't find among these. Are you sure you have n't overlooked it?"

She was quite sure of it, but after she had described in minute detail the events of the last afternoon of Farley's life, to confirm her statement that no one who could have acted as witness had visited Farley, she took the lawyer upstairs to examine the table for himself. They broadened the scope of the search, but without success.

"For the present I think it best for you not to read those wills," he said, when they had returned to the parlor. "They represent Mr. Farley's changes of feeling in regard to many things — including yourself. A little later I shall be glad to submit them to you. The important thing just now is the threat of this man Harlowe to attack your rights under the adoption. Mr. Eaton and I have already discussed that. Now that we're pretty sure there's no will, this may give us some trouble, but with characteristic thoroughness Mr. Eaton has prepared for just this emergency. His reasons for not telling me earlier about these things are sound enough — his fear of disturbing Mr.

THE PROOF OF THE PUDDING

Farley unnecessarily. He would undoubtedly have
wanted a proceeding brought to correct the adoption, but that could only have advertised the error,
and Mr. Farley might have died before we finished
it. Still, if I had known I should have taken care
that he did n't die intestate. But from what Mr.
Eaton tells me, this man is all primed to attack
any will that might have been left, on the ground
of Mr. Farley's mental incapacity — which is lu-
dicrous, of course. There was never a saner man;
and yet his eccentricities might be magnified before a jury — you never can tell. On the whole,
Mr. Eaton's silence was justified. But our next
step must be carefully considered. In the mean
time —"

He paced the floor, considering means of reliev-
ing her anxiety.

"Of course, while these things are pending we
shall arrange for your maintenance, on the old
basis, in this house. No one can pretend that Mr.
Farley did n't have every intention of providing
for you generously. It's only fair to tell you this,
that even when he seemed to waver at times he
never cut your legacy below a hundred thousand
dollars; and I know he regretted the comparative
meagerness of that — tripled the amount in the
very next will he made! You need have no fears,
Miss Farley," he went on reassuringly. "But you
are entitled to your own counsel; it's only right
that I should say this to you immediately; and

I suggest that you ask Mr. Eaton to represent you.
I hope you will confer with him at once."

He bowed with old-fashioned formality. He was
more troubled than he cared to have Nan know,
and her silence disconcerted him. But her face
expressed neither disappointment nor alarm. She
stood erect by the table, an intent look in her eyes.
Not wishing to leave her weighed down by the
uncertainties of her future, he said briskly: —

"You must n't bother yourself about these matters, Miss Farley. In the end you will find yourself
a rich woman. So —"

He waved his hand as the preliminary to a quick
exit, but she called him back. He did not like being
called back; now, he thought, there would be the
tears he dreaded.

"You don't understand," she said quietly. "I
ought to have made it clear in the first place, but
I did n't know just how — or when — to say it.
I can't — I will not take any of Mr. Farley's
money — not even if the law should give it to me."

He looked at her with the mute appeal of the
deaf when they fail to catch a meaning.

"Really, Miss Farley —"

"I won't take one cent of Mr. Farley's money,"
Nan repeated firmly.

"I can't blame you for being disappointed — for
resenting what may appear to be a lack of consideration on his part for your comfort —"

"Oh, it is n't that! I would n't have you think

that! I'm sure he meant to do what was right —
what was generous! You don't know how glad I
am that our last day together was a happy one —
we had never been on better terms. It's not that
I have any unkind feeling toward papa; it's all
myself. The Farleys were only too kind to me.
I went my own way and it made me selfish — and
pretty hard, too, I'm afraid. Papa knew it; and
you know yourself how little he trusted me. And
he was right about me: I did n't deserve his confidence. But I'm going to begin all over again, as
I could n't if I began fighting for this money. I can
see now that money can't make me happy. I'm
going to work; I'm going to stop living, as I
always have, just for myself: I'm going — I'm
going to think about the rest of the folks a lot!"

"The folks?" repeated Thurston feebly. "What
folks?"

"Oh, everybody! The down-and-outers — girls
like me who get a bad start or make mistakes!"

Thurston's brows worked convulsively. He had
been prepared for anything but this.

"Do I — do I understand you to mean that,
even if this estate could be turned over to you to-
morrow, you'd decline to receive it? It can't be
possible —"

"Yes; that's what I mean!" she cried eagerly.
"I've thought it all out and have made up my
mind about it. I don't want to be considered in
anything that has to do with papa's property."

"But, my dear child, you can't — you *can't* abandon your claims in any such fashion! It's my duty — I owe it to my friend and client to see that his wishes are fulfilled. Why —"

"Well," she persisted, "between all those wills you can't tell what he wanted — only that I was a great problem to him. I caused him a great deal of unnecessary worry and heartache. I hope this is n't going to cause you any trouble —" And she smiled in spite of herself at his consternation, as indicated by the twitching of his brows. And there *was*, she realized, something absurd in her cool statement to a hard-headed lawyer that she renounced claims whose validity he was in duty bound to support. The situation was too much for him; he must escape as quickly as possible from this young woman who brushed away a fairly tangible fortune as a waiter clears away bread crumbs.

"Really, Miss Farley —" he began; but, thinking of nothing further to say, he backed awkwardly into the hall.

She helped him into his coat and opened the street door. He hurried off without saying good-bye, clasping Timothy Farley's wills tightly under his arm.

A light snow was falling; Nan stood on the steps and lifted her hot face to the fluttering flakes. She watched Thurston until he turned the corner and then went to the telephone.

In a moment she was connected with Mrs. Copeland at the farm. "I want a job," she was saying in a cheerful tone; "yes, that's it — a chance to work. You told me the other day you needed some one to look after your business at the market-house. I'm applying for the job. Oh, no! I'm not fooling; I want that place! Well, I want to see you, too; I'll be out early in the morning!"

CHAPTER XXIII

IN TRUST

"Copeland Farm Products" in blue letters against a white background swung over Nan's head on Tuesday, Thursday, and Saturday mornings in the city market-house. On those days she left Mrs. Copeland's farm at five o'clock with the day's offerings and by six the stand was in order.

An endless, jostling throng surged by, and every sale she effected, every negotiation for the future delivery of an order, had all the joy of an adventure. Her immediate neighbors were a big-fisted German gardener and a black-eyed Italian girl who sold fruits and vegetables. When business lagged, the German chaffed her about her wares or condoled with her when some frugal marketer 'priced her butter, sniffed, and departed. Nan commanded a meager knowledge of Italian and flung a phrase at her dark-eyed neighbor now and then in the spirit of comradeship which the place encouraged. She liked her "job." She assured herself that she had never had so much fun in all her life, and that never again would she eat the bread of idleness.

But it had not proved so easy as she imagined it would be to slip out of her old life into the new. If she had left the Farley house preceded by a

301

brass band and had marched round the monument and the length of Washington Street before taking her place in the market, her flight could hardly have attracted more attention.

The town buzzed. The newspapers neglected no phase of Nan's affairs, nor did they overlook her as she stood behind the counter dispensing "Copeland Farm Products." She was surprised and vexed by her sudden notoriety. A newspaper photographer snapped her, in her white sweater and blue-and-white tam o' shanter, passing eggs over the counter. The portrait bore the caption, "Miss Nancy Farley in a New Rôle," and was supplemented by text adorned with such sub-headings as "Renounces her Fortune" and "Throws Away a Million Dollars." To be thus heralded was preposterous; she had merely gone to work for reasons that were, in any view of the matter, her own private affair. But public sentiment was astonishingly friendly; even those who had looked askance at her high flights with the Kinney crowd said it was an outrage that Farley had failed to provide for her decently.

Fanny, thinking at first it was only a joke, a flare of temperament (references to her temperament had begun to pall upon Nan!), had welcomed Nan to her house and given her charge of the market-stand; but it was not without difficulty that she persuaded the girl to occupy her guest-room and share her meals.

IN TRUST

"You'd better scold me when I make mistakes, for if I find I don't suit I'll fire myself," Nan declared. "And if I have to leave you, I'll go to clerking in a department store. I just mention this so you won't be too polite. This isn't any grandstand play, you see; I'm serious for the first time in my life!"

It was certain, at any rate, that Copeland Farm Products were sold with amazing ease. When it became known that Nan Farley had become Mrs. Copeland's representative "on market," there was lively competition for the privilege of purchasing those same "products." Fanny complained ruefully that the jellies, jams, and pickles created by the young women in her industrial house would be exhausted before Christmas and that nothing would remain to sell but butter and eggs. Nan suggested orange marmalade and a cake-baking department to keep the girls at work during the winter, and on the off days she set herself to planning the preparation of these "specialties." Mrs. Farley's cooking lessons had not gone for naught; Nan could bake a cake in which there was no trace of "sadness," and after some experiments with jumbles and sand-tarts she sold her first output in an hour and opened a waiting list.

Mrs. Copeland told Eaton at the end of the second week that she had never known the real Nan till now. There was no questioning the girl's sincerity; she had cut loose from her old life, relinquished all hope of participating in Farley's fortune, and addressed herself zealously to the business of supporting herself. She became immediately the idol of the half-dozen young women in the old farm-house, who thought her an immensely "romantic" figure and marveled at her industry and resourcefulness.

"Splendid! Give her all the room she wants," Eaton urged Mrs. Copeland. "She's only finding herself; we'll have the Nan she was meant to be the first thing we know."

"I did n't know all these nice church-going people would come to condole with me, or I'd have left town," Nan confided to Fanny. "These women who would n't let their daughters associate with me a year ago can't buy enough eggs now to show how much they sympathize with me. If they don't keep away, I'm going to raise the price of their eggs, and that will break their hearts — and the eggs! But do you know," she went on gravely, "I've never been so happy in my life as I am now! And I would n't have anybody think it was out of pique, or with any unkind feeling toward papa," — tears shone in her eyes as the word slipped from her tongue, — "but I tell you nobody ever could have made a nice, polite girl out of me. I was bound to get into scrapes as long as I had n't anything really to do but fill in time between manicuring and hair-washing dates. There's a whole lot in that old saying about making a silk purse out of a sow's ear: it can't be did!"

"If you talk that way," Fanny laughed, "I shall turn you out of my house. I don't want you to think I approve of what you're doing. I'm letting you do it because I'm scared not to!"

"You'd better be — for if you hadn't taken me in, I should have gone on the stage, — honestly, I should, — in vaudeville, most likely, doing monologues right between the jugglers and the trained seals." . . .

On Tuesdays, Thursdays, and Saturdays Mr. Jeremiah A. Amidon found it convenient to visit the market-house as early as seven-thirty (in spite of pressing duties at the store), to make sure, he said, that Nan, and the farmhand who drove her in and helped arrange the stock, had safely passed all the railroad crossings on the way to town. Jerry was a consoling person and unobtrusively thoughtful and helpful. And in his way he was almost as keen as Eaton. Jerry did not require explanations, and nothing is so wholly satisfactory as a friend who understands without being told.

"Little girl, if your eggs are guaranteed under the Pure Food Act, I'll take one — the large size."

"You'll find the hard-boiled eggs at the lunch counter in the next aisle, little boy," Nan answered. "How is John Cecil?"

"Working himself to death. You've driven him to it!"

"I hope you two are not abusing me; how about it?"

"No; not vocally. Cecil's shut up in his office every night, getting ready to clean up those cousins of Farley's down on the river, but he does n't say anything. Look here, Nan, we've got a line of cold cream and other toilet marvels — stuff you could handle here as a side line. Let us send you up a bunch to put next to that pink jelly. It's high grade and we'll make it to you at the right price."

"Not on your life, Jerry. Drugs and hand-made country butter can't associate. You'd better run down to your own little shop now and go to work."

After his morning inspection he was likely to reappear at lunch time, to see her for a moment before she left for the farm; and he assisted in balancing her cash when she confessed that it would n't "gee." His pride in her was enormous; he was satisfied that there was no other girl to compare with her.

Jerry's admiration was so obviously genuine and supported by so deep an awe and reverence that no girl could have helped liking it. And Jerry was unfailingly amusing; his airs and graces, his attempts to wear a little learning lightly, were wholly transparent and invited the chaff he welcomed. Nan's feeling, dating from the beginning of their acquaintance, that their common origin in the back streets of Belleville established a tie between them had grown steadily. In all her late perplexities and self-questioning she had found herself wondering constantly what Jerry would say, and he had supported her warmly in her rejection of the estate.

He had from the first confided his ambitions to her and they were worthy ones. He not only meant to get on, but he meant to overcome as far as possible his lack of early advantages. He steadfastly spent an hour at his Latin every night before he went to bed, with only an occasional lift from the busy Eaton. "As long as I've tackled it, I might as well keep it up," he remarked apologetically. "Cecil says my English is so bad, I'd better learn a few foreign languages to make me respectable!"

One noon Nan was munching an apple while waiting for Mrs. Copeland's man to carry out the empty crates and boxes, when Jerry appeared, looking unusually solemn.

"What's wrong with the world? You're not out of work, are you?" she demanded.

"I hoped you'd ask me," he replied, with mock dejection. "The boss has been making a few changes at the store and I've got a new job."

"Better or worse?" she asked, with feigned carelessness.

This was the first time he had referred to Copeland since her removal to the farm; and there were still vast areas of ignorance and uncertainty in his mind as to her feeling toward Copeland.

"Better for me; I don't know about the house," he answered. "Has n't anybody told you everything that's happened down our way?" He seated himself on the counter and clasped one knee with his gloved hands. "Well, we've reorganized; just about everything's changed except the sign. Boss steady as a rock; things rather coming his way now. You heard about Kinney Cement? There was never any doubt about Cecil winning the patent cases; and now the boss has sold out his interest — quit cement for good and all; concentrating on drugs. I guess he got a good price for his cement stock, too."

He waited to see how she was affected by these confidences.

"The drug business was in a bad way, was n't it?" she asked carelessly.

"Um, well; it did look for a few minutes as though we might n't pull through."

She laughed at his lightly emphasized "we."

"What are you doing now? — counting money or running the elevator?"

"Tease me some more! Say, Nan, I'm not kidding you. The boss made a new job for me; I'm sales manager — going to start out with a suitcase next week and shake hands with all our customers, just to get in touch. Not to interfere with our regular salesmen; oh, no! Just asking about the babies down the line and making the lowly retailer feel that we live only to please him. Do you get me?"

"A gleam or two. So Mr. Copeland got out of

his troubles, did he? Well, I'm glad to hear it. He's too good a fellow to go to the bad."

This was spoken carelessly, but with a note of sincerity. Her world had turned upside-down since her last meeting with Billy. She waited for Jerry to enlighten her further.

"He's all right now; you can bet on that; he's not going to fool with his luck any more. It's funny" — he was finding it difficult to conceal his embarrassment in speaking of Copeland to Nan — "but the boss and Cecil are getting chummy. When the pinch came, Cecil was right there; walked on to the scaffold and saved him after the black cap had been pulled on and tied under his chin. This is marked private — I don't *know* anything — not a thing!"

Nan nodded. She did not see very clearly what he was driving at, but she refused to ask questions.

"The boss and Cecil are lunching together every day now, and they spend an hour together. That tickles me," he ended softly. "I always wished they'd hit it off together."

He glanced at her for her approval of this new combination, which was hardly more surprising than his own manifestation of feeling. He evidently derived the deepest satisfaction from the new intimacy between Eaton and Copeland. The fleeting tenderness and wistfulness in his candid, humorous eyes touched her.

"Well!" he exclaimed cheerily, as the driver

announced that the wagon was ready, "do you fly back to the farm, or will you join me in refreshments at a one-arm sandwichorium? I've only got twenty minutes."

"I'll fool you by accepting," she laughed. "I have some errands to do and can just about catch the three o'clock interurban."

They walked to a lunch room, where he found seats and brought her the sandwich and coffee she insisted was all she wanted. He was observing her narrowly for signs of discontent, but she had never seemed happier. He understood perfectly that she wished her new activities to be taken as a matter of course, and he carefully refrained from expressing his great pride in her. As long as she continued to countenance him, he was satisfied, and she had shown in countless ways that she liked him and believed in him.

He introduced her to a bank clerk who paused in his hurried exit to speak to him and incidentally to have a closer look at Nan. A girl nodded to him across the room; he explained that she was one of the smartest girls in town — "the whole show in an insurance office; the members of the firm don't turn round unless she says so."

"Just think," Nan remarked, "I might have died without knowing how it feels to be a poor working girl."

"Well, don't die now that you've found it out! It would be mighty lonesome on earth without

you. Have a chocolate eclair," he added hastily,
— "'business girl's special.'"

"No, thanks. If I don't turn up to-night with
an appetite for dinner Mrs. Copeland will be scared
and send for the doctor."

"By the way, I wish you'd casually mention me
to that gifted lady; I'd like to hop off at Stop 3
some evening without being consumed by the dog.
How about it?"

"Oh, she'll stand for it! She'll stand for 'most
anybody who shows up with a clean face and a kind
heart. She's an angel, Jerry. She's the finest
woman that ever lived!"

"I'd sort o' figured that out for myself, just
passing her on the boulevards. I thought I'd try
for a rise out of Cecil the other night and just
mentioned her with a gentle o. k. I'd gone up to
his office to see if I could shine his shoes or do any
little thing like that for him, and he looked at me
so long I nearly had nervous prostration, and then
he said: 'My dear boy, the poverty of your vocabu-
lary is a constant grief to me!' — just like that.
I guess he likes her all right."

"She has a good many admirers," Nan replied
noncommittally, as she crumpled her paper napkin.
"She can't help it."

"Well, anything Cecil wants he ought to have."

"Well, I hope — I should hate to think he
could n't get anything he wanted in this world,"
said Nan.

THE PROOF OF THE PUDDING

Jerry had been deeply troubled at times by the fear that his adored Cecil might be interested in Nan, and the smile that accompanied her last remark was the least bit ambiguous. With all his assurance he was at heart a humble person, and he never ceased to marvel at Nan's tolerance of him. It was not for him to question the ordinances of Heaven. If Cecil and Nan —

Nan began drawing on her gloves. When they reached the street she explained that she was going to the Farley house to gather up some of her traps that she had left behind. Fully conscious of his sudden soberness and perhaps surmising the cause of it, she lightened his burdened spirit by asking him to come out soon to see her, and boarded a street car. . . .

This was her first visit "home" since she had left the house to go to Fanny Copeland's. In her hurried flight she had taken only a trunk and a suit-case, but her summer gowns and a number of odds and ends remained to be packed and moved.

The colored maid, who had only vaguely grasped the meaning of Nan's sudden departure, admitted her with joyous exclamations.

"About time yo' 's comin' back, Miss Nan. Mistah Thu'ston came up heah and tole me and Joshua to stay right along. I guess Mistah Fa'ley's been turnin' ovah in his grave 'bout yo' runnin' away. He was mighty ca'less not to fix his will the way it ought t' been. Yo' 'll find yo' room just

312

the way yo' left it. Mistah Thu'ston said fo' me to keep things shined up just the way they always was."

Nan explained that she had merely come to pack her remaining things and asked Joshua to bring up a trunk from the cellar. She filled the trunk and added to the summer frocks articles from her desk and other personal belongings that she wished to keep for their various associations.

When she had finished, she crossed the hall to Farley's room, rather from force of habit than by intention. She ran her hand across the shelves that represented his steadfast literary preferences that had never been altered in her recollection: "Pickwick," Artemus Ward; a volume of Petroleum V. Nasby's writings; Franklin's "Autobiography"; Grant's "Memoirs"; Mark Twain, in well-worn original first editions, including the bulky "Innocents Abroad" and "Roughing It." She resolved to take the "Life on the Mississippi," from which she had so often read to him in his last year. She rummaged in the closet for an album containing crude old-fashioned likenesses of Mr. and Mrs. Farley and a series of photographs of herself that marked the swift-moving years from the time she became a member of their household.

In a last slow survey of the room her eyes fell upon the portrait of Mrs. Farley that had arrested her with its kind motherly glance on the night of her temptation. She reflected that her right to remove anything from the house was questionable, but she meant to ask Thurston to give her the portrait when the house was finally disposed of.

As she lifted the frame and shook the wire loose from the hook, a paper that had been thrust behind the picture slipped over the mantel-edge with a soft rustling and fell at her feet. She laid the portrait on the bed and picked up the paper.

A glance sufficed to tell her that she had found another of Farley's wills — possibly the last, for which Thurston had inquired so particularly.

She opened it hurriedly and glanced at the last sheet. The spaces for the signatures of testator and witnesses were blank. It was only worthless paper, of no value to any one. It seemed a plausible assumption that Farley, having decided finally that he would have no use for the earlier wills, had begun to destroy them after first placing the last one behind the picture to avoid the chance of confusing it with the others.

As Nan folded it, a name caught her attention and she began to read.

I hereby give and bequeath to Frances Hillard Copeland, as trustee, the sum of five hundred thousand dollars, the same to be held by said Frances Hillard Copeland, as such trustee, with the following powers and for the following purposes: ... To pay to my said daughter upon her marriage the principal of said fund, together with all accre-

tions thereto; provided, however, that the marriage of my said daughter shall be with the approval and express consent of said Frances Hillard
Copeland. . . .

The room swayed as the meaning of this proviso
sank into her whirling senses. Farley had inter-
posed Fanny between her and Billy — Fanny,
Billy's former wife! The old man's hatred of Copeland, his warm admiration for Fanny, had thus
combined to fashion a device that was almost
malevolent in its cunning. She followed Farley's
reasoning clearly. He had assumed that his own
feeling toward Copeland was shared by Fanny, and
that she would never consent to a marriage which,
in the vague prospect, had given him so much
concern. He had presumably promoted the friendly
relations between Fanny and her with this end in
view.

As the first shock of the revelation passed, Nan
laughed bitterly.

"Poor papa!" she murmured.

He little knew how near she had come to marrying Billy! She gasped as it occurred to her that
Farley might have discussed the matter with Fanny
and persuaded her to accept the trust; but she
quickly decided against this. It was unlikely that
Farley had ever spoken to her about it; and it was
inconceivable that Fanny would have consented,
when the purpose was so clearly to make use of

her, as Billy's divorced wife, to stand between Billy and Farley's money. . . .

She told the servants she would send for her trunk and instructed them to wrap up Mrs. Farley's portrait and hold it until she could ask Thurston's permission to remove it. She hurried to the car, carrying the will with her. She must, of course, show it to Thurston, but that could wait a day. . . .

First she would tell Fanny! It was only fair that Mrs. Copeland should know. Copeland had never been mentioned in their intercourse, but she would now confess everything that had ever passed between her and Billy. She would not spare herself. She should have done it earlier — before Fanny threw the mantle of her kindness and generosity about her.

For a month she had been happy in the thought that she had escaped from all her troubles, and that she was free of the wreckage of her old life. Now it was necessary to readjust herself to new conditions, and she resented the necessity that compelled it. Her resolution to tell Fanny of this last will and of all that lay back of it remained unshaken as the car bore her homeward. It was the only "square" thing to do, she repeated to herself over and over again, as she looked out of the car window upon the gray winter landscape.

CHAPTER XXIV

"I NEVER STOPPED LOVING HIM!"

WHILE they were still at dinner, Mrs. Copeland was called to the telephone. The instrument was in the living-room and Nan could not avoid hearing Fanny's share in the conversation.

"That's fine — quite splendid!" And then, "I'm so glad! I never can thank you! Well, of course, no one knows. You're quite sure? That's good; I might have known you'd manage it just right."

There was a moment's silence after she returned to the table. She dropped a lump of sugar into her coffee and watched the bubbles rise. Then she lifted her head with a smile.

"I suppose, Nancy Farley, that God has made better men than J. C. Eaton — kinder and more helpful men — but I've never known them!"

Her lips twitched and there were tears in her eyes.

"I suppose it's his nature to be kind and helpful," Nan replied. "I've never known any one like him."

"The nice thing about him is that he does you a favor quite as though it were a favor to him. He's just done something for me that no one else

317

could have done; there's no one else I could have asked to do it!"

She lapsed into reverie, and Nan's thoughts ranged far. If Fanny and Eaton loved each other, how perfect it would be! Their telephonic communications had been frequent of late; nearly every evening Eaton called her, as though by arrangement, at the dinner hour. From the character of Fanny's responses he seemed to be reporting upon some matter, the nature of which was not apparent, but Fanny always came from these conferences in good spirits.

While Fanny was studying the produce market in the afternoon newspaper, Nan went upstairs to get the will. She had set herself a disagreeable task, but she did not falter in her determination to go through with it. She glanced through the will again, rehearsed the story as she meant to tell it, and returned to the living-room, where Fanny began reading the day's quotations from the sheet before her.

"Nan, if eggs go much higher, we'll be rich by spring. I'm going to double the poultry department next summer. They told me I couldn't make it pay, and now it's the best thing I've got!"

Nan liked these quiet evenings. Sometimes the young women from the farmhouse came in for an hour of music, and Nan occasionally gave some of her recitations, much to their delight. At other times Fanny retired to her den to write letters

or post her books, leaving Nan to her own devices.

To-night Fanny produced some sewing and bade
Nan tell her of her day's experiences.

"I hope the long winter evenings out here are
not going to bore you, Nancy," she remarked, noting the serious look on Nan's face. "Gracious!
What's that you have there? It has an official look;
we're not being sued, are we?"

"There's something I have to tell you, Fanny.
It's not a pleasant subject, and you'll see in a moment how hard it is for me to tell you. And you'll
listen, won't you; you'll let me tell you everything
I have to say about it?"

"Of course, Nancy!" said Fanny as Nan knelt
beside her. "I should be sorry if you could n't
come to me with anything! I hope nothing disagreeable has happened."

"Well, it is n't pleasant. And to think I have to
spoil one of our evenings by talking of it! We've
had such good times here. It may be that you
won't let me stay any longer after you know. I
should hate that; but I should understand it."

She touched with a light caress a fold of Mrs.
Copeland's gown, then withdrew her hand quickly,
and began fingering the will nervously.

"The sooner we get through with it the better,
Nancy," said Fanny kindly.

"Well, when I went to the house this 'afternoon
I found that other will, the last one Mr. Thurston

wrote for papa. It was stuck behind mamma's picture where he must have put it when he began destroying the other wills. It is n't signed, but, of course, I shall have to give it to Mr. Thurston. Perhaps I should n't have read it, but I did, and I knew right away that I ought to show it to you. I thought about it all the way out on the car, and I'm sure it's the best thing to do."

"You poor child! I should think you'd had enough of wills, without new ones popping out from behind picture frames. If you're sure you want me to see it, I'm ready. Let me have it."

Nan passed it to her grudgingly and rose and left the room. She waited in the dark dining-room, watching the headlight of a trolley car as it neared and passed in the highway below. The time seemed endless. She heard the rustle of paper as Fanny turned the pages. She was reading carefully, and as time passed without any sign from her, Nan knew that she was pondering deeply what she read. Nan remained at the window, pressing her forehead against the cold pane. Deep dejection settled upon her; she had made a mistake; it had not been necessary to make this revelation, which could only cause her dearest friend unhappiness. . . .

She felt suddenly the pressure of a warm cheek against her face.

"Come, Nancy! Come back to the fire and let us talk about it," said Fanny in her usual cheery tone. "Of course, I never knew of this; never dreamed of any such thing. It's a strange idea; I did n't know such a will could be made; but if it was done with Mr. Thurston's counsel, it must be all right. I should have thought, though, that they would have asked me about it. The responsibility is very great — too great — for any one to take. But, of course, as the will is n't signed, that's the end of it."

Nan turned wonderingly, doubtful whether Fanny had grasped the full significance of those phrases that touched so nearly her own life.

"It does n't say anything about my giving a bond; I might have stolen the money!" Fanny continued lightly. "And if I did n't like your suitors, I might have played the rôle of the cruel father for twenty-five years! My! but you've had a narrow escape!"

"Oh, you don't understand; you don't understand!" Nan moaned. "Don't you see; don't you *know* what it all means?"

"Yes; I think I do, Nancy. But we don't need to talk of that. It's only so much paper, anyhow, and we need n't bother. The best thing to do is to forget all about it."

"But I can't let it go this way! You are far too kind! I must tell you the rest of it — I must tell you what made papa think of this!"

"But why should we talk of it, Nancy? It's plain enough, I suppose, what was in Mr. Farley's

mind; but it's all over now. It was just a freak —
a grim bit of irony; no doubt, if he had lived, he
would have changed his mind about it. It would
have been just as well if you had n't told me; it
really was n't necessary! I'm sorry you thought it
might make any difference."

"Oh, but I had to tell you; I could never have
looked you in the face again if I had n't! He was
afraid — he had been afraid for more than a year
that — that —"

She could not say it; she could not bring herself
to the point of putting into words the intent of
Timothy Farley's last will, that was to make it
impossible for her to marry this woman's divorced
husband! The shame of it smothered her; she
wondered that she had ever had the effrontery to
eat Fanny Copeland's bread and share her fireside.
The very calmness with which Fanny had received
the news added to her discomfort.

Fanny began moving about the room with her
light, graceful step, touching a book, unconsciously
straightening the flowers in a vase on the table.
Then she walked to the fire, where Nan crouched
mutely watching her.

"Nan, dear, do you want to marry Billy?" she
asked, bending down and resting her hands lightly
on Nan's shoulders.

No one would have known that this was the
first time her former husband had been mentioned
between them.

"I NEVER STOPPED LOVING HIM!"

"No, no! That's what makes this so hard — so unjust!"

"Were you ever — did you ever think you could?" Fanny asked in the same calm tone, in which there was no hint of accusation.

"Yes; there was a time, there were times —"

Fanny was about to resume her idle wandering about the room when Nan clasped her knees.

"That's what I want to tell you; I want to tell you everything from the very beginning. Please let me! I ought to have told you before I came here; but I was so eager to come I did n't think of it; it did n't occur to me at all! You see, if I don't, — if you won't listen, — I must go away; I can't spend another night here. You must see that!"

"It is like you — it is generous and kind, Nancy, to want to tell me. But you don't need to; it's all right; it's not a thing that I should ever have asked; you know that."

She drew up a chair and clasped Nan's hands.

Nan told the story; told it in all its details, from the beginning of her acquaintance with Copeland. She took pains to fix dates, showing that she and Copeland were launched upon a lively flirtation and were meeting, usually at the Kinneys', before there had been any hint of a possible divorce. It had been her fault, her most grievous sin, that she encouraged Billy's attentions. They had tickled her vanity. She had admired "Billy"; he had been a new type of man to her. She described her deception of Farley as to their clandestine meetings; told of his wrath when he learned of her disobedience; and, coming to the frustrated elopement, she made it clear that it was through no fault of hers that she had not run away with Copeland and married him.

"But it's all over; even if it had n't been for this — this idea of papa's to put you between us — I should never marry Billy. No, no!" she moaned. "I had decided that before papa died. You know, don't you," she pleaded, with the tears streaming down her cheeks, "that I would n't have come here, I could n't have pretended to be your friend, if I 'd ever meant to do that!"

"You poor Nancy; you poor, dear, little girl!" Fanny murmured.

There was a far-away look in her eyes as she slowly stroked the girl's hair, but a smile played about her lips. She did not speak again until Nan's grief had spent itself. Then she bent to the tear-wet face and pressed her cheek against it, whispering, —

"You poor little dear; you dear little Nancy!"

"You will let me stay — you will let me stay, after all that?" faltered Nan.

"It was fine of you to tell me; you don't know how grateful I am — and glad. Of course, you will stay; it would break my heart to lose you now!"

Nan drew away and looked long into the steady, tranquil eyes. She had not been prepared for this.

"I NEVER STOPPED LOVING HIM!"

It was beyond comprehension that her story could be received with so much magnanimity, that forgiveness could be so easily won. She caught the hands that clasped her face and kissed them.

"Oh, you don't know!" she cried fearfully. "I have n't made you understand!"

"Yes, I understand it all, Nancy; I'd guessed most of it without your telling me. And it does make a difference; yes, it makes a very great difference." And then, feeling Nan's hands relax their tight hold, and seeing the fear in her face, she smiled and added, "But not the difference you think!"

"Oh, if only you don't send me away! It was brazen of me ever to come; I don't know how you came to take me without a question, when I'd done you the greatest wrong one woman can do another."

"But maybe you did n't!" said Fanny quickly, with a wistful little smile. "I'm going to ask you one question, Nancy, — just to be sure. But you need n't answer; you won't feel you must, will you?"

"Anything — anything!" Nan faltered.

Fanny turned her head, as though doubting, questioning, and her eyes were very grave.

"Then, Nancy, tell me this — and please be very honest, and don't trouble about what I may think or feel about your answer — do you — do you love Billy — now?"

THE PROOF OF THE PUDDING

"No; no! It was never love; it was never really that! His attentions turned my head, and I had n't the sense to keep away from him. It was all my fault. I'm ashamed to tell you that I was very lonely after I came home from school — it is ungrateful to be saying it; but I have always felt uneasy — self-conscious among the people here. I have never got away from the feeling that whenever they saw me they were saying, 'That's the girl the Farleys raked out of the river and did everything for — and just look at her!' I could n't help that — the feeling that they knew I was just a waif, a nobody. It made me rebellious and defiant. Oh, I know it was unjustified and that it's unkind to speak of it even to you. And that's why — one reason, at least — I've enjoyed knowing Jerry so much. Jerry *knows*, and he does n't care! He knows every little tiny thing about me and my people, and how poor and wretched we were! But Billy — I have n't any feeling about him now except — just friendliness — and pity!"

"Then I'll tell you something that will show you how very dear you are to me," said Fanny, — speaking slowly. "I think it was this that drew me to you — made me want to be friends with you when Mr. Farley first brought us together. Oh, Nan," — her voice sank to a whisper, — "I still love Billy! I never stopped loving him!"

CHAPTER XXV

COPELAND'S UNKNOWN BENEFACTOR

EATON tore March from his office calendar, crumpled it in his hand, and glanced out of the window as though expecting to see April's heralds dancing over the roofs below. It was nearing five o'clock and his big desk was swept clear of the day's encumbrances. He paced the floor slowly, his gaze ranging the walls with their ranks of file-cases. A particular box in the "C" section seemed to exert a spell upon him. He glanced at it several times, then opened a drawer in his desk, peered in, and absently closed it. He was waiting for Copeland, and as usual, when he expected a visitor, was planning the interview to its minutest details.

Since the reorganization of the Copeland-Farley Company he had been seeing much of Copeland. The winter had wrought changes in Billy — changes that at first provoked cynical comment from persons who had no faith in his reformation. But people were now beginning to say that they always knew Billy had the right stuff in him. Even the fact — which was pretty generally known — that Billy had narrowly escaped disaster did n't matter particularly. Such fellows were always lucky. If the decision in the Kinney patent case had n't come just when it did, he would have been down and out; but it *had* come. Yes; he was a lucky devil.

Eaton was breathing easier now, as days passed and Copeland seemed to have settled into a sober and industrious routine. He was even giving time to broadening the scope and effectiveness of the Bigger Business Club, and had accepted a place on the municipal reform committee of the Chamber of Commerce. Mr. Jeremiah A. Amidon pointed to his boss with pride. Jerry had risen to the dignity of a standing invitation to Sunday evening tea at Mrs. Copeland's and was the proudest and happiest of Jerries.

Three slight snarls of a desk buzzer, marked, to the attentive ear, by an interval between the second and third, spelled Copeland in the office code. Eaton raised his arm and pressed a button attached to a swinging cord over his desk. By this system acceptable visitors could be announced by the girl in the reception room and disposed of at long range. If Eaton did n't want to be bothered, he made no response. This was only one of his many devices for safe-guarding his time. When he was studying a case, he ignored the presence of his most remunerative clients on the theory that they were unlikely to have anything of importance to impart. It was a fair assumption that before he undertook any case he extracted from the client's head and stored in a file-box all the information of which that particular client was possessed. Clients resented this treatment, but as Eaton was admittedly the best patent lawyer in three States, they were obliged to humor him.

Copeland entered with a quick, springy step. Jerry had persuaded him to spend an hour three times a week at Gaylord's, and as a result Copeland was in prime condition. He nodded to Eaton and sat down in the chair the lawyer pushed toward him.

"The state of your desk fills me with envy; I never get mine as clean as that. If I turn my back, somebody throws something on it."

"Oh, my system has its disadvantages; strangers coming in think I have n't any business. You wanted to speak about those notes?"

"Yes; they're due to-morrow and I'm ready to take them up. Our merchandise bills are cleaned up, and my personal obligations are all taken care of. Our credit's A 1. The White River National is taking good care of us and they're not as fussy as the Western was."

"The Western is n't a bank," remarked Eaton; "it's a pawnshop with a third-degree attachment. About the notes," he continued, tipping himself back in his chair and crossing his slender legs, "you don't have to pay them to-morrow. They can be carried longer — indefinitely. It's just as you say, however. It might be best to accept an extension of three or six months."

"No, thanks! I've got the money to pay, and you may be dead sure it's a comfortable feeling to know I've got it! I hope I'll never have to sweat as I did for a year or two." He frowned, and slapped his gloves together. "Look here, Eaton, you're the hardest man to thank I ever saw, but for God's sake, don't ever think I don't appreciate all you've done for me! You saved me — hauled me out when I was going down for the last time! I don't know why you did it; there was no reason why you or anybody else should have done it."

"It's not I you have to thank; it's an enlightened judiciary that upheld Kinney's patents on Ivory Cement machinery."

"There may be something in that," Copeland admitted, "but there are other things I want to speak of. I insist on speaking of all of them. In picking up that Reynolds stock as you did —"

"Please stick to facts! It was our blithe gazelle Amidon who did that. I honestly did n't know it was in existence till he came to me about it. Thank Jerry!"

"Thank him! I'm going to fire him if he does n't quit working me so hard," laughed Copeland. "But you backed him, and advanced him the money. The way that boy strolled in with that certificate just as Eichberg was jamming me into a corner is the last thing I'll think of when I die."

"Strong sense of the dramatic, that Jerry!"

observed Eaton musingly. "Great loss to the stage, his devotion to commerce."

"He can sell goods, and he knows how to hypnotize other fellows into doing it. I'm giving him all the rope he wants. He's the smartest youngster on the street, and I'm proud of him. There's more than that; I'm going to tell you, because you've been mighty good to me and I want you to know just how desperate I was last November. I want you to know how near bottom I'd gone. Eaton, I tried to burn the store the night before the Western notes came due — and I'd have done it — I'd have done it if Jerry had n't stopped me! — God!" he groaned. His frame shook with repulsion and abhorrence and he turned his head to avoid Eaton's eyes.

"It's a good thing, Copeland," said the lawyer quietly, "that we're not allowed to be as bad as we want to be in this world. No man is ever that! That, for a lack of a better word, is my religion. Let's go back to the notes. You say you prefer to pay them; but that's wholly optional. It had occurred to me that you might want to keep the money in the business, and if you do it's yours, quite indefinitely."

Copeland shook his head and drew out a check.

"I made a big clean-up on my Cement stock and now that I'm out of it I'm never going to monkey on the outside again. Here you are, with interest!"

THE PROOF OF THE PUDDING

Eaton read the check, mentally verified the interest and opened the top drawer of his desk.

"There are four notes of twenty-five thousand each," he remarked, as he bent over his desk and wrote "Paid" across the four slips of paper. "They were made to me — you remember? As I told you at the time, I was n't making the advance myself, and I deserve no thanks for negotiating the loan — none whatever. You're entitled to the canceled notes, of course; but perhaps you'll be satisfied to let me destroy them here in your presence. The reason for that is that I endorsed the notes to the person who made the advance, to protect your creditor in case of my death. That person is very anxious not to be known in the matter."

"I think I ought to know," Copeland replied. "A debt like that can't just be passed over. I'd be more comfortable if I knew."

"Perhaps —" began Eaton.

Copeland shook his head and put out his hand.

Eaton bent a quick, penetrating glance upon him, then gave him the notes. Copeland's face went white as he read the endorsements.

"Fanny!" he gasped chokingly. He bent forward and grasped Eaton's arm. "This is a trick; a ghastly joke! She never would have done it; no human being would have done this after — after —"

"No human being — no!" replied Eaton, swinging round in his chair so that he did not face Copeland for a moment.

COPELAND'S UNKNOWN BENEFACTOR

Copeland's hand shook as he looked again at the endorsements.

"But, Eaton, you had no right to do it! You knew I would n't have taken her help — not — after —"

"No, I knew you would n't. And she knew you would n't. That, of course, is why she did it in the way she did."

The intentness of Copeland's thought showed in his face; he continued to turn over the notes in his shaking hands.

"But you will tell her how beyond any thanks this is — beyond anything I can do or say!" He bent his head and went on brokenly. "It would be cruel, Eaton, if it were n't so kind, so generous, so merciful!"

"I think you have done enough already to show your appreciation," replied Eaton. "I'll say to you that you've done what she expected — and what, to be frank about it, I did not expect. At least, I was n't very sanguine. You'd gone pretty far — farther than men go and come back again. You've proved your mettle. If you go on as you are, you are safe. And I'm glad — happier about it than I've been about anything in a mighty long time."

"I can't understand it. I was worse than ever you imagine. I treated her as a man does n't treat his dog!"

"Yes," Eaton acquiesced, " it was all that."

THE PROOF OF THE PUDDING

"And you can see how it leaves me," Copeland moaned, crumpling the notes in his hand, — "with a debt these things don't express; a debt that can't be discharged!"

"There's something you can do, Copeland, if you will. She has n't asked it; I have no reason to think it has even occurred to her. It's my own idea — absolutely — I want you to be sure of that. It strikes me as being only decent, only just."

"Yes, yes!" Copeland eagerly assented.

"I'm going to speak plainly, Copeland. It's about Manning. You let the impression get abroad that your wife had given you cause to doubt her loyalty. Yes; I know all about it. Manning was your friend, not hers. The injury was not only to her; it was to that man, too. Your use of him, to cast suspicion on the woman you had sworn to shield and protect, was infamous, dastardly! Manning, I have reason to believe," — his eyes ranged the file-cases, — "is a gentleman, a high-minded fellow, who admired your wife only as any friend might be expected to admire her; but you used him — made him an excuse to hide your own infamy. You had n't the courage to bring him into court; you merely let some of your new-found friends whisper insinuations that were more damning than a direct charge of infidelity. Manning cut your acquaintance, I believe, when he found what you had done. You owe him an apology, at least. And if you want to act the part of a man, you will go to Mrs. Copeland and tell her the truth."

Eaton's feelings had for once got the better of him; several times his voice betrayed deep emotion. He turned toward his desk as the buzzer sounded a cryptic message. He telegraphed a reply, and a moment later the sound of steps in the corridor was followed by the closing of a door.

"I will do it — I will do it," said Copeland. "As I began to get my bearings again, that thing troubled me; it has been in my mind to speak to you about it. God knows, I want to make reparation for all the evil I've done. I was a brute, a coarse beast. And you're right that Manning is a gentleman, and a mighty fine fellow — he never was anything else! I'll go to him and be glad to do it. But to see Fanny — that is not so easy! You can understand that, Eaton. I must have time to think it over."

"I think it best for you to see Mrs. Copeland first," replied Eaton, "then Manning."

Copeland, pondering with knit brows, nodded a reluctant acquiescence.

"Well, I will do as you say; but what if she'd refuse to see me? It's going to be mighty hard," he pleaded.

"It's conceivable that she'd refuse, of course. She never meant for you to know of her help, and I've broken faith in telling you; but I'll take the responsibility of sending you to see her. And I made this other suggestion — about Manning — with a feeling that sooner or later it would occur to you. I'm glad you've met me in this spirit. It confirms my impression of you — it satisfies me that I was right in assuming that once you got back in the straight road you would keep to it."

"I'm not going to disappoint you, Eaton. I don't intend to be pointed to as a failure in this community. The mistakes I've made have been bad ones — the very worst! God knows, I'm humble enough when I think of Fanny. It was like her to want to save me. That's what makes it so hard — that it was like her to do it!"

"Yes," said Eaton gravely; "it was like her."

He took his overcoat from a closet and drew it on, mused a moment, apparently absorbed in contemplation of the interior of his hat.

"Mrs. Copeland is here, waiting to see me. She came a moment ago and is in the next room. She had no idea, of course, that you were likely to be here — rest assured of that. My business with her is not so important as yours. Come!"

Copeland, startled, irresolute, followed him to the door of a smaller room used for consultations. Eaton opened it and stepped back.

"I shall be dining at the club later, if you care to see me," he said, and vanished.

CHAPTER XXVI

JERRY'S DARK DAYS

JERRY, who had never been ill in his life, was now experiencing disquieting sensations which he was convinced pointed to an early and probably a painful death. He went about his work listlessly, and from being the cheerfulest person in Copeland-Farley, he became so melancholy that his fellow employees wondered greatly and speculated in private as to the cause of the change. Jerry encouraged the thought of death and blithely vizualized the funeral at which Eaton's pastor (chastely surpliced and reinforced by a boy choir) would officiate. He chose the rector of Christ Church because that gentleman had not been unmindful of his occasional attendance upon services (Jerry had courageously repeated his first timid visit), and had even made a memorandum of Jerry's name and address, with a view to calling upon him. This attention clearly pointed to the rector as the minister predestined from the beginning of things to officiate at his funeral, a function about which he meditated much in a spirit of loftiest detachment.

A few people would be sorry when he died, but only a few. The boys at the store would contribute a wreath; they had done that for a drayman who had succumbed to pneumonia a short time before; and the people at his boarding-house would probably grace the last rites with their presence. Copeland would probably attend; he might even add dignity to the occasion by acting as pallbearer. One of the girl stenographers, whose lachrymose facilities had occasionally aroused his ire, would doubtless weep; she had cried when the drayman died, though her acquaintance with that person had been the most casual. Nan might attend the funeral, but he hoped to time his passing so that the funeral could be held on a market morning, thus giving her a good excuse for absenting herself. It would be a sad, pitiful funeral, with only a handful of mourners, as his only living relative was a cousin in Oklahoma whose exact address he had forgotten. The brief list of mourners included the billiard-marker at the Whitcomb. Jerry had once lent him five dollars, which was still carried as an open account and probably a permanent one; he meant to leave a memorandum of general forgiveness, including a release of the billiard-marker from any obligation to pay the five dollars. And he would bequeath him his best cuff-buttons to show that he had died with no hard feelings against him. The thought of the meager attendance and of the general gloom of the affair gave him the keenest satisfaction. No one would care particularly.

Jerry's malady was one of the oldest that afflicts

the human race. Jerry was in love; he was in love
with Nan, though he would have stormed indig-
nantly at any hint of this bewildering circumstance,
this blighting, crushing fact. His first realization
that this was the cause of his trouble fell upon him
as he sat one evening in the hotel at Madison listlessly talking to a dry-goods drummer. Jerry was
taking a run over Copeland-Farley territory to
"jolly" the trade, carrying no samples and soliciting no orders, but presenting himself as the personal
representative of the house, bent upon strengthen-
ing social ties only, and only casually glancing over
the shelves to see how much Copeland-Farley's
competitors were selling. The dry-goods man,
noting Jerry's unwonted gloom, frankly attributed
it to a love affair; and to find that his condition
was perceptible even to the eye of a dry-goods
drummer, for whose powers of discernment he had
only the mildest respect, added considerably to
Jerry's melancholy.

Nan was not for him; he knew this; there had
never been any doubt in his mind that Eaton and
Nan would marry ultimately. Any speculations as
to his own part in Nan's life, beyond the boy-and-
girl comradeship he had been enjoying, were vain
and foolish; they were even disloyal to Eaton; they
were an insult to Nan. Nan had intimated several
times that Eaton was in love with Mrs. Copeland,
but now that the black clouds had risen on his own
horizon, Jerry knew the absurdity of this. Eaton

had appeared unusually absent-minded of late, and this marked his friend as a man in the toils of love. Jerry knew the symptoms! Except for a passing attachment for a stenographer in a hardware house, who had jilted him for a red-haired bookkeeper, Jerry had never been in love. He had grieved over the hardware girl's perfidy for two, perhaps three, days. But this was the real thing and a very different matter; he meant to win the martyr's wreath by going to his death so heroically that no one would ever know how he had suffered.

Returning to town Saturday evening he checked his grip at a hotel and went to the theater, not for pleasure, but to lose himself among strangers and enjoy his misery. As he moodily surveyed the assembling audience a cold hand gripped his heart. Eaton, followed by Mrs. Copeland, Nan, and a lady he did not know, filed down to the second row where Eaton always sat.

Since Farley's death Nan had attended no entertainments of any kind; she had refused to accompany Jerry to a concert only a fortnight earlier. Her presence at the theater with Eaton confirmed his worst suspicions. Their engagement would doubtless be announced in a day or two; he must steel himself against this and prepare to offer his congratulations. The comedy presented was one of the hits of the season, but its best lines and most amusing situations failed to evoke a smile from Jerry, who clutched his programme and stared at

the back of Nan's head. Nan was enjoying herself;
from his seat on the back row he was satisfied of
that, and he assured himself that he was glad of
her happiness. At the end of the second act, he
left and went to his room to spend a wretched
night.

Jerry found on his desk Monday morning a note
from Eaton, written several days earlier, asking
him to join his theater party and go to the club
later for supper. His sister had come down from
Cleveland to make him a visit, Eaton explained,
and he wanted Jerry to meet her. For an instant
the world was the pleasant, cheerful place it had
been in the old days before love darkened his life.
Eaton was still his friend; but only for a moment
was the veil lifted. The clouds settled upon him
again, as he grasped the motive behind Eaton's
friendly note — as though at any time in their
intercourse there had been the ghost of a motive
back of anything John Cecil Eaton had ever done
for him except a perfectly transparent, generous
wish to be kind to him! But the coming of the
sister (who had never, so far as Jerry knew, visited
Eaton before) could only mean that Eaton wished
to introduce Nan to her as a prospective member
of the family. And, proud of his logic, Jerry rea-
soned that he was to have been given an opportunity to offer his own congratulations.

For a week Jerry kept away from the market-
house; Nan knew he had been out of town, and,

failing to see him, would assume that he was still away. He could not face her; it would be a merciful thing if he never saw her again. Eaton he would avoid; his friend must never know of his hopeless passion. Nan and Eaton must begin their married life wholly ignorant that he had ever looked upon Nan as anything more than a good friend. Phrases out of novels he had read assisted him in the definition of his attitude toward her and Eaton. "Unworthy of the woman he loved," and "climbed slowly, painfully, to the sublime heights of a great renunciation." He *was* unworthy; he had known that all along; and he would give her up to his best friend with a beautiful magnanimity. The fiction with which he was familiar had not lacked in noble examples of just such splendid sacrifice. If death failed to end his misery, he would live on, sadly, but manfully, and on every anniversary of their meeting on the river bank, he would send her a rose — a single beautiful rose — always exactly the same, and it would puzzle her greatly and make her wonder; but she would never guess that it was from one who had loved her in the long ago.

He had made no sign to Eaton, not even to acknowledge the theater invitation; and when one day he ran into the lawyer in the bank lobby he was about to pass him hurriedly when the familiar "Ah, Jerry!" arrested him. He swallowed hard; it was not easy to meet his friend with the air of sweet resignation and submission to inexorable fate that he had been cultivating.

"An overdraft?" Eaton suggested in his usual tone. "Nothing else could account for your woeful countenance! I did n't know you were in town. Just in, I suppose, from a flight into the remoter recesses of the Commonwealth."

"Well, I 've been back a few days," Jerry confessed reluctantly; "but I 've been too busy to come around. I meant to call you up about that invitation; I did n't get it until after the show."

"We missed you; I had wanted you to meet my sister. In fact, I 'd rather prepared her for the meeting — led up to it, warned her of your native flavor. She 's still with me. You 're working yourself to death; it 's in your eye. Can't you come up Tuesday night and dine with us? I 'll see if we can't get Mrs. Copeland and Nan to come in. They 've been seeing something of Florence. You 've seen Nan —"

"No; I have n't seen her," Jerry replied, a little resentfully, as though Eaton ought to know why Nan had become invisible so far as Jeremiah Amidon was concerned.

"She 's another victim of overwork," Eaton remarked carelessly, but behind his glasses there was a gleam of humor. "Not quarreling, I hope? I confess that at times Nan is a trifle provoking, but she means nothing by it. You must give the benefit of all doubts to a girl who is just emerging from a

343

severe ordeal — settling herself into a new manner of life. It's wonderful; really amazing how she's coming on. We shall be dining at seven. Please don't make it necessary for me to explain a second scorning of my hospitality to my sister. She'd begin to think you a myth, like Jupiter and the rest of the immortals."

"Thanks; I'll be there," Jerry answered solemnly. Then he watched Eaton's retreating figure shame-facedly. He was acting abominably toward Eaton.

The Pembrokes had gone to Florida for the spring months, and Eaton had taken their house that he might indulge in a round of dinners and a ball that proved to be the season's smartest event. These social activities Jerry had taken as another sign of Eaton's approaching marriage. And Jerry had resented, as an attack upon his personal rights, Eaton's transfer from the rooms where he had always been so accessible, to the big house where visitors were received by the Pembrokes' butler — a formidable person who, he fancied, regarded him with a hostile eye.

Jerry presented himself at the hour appointed, wearing the crown of his martyrdom, which, if he had known it, was highly unbecoming. As he had walked around the block twice to prepare himself for the ordeal, he was late, and stood uncomfortably in the drawing-room door, quite unnoticed, while the sister (whose back he distrusted) finished a story she had been telling. But spying him, Eaton rose and greeted him cordially.

"Florence, Mr. Amidon; my sister, Mrs. Torrington, Jerry."

Mrs. Torrington, a tall, dark woman in her early thirties, graciously assured him that she had delayed her departure from town until he could be produced for her edification.

"I guess you would n't 'a' missed much," said Jerry, hating himself at once for employing a contraction from which he had honestly believed himself permanently emancipated. He shook hands with Mrs. Copeland and then with Nan — without looking at her. The butler announced dinner, and he found himself moving toward the dining-room beside Mrs. Torrington. In her ignorance of the darkness in which he had immersed himself, she treated him quite as though they were in the habit of meeting at dinners. It was to his credit that he saw at once that she was a superior person, though he did not know until later that, as the wife of a distinguished engineer, she was known in many capitals as a brilliant conversationalist, with a reputation for meeting difficult situations. On the way down the hall she spoke of Russia — she had been telling a Russian story at the moment of his appearance — and her manner expressed a flattering assumption that he, of course, was quite familiar with the social life of the Russian capital.

THE PROOF OF THE PUDDING

It was the most informal of dinners; Jerry found himself placed between Mrs. Torrington and Mrs. Copeland, which left Nan at Eaton's right. This arrangement had not been premeditated, but he saw only the darkest significance in Nan's juxtaposition to Eaton. She seemed unwontedly subdued, and averted her eyes when their gaze met.

"This is the nicest party you've had for me, Cecil," Mrs. Torrington was saying, — "cozy and comfortable so everybody can talk."

Jerry hoped they would talk! (He was watching Mrs. Torrington guardedly to see which fork she chose for her caviar.) Eaton was unusually grave; Mrs. Copeland seemed preoccupied; Jerry's heart ached at the near presence of Nan. But at a hint from Fanny, Mrs. Torrington returned to her experiences abroad, and soon had them all interested and amused. Jerry quickly fell victim to her charm; he had never before met a woman of her distinction and poise. Even her way of speaking was different from anything he had been accustomed to — crisp, fluent, musical. Her good humor was infectious and she quickly won them all to self-forgetfulness. Mrs. Copeland described an encounter she had witnessed between a Russian and a Frenchman in a Roman *pension* where she had once spent a winter — an incident that culminated in a hasty exchange of wine-glasses across the table.

"Ah, Jerry," remarked Eaton casually; "that leads us naturally to your pleasing adventures down the road. Florence, if you urge Mr. Amidon he will tell you of most amazing experiences he has had right here at home in the pursuit of food."

Mrs. Torrington's fine eyes emphasized her appeal. They would all tell of the worst food they had ever eaten, she said; she had spent years collecting information.

"You may lapse into the vernacular, Jerry," Eaton added encouragingly; "we will all understand that you are falling into it merely in a spirit of realism."

"This is tough," said Jerry, turning to Mrs. Torrington. "Your brother has told me a hundred times to cut out those stories."

"That was only after he had heard them all! And he has been boasting that he could persuade you to tell them to me. Please! I want to add them to my collection."

"Well, you understand this is n't my fault —" he began. . . .

They were still demanding more stories after the dessert plates had been removed. He had so far yielded to their friendliness that he appealed occasionally to Nan, and finally asked her to tell one of Farley's stories about the river, which he said he had forgotten. They remained at table for their coffee to avoid disturbing the good cheer that now prevailed.

"Mr. Amidon is up to my highest expectations," Mrs. Torrington remarked when they rose. "I 'll stay another week if you'll give just this same party again!"

"We've missed you at the farm," said Mrs. Copeland, as Jerry seated himself beside her in the library. "And I was just beginning to feel that we were acquainted! But, of course, you've been away. I heard that from Mr. Copeland."

As she mentioned Copeland, she smiled gravely.

"Well, I have been away, and we're busier than usual just now," he replied, realizing that something had happened in her relations with Copeland to make possible this careless reference to him. "I guess Mr. Copeland is working harder than any of us," he added warmly.

"Oh, we're all happier when we're busy," she said lightly.

"Not smoking, Jerry?" asked Eaton, proffering cigars.

"I've quit," Jerry replied, remembering that he had given up smoking in his general abandonment of the joys of life.

Mrs. Copeland left him, making it necessary for him to join Nan, who had moved a little away from the circle they had formed before the fireplace.

"It's too bad you don't tell your friends about your troubles," she remarked after a moment's silence. "So many things have happened that you ought to be very cheerful."

"I haven't been feeling very well," he answered doggedly.

"You do look utterly fagged out," she retorted. "But if I were you I would n't cut all my friends."

"I have n't cut anybody," he replied. "I guess I know when to drop out. I want everybody to be happy," he said plaintively, feeling his martyr's crown pinching his brow.

"That's very sweet of you, Jerry. The policeman at the market asked Saturday what had become of you. Your absence seems to have occasioned remark, though I had n't noticed it myself."

"I did n't suppose you would," he said, with an effort at bitterness that was so tame that she laughed.

"Of course, if you've lost interest, it's all right. I never meant to bore you. And I'm not complaining. But you have n't been kind to Mr. Eaton. I suppose it never occurred to you that he's taken a good deal of pains to be nice to you. And just now, just now," — she added, lowering her voice, — "we should all be as good to him as we can."

He frowned at this. If she and Eaton were in love with each other, he saw no good reason why he should be sorry for either of them.

"If I had a chance I could tell you some things," Nan continued, "but I suppose it's just as well to let you read about them in the papers."

His spirits sank; he had been scanning the society columns daily expecting to see the announcement of her engagement.

349

THE PROOF OF THE PUDDING

"When I'm an old, old woman and living all alone with my chickens somewhere, I suppose you may come to see me again and tell me about your troubles."

"I won't," he replied with a smile he meant to be grim, "because I'll be dead."

She regarded him with knit brows, puzzled, slightly disdainful.

"Just when things were a little hard for me, and I have been much troubled because one of the kindest friends either of us ever had or could have—"

She shrugged her shoulders impatiently, and rebuke and indignation were mingled in the glance she bent upon him.

"I guess we're not talking about the same thing," he said huskily. "You know I mean to do the square thing, Nan."

He was so pathetic that she changed her tone, sorry that she had been so hard on him.

"I think you do — usually, Jerry."

"And I'll be out to-morrow night if you're going to be at home," he suggested timidly, her reproach still upon him.

"Well, if you're not too tired, or ill, or anything, and can't think of anything else to do, come along," she said.

Mrs. Copeland called to Nan that it was time to go. They had come in on the interurban, but Eaton announced his intention of taking them home in the Pembroke car.

"There's no use of my living in all this borrowed splendor unless I use it. Jerry, please keep the fire burning till I get back."

Nan's smile as she gave him her hand conveyed an apology for her harshness and sent his spirits soaring.

"I hope," remarked Mrs. Torrington, as they heard the car leave the door, "that you know how fond my brother is of you. You've been a great resource to him; he's mentioned you often in his letters. You know Cecil and I are very close, unusually so; and it breaks my heart to see him —" She waved her hand with a gesture that expressed the futility of explanations.

She was taking him for granted as her brother's friend, not a mere beneficiary of his big-heartedness. He was aware of something spacious in her nature; she would brush little things away with a sweep of her eloquent hands. A wonderful woman was John Cecil's sister. She was addressing him as though he were a gentleman, a man of her own world, instead of the miserable ingrate he knew himself to be.

"She's lovely, quite adorable," Mrs. Torrington continued, as though speaking of matters they had often discussed before. "I'll say quite frankly that I'd been afraid to meet her after what he had written."

Jerry sat silent, wondering. Nan had left him mystified. He did not know what Eaton's sister was talking about unless it was his love for Nan.

"I shall be leaving in a few days; my husband's business calls him to China. I want you to keep an eye on Cecil; don't let him be alone too much," she went on. "A man with a sorrow like that in his heart ought n't to be alone. I came here on purpose to see just how the land lay; I suppose you understand that."

He muttered incoherently, touched by her assumption of his sympathy, her direct, intimate appeal.

"I felt that I could speak to you quite frankly," Mrs. Torrington continued. "No one else seemed quite so accessible, no one really quite so close to him."

"Of course, he has a lot of friends," said Jerry humbly, and anxious to respond to the demand this fascinating woman was making upon his generosity.

"She's going back to her husband; of course you know that."

There was a degree of indignation in her tone, as though the person of whom she spoke was doing an unpardonable thing.

Jerry felt himself shrinking; his hands clutched the arms of his chair as it dawned upon him that it was Mrs. Copeland — not Nan — of whom Eaton's sister was speaking. He was struck with fear lest she should read his thoughts as he realized how dull, how utterly selfish and contemptible, had been his apprehensions.

"I suppose," said Mrs. Torrington, "that a man as fine as Cecil is doomed to just this kind of calamity."

"I thought maybe it would be Nan," he faltered. "I know he likes Nan, and he's done a lot for her."

Mrs. Torrington had been staring musingly into the fire. She turned toward him absently, and then, catching his meaning, her eyes widened with surprise.

"Nan," she repeated slowly; and then, in her usual brisk tone, "A man like Cecil can't be passed on from one affair to another so easily. And, besides," — she smiled her charming, irresistible smile, —"that child is in love with you, you silly boy! It's in her eyes! That's the one hopeful thing about the situation — that together you two will take good care of him!"

CHAPTER XXVII

"JUST HELPING; JUST BEING KIND!"

NAN crossed a pasture, whistling. The Holsteins, nibbling the young grass, lifted their heads and bent their slow, meditative gaze upon her. She paused to pat one of them on the nose. Nan was growing wise in dairy lore and knew at sight the heaviest producers of the herd. She resumed her whistling and went on toward the house, with a pair of robins hopping before her. June had come and summer sounds and scents filled the air.

As she neared the bungalow a motor swept into the driveway and discharged Eaton and Thurston.

"A child of the pastures! The daughter of Cincinnatus tripping in from the fields!" observed Eaton, as he shook hands.

"Just been tinkering an incubator, if you want the facts — counting chickens before they're hatched," laughed Nan, brushing a straw from her skirt.

"We have a small business matter to discuss with you, Nan. We'll fall upon it at once if you're agreeable."

"Business!" Nan mocked. "I hoped you'd come to look at the dairy."

This was a very different Nan, Eaton reflected.

from the Nan of a year ago. Exposure to wind and sun had already given her a becoming tan. Her old listlessness, the defiant air she had sometimes worn, had vanished; she had become alert, self-reliant, resolute. Within the bounds of her self-respect she meant that the world should like her. A democratic young person — this new Nan, on good terms with truck farmers, humble drivers of grocers' wagons, motormen, and market-house policemen. In her short skirt and plain blue blouse, she looked less than her years to-day.

"We can sit on the veranda if you gentlemen are not afraid of the country air."

"I would n't dare go in after that," remarked Thurston dryly; "Eaton already refers to me as his learned senior."

"Mr. Eaton is the youngest and the oldest man in the world!" Nan declared.

"Well, Miss Farley," Thurston began, as they gathered about a wicker table and he drew a formidable bundle of papers from a leathern pouch, "as we telephoned you yesterday, the opposition of Mr. Farley's relatives has been disposed of and your adoption was upheld by the court. To prevent an appeal, and get rid of them for good, we've agreed on your behalf to pay the two cousins ten thousand dollars apiece. Mr. Eaton would have preferred to fight it clear through, but I prevailed on him not to make Brother Harlowe work too hard. You may not know it, but Eaton is a remarkably belligerent person. There's no compromise in him. He'd fight to the last ditch."

He looked from Eaton to Nan over his glasses with a twinkle in his eyes.

"I never saw a fellow I wanted to smash as badly as I do Harlowe," Eaton remarked. "He's the smoothest rascal I've ever known."

"I don't see that you've been very generous," said Nan. "How much will he get as a fee?"

"About nine tenths of the twenty thousand," replied Thurston grimly.

"Rather less than that," said Eaton, with one of his elusive smiles. "I started the secretary of the White River Trust Company down to see the esteemed cousins before we signed the agreement; told him to persuade them to confide their ill-gotten gains to the company and advised them to cut off Harlowe with a niggardly ten per cent for his services. I was afraid to tell you that, Thurston. I knew you would scold me."

"Eaton, for combined ingenuity and malevolence, you have n't an equal!" declared Thurston, chuckling.

"I don't believe it," cried Nan, glad that the interview was progressing so cheerfully.

"Now, Miss Farley," Thurston resumed, "if there's anything a lawyer does n't like, it's an ungrateful client. Mr. Eaton and I have a sneaking feeling that we've done pretty well with this case. The credit is chiefly his — and I take off my hat to him. We've come here in the hope that we shan't have to argue with you, but just tell you. Your scruples against accepting any share in Mr. Farley's estate, expressed after his death, did you credit — in a way. But now it's all yours; there's no escape. A considerable amount of income has already accumulated, and we can arrange payments necessary for your support to begin at once, though the estate can't be closed till the year of administration is up. So far as your ability to earn your own living is concerned, you have demonstrated that. You have shown a plucky spirit, and I admire it. I will go further, and say that the community has supported you strongly, and that your attitude has made many friends for you. But now — now, we must have no more of this nonsense!"

He waved his hand to indicate the fields, and glanced meaningfully at Nan's heavy walking-shoes, which were disgracefully muddy.

"But that was settled — once and for all!" Nan replied firmly. "You mustn't think me ungrateful for what you've done; but I thought that all out before I came here, and I haven't had a single regret. If it isn't impolite, I'll say that all I want is to be let alone!"

"Thurston and I are not sentimentalists," said Eaton. "We've given you free rein to indulge your whims; but now we've come to a point where we've got to take a hand."

THE PROOF OF THE PUDDING

"But you can't make me, if I won't!" laughed Nan. "Just think how humiliating it would be to back down now after I said I would n't! Worse than that, think of the effect on these girls we have at work here; they'd lose their respect for me if they found I was n't really as poor as they are! And there are other reasons, too," she went on soberly. "I don't like to go over this again, but I never deserved anything of the Farleys. I've got my conscience to live with, and I could never get on with it if I allowed myself to take money which papa knew it was best for me not to have. I'm serious about this. He knew me better than I knew myself. You understand what I mean —"

"I don't understand it in the way you mean, Nan," Eaton answered; "but let's not argue it. Let's be practical. Has it occurred to you that something has to be done with this property? The lawful heir can't just walk off and leave an estate like this. It will be confiscated by the State — thrown into the treasury and spent by a lot of politicians if you refuse it. Take the money and buy a lot of farms with it or spend it on working girls as much as you like — but please don't talk any more about refusing it."

Eaton had spoken lightly, but she saw that he was very much in earnest. The contingency he suggested had not, in fact, occurred to her. She had assumed from the beginning that the adoption would be nullified and that Farley's money would be divided among the obscure and shadowy cousins; and this abrupt termination of the case brought her face to face with an unforeseen situation. Thurston was quick to take advantage of her silence.

"You have to consider, Miss Farley, what your foster father's feelings would be. He was a just man, and all the wills he considered from time to time prove that he never had the slightest intention of disinheriting you. Even in the last will creating the trusteeship, he made you his sole heir; it was really the most generous of all! Oh, yes," he exclaimed hastily, as Nan colored deeply, "there was, I suppose, a certain bitterness behind that. I want to say to you again that I did my best to dissuade him from that step. I was confident he would change his mind about it, as he had about so many other things in his varying moods and tempers; and that he would realize its unkindness. We have no right to assume that when he hid that will behind his wife's picture, he had any intention of executing it. It's an open question and it's only fair to give him the benefit of the doubt."

"That's true enough," Nan assented; "but when I read that will and found how bitter he had been, I knew I had done the right thing in refusing to take anything!"

"I don't agree with you," Thurston continued patiently. "You must be just; you must remember that that was the act of a man near his death —

nearer than any of us imagined. He did n't have a chance to change his mind again. It's unjust to his memory to leave him in the wrong utterly, as you will if you persist. There has already been a great deal of talk about this attack on the adoption — people have been blaming him for not guarding against the possibility of any such thing. You see public sentiment is behind you! And in spite of anything you may say, your act would have the appearance of pique; it would be like slapping a dead man in the face!"

"Mr. Thurston is right, Nan," said Eaton. "There is not only Mr. Farley's memory as a kind and just man to protect, but you must guard yourself against even the appearance of resentment. The only thing you have to consider is Mr. Farley's conscientious desire to provide for you, which was manifest at all times. As Mr. Thurston says, that last will gave you absolutely everything, cutting out all the bequests he had made at other times to benevolence and charity. My dear Nan, your scruples are absurd! You have n't any case at all! The idea of letting the property Timothy Farley spent a laborious lifetime accumulating go to the State is horrible. I can readily imagine what his feelings would be! Why, my dear Nan, rather than let that happen, Thurston and I will steal the whole thing ourselves!"

She received this with a grudging smile. What they said about the injustice to Farley of a refusal impressed her, but her resolution was still unshaken. And there was a stubborn strain in her of which she had only lately been aware.

She reached for a pencil, and Eaton pushed a pad of paper toward her. She began jotting down Farley's various bequests to charity, as provided in the series of wills, pausing now and then to refer to Thurston for items she only imperfectly remembered.

The total was three hundred and fifty thousand dollars. She tapped the paper reflectively.

"Of course," remarked Thurston anxiously, as he saw what was in her mind, "you are not bound by any of the legacies in those unsigned wills. Not one of the wills contained all those bequests, so your total doesn't represent what he meant to dispose of in that way. And his last will is evidence that he had wholly changed his mind about them."

"We are bound to accept that last will as convincing proof of his very great confidence in Miss Farley," said Eaton quickly, "rather than as an expression of distrust."

"We all know perfectly well what he meant by that," Nan replied. "But I don't want you to think I have any feeling about it."

They nodded gravely as she glanced at them appealingly.

"I can see," she went on hurriedly, "that my refusal to accept anything at all might look like resentment; that it would be in a way unjust to him." She turned for a glance over the fields, as though seeking their counsel. "Papa really wanted to help people who had n't a chance; he was only hard on the idle and shiftless. If he had n't been big-hearted and generous, he never would have taken me up as he did. And mamma was like him. I feel strongly that even if he did change his mind sometimes, his wish to help these things — the Boys' Club, the Home for Aged Women, and all the rest — should be respected."

"That can't be done unless you take the whole," said Eaton quickly. "But you need n't decide about it now."

"Yes; you should wait a few years at least!" added Thurston, crossing his legs nervously.

"And since I've been out here and have learned about the girls Mrs. Copeland is training to take care of themselves, I've thought of some other things that might be done," said Nan, ignoring their manifest unwillingness to acquiesce in the recognition of Farley's vacillating benefactions. "There ought to be, in a town like this, a home and training school for girls who start the wrong way, or make mistakes. We have n't anything that quite fills that need, and there are a good many such girls. A hundred thousand dollars would provide such a place, and it ought to have another hundred thousand for endowment. Mrs. Copeland and I have talked of the need for such a school. It would be fine to start something like

that! And you know," she added, "I might have
been just such a girl myself!"

Thurston turned to Eaton helplessly.

"It's as plain as daylight," Eaton remarked,
amused by the despair in his associate's face, "that
you will soon pauperize yourself at this rate. It's
only fair to tell you that the estate shrank on a
rigid appraisement of Mr. Farley's property. The
million the newspapers mentioned has dwindled to
about eight hundred thousand. If you give away
all that's mentioned in those wills and start this
girls' home, you won't be able to keep more than
three automobiles for yourself."

"Oh, the proof of the pudding is in the eating —
and I know it's good!" Nan laughed. "I stuffed
myself so long without thinking about my hungry
neighbors that it won't hurt me to pass the plate
down the table!"

"Well, the main thing," said Thurston, "is to
get your assurance that you'll accept the estate
under your rights as Mr. Farley's adopted daughter. I suppose we can't prevent your giving it away
without having you declared insane!"

"I dare you to try it!" Then, more serious than
at any time during the interview, she said: "You'll
have to let me reason it out my own way. It was
only a piece of luck that I wasn't thrown into an
orphan asylum or left to die on the river bank
when the Farleys gave me a home. I shall never
forget that — never *again*," she added with deep

363

feeling. "The least I can do is to pass my good luck on. I've thought all that out, so please don't make me talk of it any more!"

Then, as the men rose to leave, Fanny appeared, and urged them to remain to dinner. Thurston pleaded an engagement in town; Eaton said he would stay.

"You've broken that man's heart, Nan," Eaton remarked, as Thurston rolled away in his machine.

"What did you do to him, Nancy?" asked Fanny.

"She scared him to death! He's convinced that she's headed for an insane asylum — that's all," chuckled Eaton. "Mere altruism does n't interest Thurston; he thinks it just a sign of weak character — worse than a weak chin."

"I've always thought," said Fanny, as her arm stole around Nan, "that Nancy has a very nice chin."

"I might go further," Eaton remarked daringly, "and say that the face in its entirety is pleasant and inspiring to look at!"

"Stop teasing me!" cried Nan, "or I'll run out to the barn and cry."

They were still talking in this strain when Copeland's machine appeared in the driveway.

"I did n't tell you that we're having a party to-night," said Fanny. "Unless I'm mistaken, Mr. Amidon is driving that machine."

"JUST HELPING; JUST BEING KIND!"

She walked to the veranda rail and looked expectantly toward the approaching car. Though Billy had lately paid a visit to the farm, Nan had not met him. Fanny, with her usual frankness, had warned Nan of the expected visit, and Nan had carefully kept out of the way. She had not seen Billy since the night he proposed the destruction of Farley's will.

Copeland jumped from the machine and ran up the steps, while Jerry disposed of the car. He shook hands with Fanny, and then turned toward Nan inquiringly.

She was already walking toward him.

"I'm glad to see you, Billy."

"I'm glad to see you, Nan," he said, and added in a slightly lower tone, "I'm glad to see you *here*."

"And I'm glad to see you — here!"

Both knew what was in the other's thoughts. Copeland bowed slightly, and crossed to Eaton, who was gazing fixedly at the gathering glories of the sunset.

Jerry, in a gray suit, and the very tallest collar he could buy, now added himself to the group. He bent over Mrs. Copeland's hand with his best imitation of Eaton's manner, and then, as he raised his head, looked around furtively to see whether his mentor was watching him.

The laughter that greeted this had the effect of putting them all at ease.

"I knew Jerry could do it," said Nan, "but I

did n't suppose he would dare try it in his Cecil's presence."

"I don't know what you're talking about," remarked Eaton, feigning indignation at their treatment of his protégé. "If you're not satisfied with Jeremiah's manners, we'll both go home."

Nan ran away to change her clothes and reappeared just as dinner was announced.

"Please sit wherever you happen to be," said Fanny, as they reached the dining-room; and then, as they sat down, she bit her lip and colored, finding that it fell to Copeland's lot to sit opposite her. Eaton, noticing her embarrassment, immediately charged Copeland Farms with responsibility for the high cost of living.

"You must watch Nan carefully, Mrs. Copeland. She's grinding the face of the poor. I heard Mrs. Harrington complaining bitterly last night about the price she has to pay for such trifling necessities as eggs and butter. You're going to bring a French Revolution on this country if you're not careful. And there will be eggs thrown that don't bear the Copeland Farm's stamp."

"I refuse to have this suit spoiled with any other kind," Jerry protested. "Speaking of eggs —"

"No, you don't!" Nan interrupted. "You can't tell any of your country-hotel egg stories here. I refuse to hear them."

"All right, then; we'll drop the eggs. I was shaking hands with old friends on the lower Wabash last week and struck three slabs of cocoanut pie in three days. I'm going to make a map of the pie habits of the Hoosiers and send it out as a Cope-land-Farley advertisement. I've been all over the State lately, and I've never found cocoanut pie north of Logansport, and you never find it east of Seymour going south. Down along the Ohio you can stand on hotel porches in the peach season and see thousands of acres of peaches spoiling on the trees, and you go inside and find dried-peach pie on the programme. And you have to eat it or take sliced bananas or hard chunks of canned pineapple. No wonder traveling men go wrong! I wonder at times at my own pure life!"

It was evident that they liked Jerry. They encouraged him to talk, and he passed lightly from Praxiteles, whom he had just discovered in a magazine article, to the sinfulness of the cut-price drug store, which he pronounced the greatest of commercial iniquities.

After coffee on the veranda, Eaton quietly disappeared. Then Jerry and Nan went off for a stroll, leaving Copeland and Fanny together.

"I guess that's coming out all right," remarked Jerry, indicating the veranda with a wave of his straw hat. "But it's tough on Cecil. I've been wondering whether *she* knows how it's going to hit him."

"Oh, I hope not! But that's something we'll never know."

THE PROOF OF THE PUDDING

"Of course, Cecil need n't have done all the things he did to bring them together again. He might have let the boss go by the board. It was n't just money that saved the boss! it was John Cecil's strong right arm!"

"And yours, too, Jerry! Oh, yes; I know more about it than you think I do. You helped — you did a lot to save him."

"Well, if I did," he admitted grudgingly, "that was Cecil, too. I'd been busy rustling for myself — never caring a hang for the other fellow — till Cecil got hold of me. I've wondered a good deal how he did it — a scrub like me!"

"Don't be foolish, Jerry; it had to be in you first. But he does make people want to be different. He's certainly affected me that way."

"Oh, you!" he exclaimed disdainfully.

"Well, don't you ever think I'm proud of myself, Jeremiah Amidon!" She paused abruptly at the edge of a brook that tinkled musically on its way to the river. "I'm only just beginning to try to be self-respecting and decent and useful; I think it's going to be a lot of fun if I ever get started."

"Well, I hope to see you on the cars sometimes. I've got the same ticket, but I'm not sure it's good on the limited. I'm likely to be chucked at the first tank."

They jumped the brook and followed a cow path across a broad pasture, talking of old times on the Ohio, and of Farley, of whom Jerry always spoke in highest reverence, and then of his own prospects.

Both were subdued by the influences of the night. The stars hung near; it seemed to Jerry that they had stolen closer to earth to enfold Nan in their soft radiance. A new idea had possessed him of late. His heart throbbed with it to-night.

"In a place like this," he began slowly, "you think a lot of things that would n't strike you anywhere else."

"It's just the dear country lonesomeness. I come out here often in the evenings; used to in the winter, when the snow was deepest. I love all this —" She stretched out her arms with a quick gesture comprehensive of the star-hung fields.

Jerry's dejection increased. The more he saw of Nan the less he seemed to count in her affairs. A Nan who tramped snowy fields and took counsel of the heavens was beyond his reach —immeasurably beyond.

"I don't take hold of things the way you do, Nan. Being out here just makes me lonesome, that's all. I've got to be where I can see electric signs spelling words on tall buildings. Just hearing that trolley tooting away over there helps some; must be because it's going toward the lights."

"If you feel so terribly, maybe we'd better go back!" she said tauntingly and took a step downward.

"Don't do that again! If you leave me here in the dark I'll be scared to death."

"That *would* be a blow to the human race," she mocked.

"Well, I've had blows enough!"

"You hide the scars well — I can say that!" she flung back.

"Listen, Nan — "

"I thought John Cecil had broken you of the 'listen' habit."

"Forget it! You know perfectly well what I want to tell you!"

"Then, why do we linger? We really must go!"

"My business is selling goods and it's a rule of the game never to let a customer turn his back on you."

"All right; you go first!"

"Nan" — he drew nearer and planted himself in her path — "you can't go — not till I've promised to marry you!"

This reversal of the established formula evoked a gay laugh; but she did not attempt to pass him.

"I never meant to ask you; I was afraid you'd marry me for my money and I want to be loved for myself alone! And don't think I'd be mentioning it now if I wasn't so lonesome I could cry! If you're going to take that money, it's all off, anyhow. I can't afford to have anybody questioning my motives. As far as loving you's concerned, I started full time that first day we met on the

river bank, when you pulled my fly out of the tree.
I might just as well have told you then — and I
wish I had!"

"Well, you need n't scold me about it now!"

"I'm not scolding. I'm just telling you what
you missed!"

"Why don't you give me another chance? I
know I'm only a poor working girl —"

"Nan, I wish you were that!" he cried earnestly.
"But all that money's coming to you now. I
would n't have the nerve —"

"It would be the first time your nerve ever
failed!" Then, fearing she had wounded him, she
added quickly, "Of course, I did n't mean that."

"Nan!"

"Well, don't cry, little boy!"

"Nan!"

"Yes, Jerry."

"I love you, Nan!" he said gently. "I wish you
cared even a little bit."

"It's a good deal more than that, Jerry."

He took her hands and kissed them. There was
a great awe in his heart.

"Nan, this does n't seem right, you being you;
and you know what I am!"

"I think I know what you are, Jerry, — you're
fine and loyal and good!"

"I'm going to try to be," he said humbly.

"And you've helped me more than I could make
you understand, from that very first day we met,

when I hated myself so! You brought back the old days; everything that has happened since has made me think of you. You were the only person around here who really knew all about me — just what I came from, and all that. And it helped me to see how bravely you were fighting your own way up. I had the chance forced on me that you made for yourself. And I made a mess of everything! Oh, Jerry!"

She clung to him, crying. As he kissed away her tears, the touch of her wet cheek thrilled him. . . .

"We must n't be so happy we can't remember other people," she said as they loitered hand in hand toward the house.

"I guess that 's the only way, Nan. That 's what Cecil 's always saying. And I guess he 's about right about everything."

Eaton passed them, unconscious of their nearness. He walked with head erect, as one who has fought and won a good fight. A sense of all his victory had cost him was in both their hearts. There was an infinite pathos in his figure as he strode through the dusk, returning to the woman he loved and to the man he had saved and given back to her.

"It 's tough on Cecil," said Jerry chokingly. "It does n't seem quite square, some way — I mean the Copelands hitting it off again."

"Well, we may be sure he does n't feel that way," Nan answered. "It 's all come out the way he wanted it to. He brought them together."

" JUST HELPING; JUST BEING KIND! "

"It's funny, Nan; but I'm never dead sure I catch Cecil's drift — the scheme or whatever it is he works by. I can't find it in the books he gives me to read."

"It is n't in books, Jerry; it's in his heart — just helping; just being kind!"

THE END